The Nudge Man

Harrison Vaughan, Volume 1

Keith Nixon

Published by Gladius Press, 2019.

The Escape Clause

F ive Years Ago
         Battersea, South London

Thirty minutes.

That's all they had. Half an hour. For Elizabeth Vaughan and her children to collect whatever possessions they could from their house before leaving for who knows where for who knows how long. A week? A month? Perhaps permanently.

One of the three cops guarding them, Detective Sergeant Noah Maddox, had woken Elizabeth. She'd fallen into a restless doze in front of the television, a three-quarters-finished bottle of wine and an empty glass at her elbow.

"Shaw's just called," said Maddox.

Chief Inspector Andrew Shaw was Maddox's boss, and running the operation. They'd assigned a name to it too – Mandrake.

Elizabeth blinked, checked her watch. It was gone 1am. "Why?" She felt shabby, her clothes wrinkled, pungent with body odour. Alcohol on her breath that she was certain Maddox could smell. She felt a tinge of shame because Maddox was tee-total and non-judgemental. She'd been drinking a lot lately. Because of the stress.

Maddox delivered the sucker punch. "Hennessey knows you're here."

Elizabeth sagged, a buzzing in her ears.

1

"Are you listening?" Maddox had hold of her arm – was staring intently at her.

"Sorry, what?"

"Shaw wants you all out of the city immediately."

"Where?"

"I don't know specifics. But it'll be a safe house. And a new name. We need to wake the children. There isn't much time."

"What about my mother?" asked Elizabeth. "Our friends?" She tugged at her sleeve. She stopped when Maddox noticed the nervous tic. "What do we say?"

"You can't tell them anything. It's too dangerous."

"And Harry?"

"*Nobody*, Elizabeth. Not a soul. Remember, the more people who know, the greater the risk to them – to you. And, most importantly, to Jack."

"Oh God."

"Once this is all over, maybe then you can get back in touch with everybody," said Maddox as a salve.

"When will that be?"

"Hopefully, after the trial."

"*Hopefully?* That's the best you can do?"

"The law has to take its course. Until then, Shaw wants you in the witness protection programme. The system will look after you."

The system. It sounded impersonal at best.

"I can't do this to the children."

"These are very bad men who'll stop at nothing. Hennessey would happily stand over all our dead bodies if it meant he stayed free. What would you rather have, Elizabeth?"

She wasn't going to be pushed into another bad decision, be used by the police again. "I need to think." Elizabeth headed into the living room, the space lit by the flickering TV screen, a repeat of *Top Gear*. She poured some of the wine, drained the glass. Vinegar on her tongue.

Maddox had been with them throughout. At first, she hadn't liked him at all; it was the hard eyes, the flat mouth. In fact, Elizabeth complained to Shaw and asked for somebody else. He refused. It was Shaw's way, always. However, over the weeks, Maddox softened and Elizabeth began to appreciate and even value his quiet strength. She needed that right now.

"Do you believe Shaw?" she asked. "That Hennessey's coming for us?"

"It's a distinct possibility. This is the closest we've ever been to putting him away. But most importantly, he's a killer. If we don't take this seriously the outcome could be catastrophic."

Catastrophic.

Three dead bodies. Two disgraced cops. One grieving ex-husband and father.

Maddox was right. Shaw was right.

"Will you be with us?" asked Elizabeth. Maddox was the only one of them she trusted.

"All the way."

Which made Elizabeth's decision final. "I'll get the children."

Energised, she ran upstairs, roused fourteen-year-old Maddie and twelve-year-old Jack. Avoided the inevitable questions, told them to get sorted.

So here Elizabeth stood. In the master bedroom, trying to figure out what the hell to pack while Maddie and Jack did the same. Thirteen years in one place meant an accumulation of possessions. Now it was up to her to choose what was important. Enough to fit into one suitcase. Elizabeth opened the wardrobe doors. In the scheme of things, it was just stuff. Pieces of coloured material.

She grabbed an armful of clothes and tossed them into the case. Snatched underwear, a couple of pairs of shoes. The resultant outfits would be mismatched, but the urgency had gripped her, a cold fear was squeezing her heart and she just wanted to be gone. Hennessey was on his way.

Finally, she picked up a framed photo that stood on the bedside cabinet. It was of her and Harry on their wedding day. They'd never been happier. She placed it carefully into the case – she needed something to root her in the past – flipped the top down and zipped up.

Maddie and Jack waited on the landing, Maddox at the top step. Maddie was trying to be tough, but Jack appeared about to burst into tears.

"It's not your fault, Jack," said Elizabeth. Just a case of wrong time, wrong place.

In fact, Elizabeth blamed herself for all of this. She should have said no to the police at the outset. Let somebody else take the weight. But it was too late for recrimination. They couldn't go back.

"Are you ready?" asked Elizabeth. She received two nods in response. "Come on then."

"Let me help," said Maddox.

"We can manage." Elizabeth allowed the children to go first, then hefted her own case down the stairs. Maddox followed. Once outside Maddox closed the door behind her, the click of the Yale lock loud on the quiet street. There was a faint buzz of traffic from a nearby main road, people moving around, even at this hour. She felt eyes on her. A silver-haired guy with a Labrador walked with a stick on the other pavement. He stared at them. Was he one of Hennessey's men? Her heart skipped. Two unmarked cars waited, parked on double yellows, engines running.

The cases went into the boot of the front car. Maddox slid behind the steering wheel. The Vaughans took the rear. Elizabeth in the middle, Jack and Maddie either side of her.

Car doors closed and then they were moving. As they pulled away, Elizabeth glanced over her shoulder; watched the house recede. She hoped to be back soon. Able to take up where they were leaving off.

Then she returned her gaze to the windscreen, looked forwards, to whatever faced her family. She placed an arm around both her children, drew them tight towards her. With Maddox at her side she had to believe Hennessey would never, ever reach them.

Elizabeth was wrong.

The English Flag Flies

N^{ow} **Manston, Margate**

Before you and I can get properly started on this journey together there's a dog to deal with. A big one. All muscles, teeth and slobber. It's staring at me through narrowed eyes beneath a furrowed brow, a still life of temporarily restrained loathing. I'm to be a late dinner, it seems.

This wasn't meant to happen. Then again, that's the story of my existence. I, Harrison Vaughan, was never supposed to be here. A reporter – "freelance" because no-one will employ me – by now I should be successful, with a happy family and regular, sun-kissed holidays. But I'm divorced, estranged from my children, existing on the Isle of Thanet in deepest Kent, scratching around in the dregs for a few scraps of paid employment. Tainted by a past event that stretches well into my future.

Actually, we need to go back a step, before the dog.

To Les.

Occasionally I'm thrown a job by the aforementioned Les Garrett, editor of the local newspaper, circulation: the square root of bugger all divided by zero to the power ten. Les doesn't pay much, puts more notes on the nags down the bookies than he pays me.

We were in a Margate pub when he made his proposal. The English Flag, a run-down dump on the edge of the up-and-coming fashionable Old Town. The Flag stood in dilapidated splendour, resisting the general onslaught of gentrification by enthusiastic hipsters gripping the area. Inside, it was a melting pot of aggression and xenophobia, right down to the George Cross hanging behind the bar.

A certain type of clientele gathered here. The disaffected, the angry, the tired. The Flag didn't do music, there wasn't a TV and bar snacks were restricted to nuts. And the beer was crap too.

Being a regular was a tenuous status. Like life, having your own tankard behind the bar was only a temporary possession, as was breathing in the foetid air of desperation and decay, until the time came to pass on to a better existence (i.e. die) and become a faded memory in the addled minds of the remaining drinkers.

It was one of those places which never shuts. During the beginnings of the morning and the depths of night there was always at least a single patron outside, cigarette in one hand, glass in the other, glaring at the unfair world passing by.

However, recognising everybody in the Flag was a benefit. Briefly, I was able to shake off a nagging feeling that I was being followed. It had been going on for a couple of days. A shadow tracking me. Or maybe it was my imagination.

Anyway, when I found Les he was taking a major risk by perching on a tall stool at the bar. The seat was one of those constructs where everything's undersized except for the legs, which were long and spindly. Les was bent over, studying a newspaper that lay between his hairy forearms, a pint of lager at his fingertips. He looked like a hunched-over gorilla in wrinkled clothes.

I stood at his shoulder but Les didn't notice, he was reading so intently. I glanced at the article in one of the left-wing red-tops. Another secret data leak; apparently it was dangerous, and we should all be extremely worried. The new US President said so. The particular paper Les was reading had fired me, so I'd refused to go near it since, and anything the President had to say I immediately classified as bullshit. He was that kind of fake news guy.

Once I'd ordered my drink, and sunk half of it, Les finally sensed my presence. He turned, said, "Ah, H. Nice to see you. Thanks for coming." He grinned, displaying yellowing square teeth.

"It's Harry," I reminded him for what must have been the millionth time in just a few short months. "Not H." I was Harrison to anyone in a position of responsibility, Harry to a handful of acquaintances and H to Les only. He frowned, I'd confused him. "You wanted to talk," I said.

"Not here." Les nodded to the landlord called Dick, because he was. A man of lofty expectations, but basement-level accomplishment. Ex-public school, with barely a remaining whiff of the posh, and with a ridiculous combover, Dick could always be found behind the bar. Unless there was a fight on, then he'd be in the cellar with the hatch closed. Dick was hovering a few feet away, pretending to be unobtrusive, but he had sharp ears and a loose mouth.

Les finished his pint – rolled up the paper. With evident difficulty, he shifted his weight off the stool. Les was a big lad, with a gut the size of an eight-year-old child. He never seemed to eat much but drank to excessive excess. And he sweated, constantly. Like we were in Antigua in August rather than Margate in March.

He walked as if pregnant, accompanied by a pronounced limp and a grimace of pain. Les slowly led me to a table as far away from the bar as possible, the newspaper clutched in his fist. He sat, sighed in relief as the pressure came off his knees. "I need a holiday," he said. "Somewhere warm to ease my joints." Les patted the space beside him.

When I'd taken the seat opposite, Les leaned across the table, got closer to me before murmuring, "A mate of a mate whispered in my shell-like." He tugged his ear lobe.

"Everyone's your mate," I said.

"That's right," he replied with the solemnity of a priest at a funeral. Sarcasm was a companion who knocked at Les's door only on high days and holidays.

"Your 'mate' has a story for you."

"Yeah, how did you know?"

"Lucky guess."

"Lucky is exactly what it is, H."

"It's Harry," I sighed. "And is it risky?"

"Unlikely. This is Thanet, not Syria. Although you might have to do a bit of burgling."

I raised my hands, palms out. "Not a chance." Bending the rules, no problem. Breaking the law was a different matter. I'd spent enough time inside a cell, thank you, and had no desire to give the cops the slightest opportunity to throw me back there.

I made to rise; Les placed a damp restraining palm the shape of a stoker's shovel on my shoulder. His expression of false reassurance would have shamed a Westminster politician.

Les had lost me. Despite appearances to the contrary, he was one of the most astute people I'd ever met. He waited until the climax to play his trump card and produced a chunky roll of brown notes, to nudge me in the direction he wanted. "Of course, you'll be well remunerated for your efforts."

"I'm not interested."

Les licked finger and thumb. "Are you sure?" He began to peel cash off, dirt evident under his nails, placing one note after another on the table between us, the prod becoming a shove. "Fifty quid is fifty quid, after all."

Ultimately, money actually is money and I didn't have any.

"I'm not that cheap," I said when Les paused. Les knew he'd got me and he bared his teeth in an approximation of a grin.

Exactly like the dog was doing right now.

Bonzo Dog

A Cabbage Field Outside Broadstairs

I yawned.

It was early, or late depending on your perspective. Approaching 4am. My objective was a breaker's yard called O'Neal's; an isolated, rectangular chain-link and razor-wire-fenced space out in expansive farmer's fields, located between the edge of Broadstairs and the now-defunct Manston airport, which dated back to World War Two. O'Neal's would have been under the flight path, back in the day. However, the concrete of the second-longest runway in England was now being split apart by weeds, while owners and council wrangled over its future.

The breaker's was located on a long, straight road. I paused outside the gated entrance. A high wire fence disappeared into the shadows in both directions. I stepped out of the car. No headlights left or right, but I retained a nagging doubt that I wasn't alone.

Realising my car would be obvious if parked anywhere near, I got back in, performed a three-point turn and crawled back the way I'd come until I found a rutted farmer's track a hundred yards or so beyond the compound. I turned onto the track and bumped along, wheels lurching in and out of potholes that would be nothing to a tractor but potential death for my rusty suspension.

The surrounding area was a no man's land of rotting brassica stubs where last year's cabbages had grown; wrested from the ground and the remnants left to rot. I cut across the compacted ground and got as near to the fence as I could, turned the engine off and got out. The accumulation of eggy farts from decomposing cauliflowers tainted the air.

Breathing through my mouth, I examined the yard's interior. Huge, teetering piles of scrap, some rectangles of crushed metal, their original form unrecognisable. Others, car bodies awaiting treatment; engine, tyres and glass removed, simply empty husks. A compactor lay idle. Above hung the open claw of a crane, just as immobile.

Pretty much central to this alloyed randomness, a single-storey prefabricated unit stood, picked out by a couple of spotlights at each corner. The building was arranged in one long strip, probably the kind of place which would be inhospitable most days of the year; freezing in winter yet roasting in the summer.

Les wanted me to get hold of a document, apparently buried within a filing cabinet in an office inside that building. He'd simply said, "It'll be obvious." He hadn't revealed what the contents were, and I wasn't asking.

A sign fixed to the fence at nose-height warned me about guard dogs. I walked two sides of the perimeter, rattling the links and throwing stones over in an attempt to attract the danger towards me. Despite all the noise, nothing four-legged responded so I decided the notices must be fraudulent, more fake news, to deter the casual passing thief. A few pence spent on a bogus placard to save many pounds on dog food.

I headed back to my car, popped the boot and grabbed a piece of carpet and a torch (a neat bit of forward thinking, even if I say so myself). I threw the former over the barbs (which took several attempts to get right), shoved the latter in a shallow pocket, before inelegantly shinning over. At the apex I paused once more, one leg either side of the boundary, steeling myself to break the law. Strictly, I was already over the line, but I could easily withdraw. Until the torch fell out of my pocket and rolled away a few feet.

"Bollocks," I said.

My fingerprints were on the casing and I possessed a police record. And Les had handed over a twenty quid down payment as my car was running on empty. I'd only get the balance of eighty once I gave him what he wanted. Plus, if I failed, he'd insist on the advance being returned; money I didn't have any more because it was unleaded in the fuel tank.

So, now I was committed. I figured I could have a quick look around, at least. Where was the harm?

I swung the other leg over, slid off the carpet and landed on the muddy ground in a sprawl, tweaking my ankle in the process. I swore a lot, holding myself where it hurt – my backside in a puddle. All this for a hundred quid. After a couple of minutes, the pain receded. I pushed myself up and gingerly attempted a hobble. I wouldn't be going anywhere fast.

Leaving the carpet where it was, I retrieved the torch, clicked it on and off a couple of times. It still worked. Manfully, I made my way over to the building at a little above tortoise pace, trying to ignore my wet arse. Within the yard the rotting brassica odour was tainted with oil and fuel and the metal piles threw long shadows. I paused at the edge, at the point where

k became harsh brightness because of the spotlights. I didn't
ke the thought of being exposed, but I had little choice. There
was only one way into the building. I crossed the Rubicon and
hustled to the door, grimacing at the shooting pain from my
ankle.

The door proved to be unlocked. I took a few steps inside,
breathed a sigh of relief in the relative darkness and flicked on
my torch. When the beam illuminated a pair of yellow eyes, I
realised why entry had been so straightforward.

Who needs a lock when you've a bloody great big dog?

It was one of those rip-your-throat-out, piss-on-your-
corpse breeds. I'm no expert on dogs so I couldn't tell you exactly what it was, and I wasn't about to ask Google. The beast
was standing about half way along the corridor, partially in
shadow as the torch batteries were old, the beam weak.

Uninjured, I reckoned I could back through the door and
have it shut behind me by the time the dog covered the distance. But with a sprain? Very unlikely.

Meaning there was only one course of action.

I turned off the torch, plunging the interior into relative
darkness. The dog's eyes still shone, though. Pale orbs of hate.
I felt for a switch, assuming there would be one sensibly placed
by the door as there is in every habitable construction. I was
right! Strip lights flickered into life along the corridor in series,
one after the other. Me first, dog last. It stood totally still. I
wondered if it was stuffed, until saliva dripped from its jaw onto the floor with a wet plop. No, it was very much alive.

Now is a good time to reveal an inner secret. I genuinely
don't care about life. *My* life, anyway. I have no value to anyone.
Not since *the accusation*. When I'd scraped bottom and stayed

there – each event after *the accusation* a further body blow which kept me low.

So I had to confront the hound. If it ripped me to shreds, then that's how it would be. Before what limited good sense I retained could argue, I took a step towards the dog. Not fast, not slow, but with a suicidal confidence. Worn-out heart in agreement with jaded mind.

Two steps: the dog growled, took a pace forward itself. I growled back. What if the dog attacked? There was an office door nearby, a few paces away. Maybe I could dive in there and slam the door?

Six steps, the animal tilted its head, probably as confused as I was at my progress, trying to make sense of what was going on. Another growl.

Twelve steps, the mutt barked, deep and low. I paused. Tried to calm my fast, shallow breathing. I was beyond my escape route. Closer to the dog than safety. What part of my body would the animal maul first?

Thirteen steps, the dog sat. Growled again, but quietly this time. All this for £100. I must be mad.

When I reached the dog it was lying down, head between its paws. I squatted, put my hand out, paused above its skull, ready to snatch back my hand should he go for me. Another growl. I softly patted his head. The hound flattened his ears. Looked like I was going to survive. I was some sort of dog whisperer. Like Mel Gibson in *Lethal Weapon Two*, or *Three*, whichever. A small part of me exulted in having survived; most of me sulked like a bastard for the same reason.

Anyway, better get searching.

Seventeen minutes of effort was what it took to make me realise I was wasting my time.

The building was organised around a central open-plan office – the walls removed at some point to produce an enlarged area. Tables and chairs were squashed together – space at a premium, although junk was not. I guessed it was mainly an area for the drivers and workers. Otherwise there were a couple of smaller offices with a single desk, chair and cabinet within; and a single, presumably unisex, smelly toilet cubicle (but no sink).

I found that every cabinet and every drawer in every room was unlocked. A careful rifling revealed absolutely nothing of interest. It was invoices, bills, brochures and porn mags. Frustrated, I left the main office and returned to the dog. I patted the beast once more, just to ensure the animal remained on the right side of friendly, then read the engraved tag on its collar.

"Hello, Bonzo." I scratched behind his ears. Poor bastard, being stuck with a name like that. It said, cuddly cat, not vicious dog. Then again, maybe he wasn't so tough after all.

Bonzo sat up and wagged a long, fluffy tail the length of my forearm, in an outward demonstration of shared disappointment. As if he'd known I'd be as unsuccessful in my hunt as the England football team was at winning trophies. But I wasn't really an animal lover so Bonzo's outward affection meant little.

I was about to leave Bonzo and the building, but something niggled at me. An irritating little tap somewhere in my tiny mind. I returned to where I'd started, accompanied by the sound of clicking claws. Bonzo was on my heels this time. Perhaps he could feel the anticipation too.

In the far corner was a desk, crammed against the wall, laden with the paraphernalia required to make cheap, unappetising hot drinks. The desk had drawers, but access was impossible because it was pushed up against the wall, wrong way round.

I knelt down, brushed my fingers across the floor. There were scrape marks where the desk had been moved, and more than once. I stood. Careless of the stuff on the surface I dragged the desk a few feet across before pivoting it, like a door on hinges. The drawers wouldn't budge. Locked.

A clue!

"What do you think, Bonzo?" I asked. The dog barked, a deep huff from the chest, another tail wag.

Dealing with the lock was pretty straightforward. In a junkyard there is a multitude of metal lengths available. Frankly, I was spoilt for choice. I selected a sturdy looking piece, returned to the desk and wedged it into the gap between drawer and lock, and leant on the makeshift bar. Ultimately, the security held firm and the laminated wood gave way.

Inside was a folder, just one, pushed towards the rear. It contained a couple of pieces of paper. They were related to planning applications for a huge housing complex on the airport land. I photographed both, emailed the images to Les. Then deleted everything; pictures and message. I didn't care what this was about, nor did I want to know. Capitalist bastard, I was simply in it for the money.

I returned everything to its previous state. Well, as much as I could. The broken drawer would be obvious when somebody shifted the furniture, but by then I'd be long gone. Time to leave for sure now. I told Bonzo I was off when we were back in the corridor. He wasn't happy. Maybe it was the lack of company he'd miss.

"Sorry, mate," I said with my palm on the handle. His eyes were still burning when I flicked off the light. When I closed the door, Bonzo howled like a werewolf.

The sky was beginning to brighten as I tramped back across the metal-strewn wasteland, still a bit of pain from my ankle, though not as bad. Getting back over the fence was simple. I landed – favouring my good leg – on the other side. I reached up for the carpet, but the fabric was stuck on the sharp points and I had to yank at it a couple of times.

"Would you like a hand there, sir?"

I replied, "That would be good, thanks."

The penny hit and hard. I should be on my own. A glance over my shoulder revealed a man grinning at me. He held up a warrant card.

"You're nicked, my son," he said.

"Bollocks," I replied.

Framed

Interview Room 4, Margate Police Station

In the past, when I'd been a journalist of average abilities and before the days of being able to access a dictionary via my phone, I'd been expected to be a kind of walking thesaurus. However, there were some expressions carved into the table's surface that were new to me.

Several were, without doubt, foreign and more than likely calling the police into blunt disrepute. Others, for sure, were made up – drunken convulsions combining multiple expletives to create new and interesting forms that were worth future use. I wished I had a pen to write them down.

Other than the defaced table, four stunningly uncomfortable chairs (my backside in one) and a clock on the wall, the interview room in the Margate police station was entirely empty. Not even a two-way mirror or the lens of a CCTV camera for company (too expensive, I guess).

Forty-one excruciatingly dull minutes they made me wait, during which I wondered how I was going to get my car back from the field next to O'Neal's where it was still parked, examined the cracks in the wall and, eventually, resorted to counting the number of tiles on the ceiling. The clock face didn't even have a second hand to watch crawl around. Just a faint, drawn-out tick from the mechanism indicating the passage of time.

The door, at last, opened. In walked a copper so haggard he must have pulled a long shift. Dishevelled brown hair, twenty-four-hour stubble and bloodshot blue eyes. Average height, average looks. First a folder hit the defaced surface of the table, then he drew out one of the chairs; wilted into it. By the sigh that slipped from his lips, the seat was a welcoming hug. He hung his head back, actually drifted off for a minute until he jerked into consciousness. I noticed my name on the cover of the folder, printed onto a label in a nice Copperplate font.

"Tired?" I said.

"You've no idea," he replied.

"I know you."

The cop nodded. "Bet you can't remember my name."

"Sorry."

He shrugged as if it was no consequence, though I'm sure it was. "Detective Sergeant Guy Gregory," he said.

"Of course. One of Margate's finest."

By the grimace on Gregory's face he knew that to be a lie.

"Sorry to keep you waiting, we've been busy."

"Right."

He flipped open the file. It wasn't particularly thick. I was unsure whether to be insulted. "Do you know who owns O'Neal's?" he asked, the paperwork before him ignored.

"O'Neal?"

"Funny. He was just a front. And O'Neal is deceased. Any idea how?"

"Never met the man."

"Debts."

"Owing money can kill you?"

"Depends on the size of your liabilities. And who you're obligated to."

"I'll take your word for it."

"O'Neal was crushed to death in his own compactor. What we found of him could have fitted into a jam jar."

"Raspberry?"

"That's not funny."

"One of my biggest failings, if I'm honest."

"Honest. Interesting word," said Gregory. I kept my mouth shut for once. Gregory continued. "The coroner ruled O'Neal's death a tragic accident. He managed to fall inside the machinery during operation. The safety mechanism had been disabled. Several employees swore O'Neal deactivated the emergency stop himself. However, we kept the case open."

"The coroner was wrong?"

"Maybe a better way of putting it is 'influenced.'"

"Why are you telling me this?"

"Think of it as context."

"Okay." I wasn't sure where this was all leading.

"Why were you on private property?"

"Bonzo looked lonely."

"Bonzo?"

"The desolate dog."

Gregory made a show of reading the details slowly and line by line. I expected his lips to move silently. I was disappointed.

"There's no mention of a dog in the arresting officer's report."

"I locked Bonzo in the building."

"So, you're admitting that as well as climbing over a fence you broke down a door?"

"It was already open."

"You said locked."

"Turn of phrase. Dogs can't use handles." I was getting irritated with Gregory's relentless prodding. It was like watching a child fumble around in the dark, periodically banging their shins.

"What were you after?"

"I told you, it was compassion for an animal." It was the best I could think of while being driven over to the station in the back of the cop car, okay?

"And you just happened to be passing by?"

"Yes."

"Your vehicle was found in the middle of a field."

"I lost my bearings."

"There was carpet over the wire fence and you had a torch in your possession. That strikes me as pre-meditation."

"The carpet was already there."

"And you were carrying a torch."

"I get scared in the dark."

"Is this how you want to play it, Mr Vaughan?"

"Play what?" I do a good line in innocent. Lots of practice with the ex-Mrs Vaughan.

Gregory regarded me for a long moment. Pity or frustration, I wasn't sure. Equally, it could have been indigestion. "I'll get your lawyer then."

"What lawyer?"

"You didn't request legal counsel?"

"Maybe." I hadn't.

"There's a man outside, says he's here to represent you."

"Oh-kay."

"So, you don't want him?"

"Should I?"

"I can't advise you either way." Gregory didn't bother to hide his inner thought – that I was an idiot. "I can tell him to leave if you'd prefer."

"What's his name?"

Gregory pushed a business card over. I took it. Thick, black letters printed onto a heavy paper stock said:

Aaron Conn. Attorney of Law. At Challinor, Lockheed and Conn.

Then a central London address – whose rent would be similar to the annual GDP of a decent-sized tropical island – along with phone numbers, landline and mobile.

"What I'd like to know," asked Gregory, "is how Conn got here from London so quickly. You were arrested less than ninety minutes ago."

"Oh, *him*. Aaron's an old friend."

Gregory stared at me. I kept my mind as blank as possible, so nothing would register on my face, which was easy.

Eventually Gregory said, "I'll have him brought in."

I didn't have a clue what was going on or who Conn was, but I had to go with it.

Snatch

Interview Room 4, Margate Police Station

Aaron Conn totally conformed to my expectations. A heavy pinstripe suit hung off a lean frame. Slicked-back thinning hair and a Home Counties accent laced with money and connections. In his left hand was a thin leather briefcase. Bonzo-like, my hackles rose the instant he entered the room. I bloody loathe the arrogance of privilege by birth. After all, it's just comparative luck.

"Good to see you again," said Conn as he sat. He held out a pampered hand for me to take. Presumably to peck the gold ring on his pinkie. Or to check if I was a Freemason.

I didn't kiss or shake, crossed my arms instead. Unaffected by the snub, Conn nestled himself in the chair and placed the briefcase on the floor. Gregory threw me a suspicious look which I batted back with a raised eyebrow.

"Sergeant Gregory," said Conn, locking eyes with the cop, "I need some time alone with my client."

"He's all yours," said Gregory.

The moment we were alone Conn said, "What have you told them so far?"

"Just about Bonzo."

"Who?" asked Conn.

"The dog."

"What dog?"

"The one I saw inside the compound," I said. "He didn't seem happy. I said I entered to save the animal."

"Okay." Conn shook his head. "Now, ahead of an explanation, I need your pledge that you will trust me entirely and not contradict the argument I'll be presenting to Sergeant Gregory. Behaving like an ignoramus simply makes my objective near impossible and your predicament more precarious and I can't effectively represent you under those circumstances."

"You can get me out of here?"

"Indubitably."

"Then yes, I'll behave."

Conn appeared relieved. "Good, because I was told you can be challenging."

"I'll take that as a compliment."

"If you wish. Now, I'll be presenting substantive evidence that you are, in fact, a valued employee of the firm of O'Neal and Partners and were simply undertaking a security assessment as part of your day-to-day responsibilities."

That had some plausibility. "I'm impressed," I said. And despite myself, I was. But there was one important point I needed confirming. "I hope this is pro bono, Aaron. I don't have two pennies to rub together."

"Actually, you have precisely one hundred and thirty-nine pence, Mr Vaughan. Unless there are a few coins which have fallen down the back of your sofa at home."

For a moment I was lost for words. Conn knew my bank balance precisely. "Who's paying your fee then?"

"A friend."

"I don't have any friends."

"We need to discuss that later. For now, we must concentrate on the job in hand, Mr Vaughan, which is getting you back out onto the mean streets of Margate."

While my brain was rotating like a washing machine on a rapid spin, Conn called Gregory back.

The sergeant regained his seat and said, "Let's get this charade back on the road, then."

"You must release my client immediately."

"Must, Mr Conn? On what basis? Your client was trespassing on private property and has so far failed to provide a reasonable explanation for doing so."

"Bonzo," I said.

"Not this again," said Gregory. My legal eagle picked up his briefcase, laid it on the table and popped the catches. Inside was a laptop, a single sheet of paper and a glasses case. He passed the document to Gregory. While the cop was reading, Conn placed the spectacles on the end of his nose before reversing the process with the case.

"What am I looking at?" asked Gregory.

"A contract of employment," said Conn. He repeated the lie regarding the purpose of my presence at O'Neal's.

I stole a glance at the document. There was a signature at the bottom that appeared suspiciously like mine.

Gregory turned to me. He didn't look happy; in fact, it seemed anger was playing across his features. "Is this correct?"

"Apparently so."

"You work for *him*?" asked Gregory via gritted teeth.

"Words don't lie," I lied, not sure what I was lying about.

"Unbelievable." Gregory blew out some air through pursed lips. He stood, strode across the interview room, paused at the door. "Do you remember the guy in the compactor?"

"The one who became raspberry consommé? I could hardly forget him."

"He fell out with the yard's real owner."

"Who is ...?"

"You don't know?"

"Why would I?"

"You're right, why would you?" The sarcasm was obvious in Gregory's tone. "Plausible deniability."

"Sergeant, this is getting tiring," interjected Conn. He removed the glasses and put them into a jacket pocket.

"I agree. You're free to go, Mr Vaughan."

"Just like that?" I asked.

"Mr Conn here has given me no reason to hold you. In fact, I just want you gone." Gregory yanked the door open, leant out and crooked a finger at a police constable. "I thought better of you, I really did," said Gregory in a final riposte before he disappeared.

All irritation banished, replaced with the flush of success, Conn turned to me and shook my hand. "I'll see you outside. We can talk more then. I hope there's a decent establishment we can subsequently proceed to. I fancy something with a hint of fizz to celebrate. Now, where are my glasses?" Before I could tell him he was probably going to be disappointed in the local offerings, Conn was gone too, leaving behind a whole heap of questions in my mind.

The uniform processed my release in double-quick time. Incredibly soon afterwards, I was heading out the front door, into salt- and seaweed-laden fresh air and precious liberty. Conn was standing across the road, facing the station, his back to the briny. He tipped his head, implying I should join him.

Before I could cross over, a black Mercedes Benz drew up kerbside immediately opposite me. The passenger doors, front and back, opened with precision and two rather large men stepped out. Within a couple of steps, they had me by each arm and were throwing me inside. The doors slammed shut and I was squeezed between tattooed thugs like a chipolata in a crusty baguette. I looked over my shoulder, saw Conn staring at the car, his mouth open.

Kidnapped, right in front of the police station. Where was a bloody copper when you needed one?

Blessing's Entrance

Somewhere Over Ireland

Melody Blessing reacted to the personal contact. A mere touch on the arm, but enough to make her jerk away. Interaction was strictly prohibited. Under any circumstances. She'd made that very clear before the flight departed. Blessing didn't exist and was to be treated as such.

Blessing blinked in the early morning sunlight that filtered its way through small windows inset along the fuselage. She must have nodded off, despite the roar of the engines. Surprising, given the stress she was under. Sleep had been a rare commodity of late.

The transgressor, a female private in masculine-green fatigues, hair tucked under a peaked cap, stepped back under Blessing's glare. There was a name printed onto a badge affixed to the private's chest, but Blessing didn't bother to read it. There was no point. They'd never meet again as, officially, this trip wasn't happening.

The plane was a military transporter, a wide-open space in the fuselage for bulky items, like crates packed with supplies or a jeep or a tank. Passengers were peripheral, dealt with by the manufacturers fixing uncomfortable benches around the circumference of the fuselage.

The transporter had been the first flight she could board to get her the right side of the Atlantic. A civilian route would have been far more comfortable, but also very visible. She knew the British were sticklers for the rules. In this fashion, Blessing could gain access to the UK without revealing her presence, courtesy of the "Special Relationship" which allowed the US military only minimal fettering.

"You've a call, ma'am." The private had to shout to make herself heard, such was the racket.

"Who from?" asked Blessing.

"The President's office, ma'am." The private was a Southern hick by the drawl – Texas maybe, where race was still an issue. The accent made the private sound dumb. Which was why Blessing had buried her own heritage years ago. No contact with friends or family, the optimum choice for her career.

The private held out a large, clunky satellite phone. Blessing waited for her to retreat before she pressed the phone to one ear, covering the other with a hand. "This is Blessing."

"One moment." A woman's voice which was gone immediately. Blessing waited impatiently. Her watch told her they'd be setting down momentarily at RAF Croughton, America's major air force base in the UK, located north-west of London. But the President got what he wanted, when he wanted. He was that kinda guy.

After a long minute POTUS came onto the line. "Melanie, hi. How are ya?" He spoke as if they were friends. In fact, the pair had never met. But 45, as he was referred to, was infamous, even before he was elected.

"Fine, sir. Thank you for asking. And it's Melody, sir. How can I help today?"

"I wanted to see, to see if you'd got him? This Nudge guy. Not that I'm concerned about him in any way, you understand. But I just wanted to see."

"Not yet, sir, I'm just entering the UK. I doubt it will take me long to acquire the target."

"That's just great. I'm glad you went with my excellent advice."

Blessing closed her eyes. 45 had proposed a covert operation on the soil of an ally. She'd shuddered when she'd learned of the proposal. The few remaining level heads in the White House had pushed back. Advised against it. Said that if their action was ever discovered, even years later, the fallout out would be immeasurable. Their response simply made 45 more intransigent. He insisted the manoeuvre go ahead.

"You gave the order, sir."

"Damn straight." The plane banked. Blessing braced herself in response. "Who's on your team, Melanie?"

Blessing didn't bother to correct him this time. "Special Agent Six, sir."

"Good guy, one of our best. Extra special, wouldn't you say?"

"Certainly, sir."

"With Six on board I'm sure you'll succeed."

"I hope so, sir."

"You need faith, not hope, Melanie. Forty-eight hours, his head on a platter. Forty-eight, that's what I want."

"Sir."

"'Cos you know how I feel about people who disappoint me, don't ya, Melody?"

Typical of 45 to focus on the negative. "I do, sir."

"I'm glad we're clear."

"I won't let you down, sir." But POTUS was gone.

She placed the phone on the bench, left a palm on it to stop the handset from moving. The private had strapped herself in already. Two days, there was no way. 45 was setting her up to fail.

From beneath Blessing came the whine of the landing gear extending, then a thud as the metal legs locked into position. The aircraft slowed as the pilot throttled back. A few seconds' pause before wheels hit the ground. The landing was anything but soft and Blessing's spine took the pounding with bad grace. She'd ache for a while but, it was worth it for the anonymity. The engines roared with reverse thrust.

Special Agent Six couldn't be more different from Blessing. Six's politics were far, far to the right, an ardent admirer of the Tea Party movement. Six had lurked on the lunatic fringes of the Grand Old Party until POTUS gained office. POTUS had legitimised people like Six and in return Six was an open and honest admirer of POTUS, which curried favour.

Blessing was a Democrat, leaning towards the centre; a progressive. Six hated just about everything Blessing valued, including Blessing herself. Because Blessing was female and a person of colour. But Blessing had always given everything her best shot and she'd do so again, despite POTUS's threats. She needed Six to do his utmost too, so she'd grit her teeth, knuckle down and continue to keep her mouth shut.

And all this over an innocuous tweet which POTUS felt made him look bad. The most powerful man in the world raging over a handful of letters from an underground activist who called themselves the Nudge Man. Really, POTUS should just let it go. But he couldn't. He was that kinda guy. Narcissists. Who'd have them?

"Welcome to England, ma'am," said the private as they drew to a halt.

A Message from Above

An A Road, Thanet, Kent

"Where are we going?" I asked. I was ignored by all four of my erstwhile kidnappers. Not even a glance. It was as if I didn't exist. Maybe I wouldn't for much longer.

There were more rings on show than a swarm of homing pigeons, bigger muscles than in a prison exercise yard, more ink than at a tattooist convention. And plenty of cigarettes.

"Isn't it illegal to smoke in confined spaces when accompanied by a minor?" My question came out as a bit of a squeak due to my lungs being constricted by the lack of space and the grey clouds. Normally I'm able to irritate anyone into a response. Not this lot, though.

I couldn't reach over to open a window, my comparatively narrow frame squashed between oversized geezers. Arm outstretched, I could just about get my fingertips to an air vent positioned between driver and passenger seat. A cool breeze rippled over me which helped somewhat until one of the thugs shut the outlet.

The only other option available was to stare out the window at the fast-moving countryside. We were heading away from the coast and off Thanet. Miles and miles of flat fields and marshes reclaimed from the sea. Dull, dull, dull.

So, I decided to sleep.

I was rudely awakened from my doze when the BMW jerked to a halt. I checked my watch, a black Casio that would be considered retro these days, but I know is just cheap. Only twenty or so minutes had passed, so we were somewhere out in those marshes I'd spied earlier.

The geezers got out. I assumed I was required to do the same. I slid out of the car, which was parked on a gravel drive before a large, Jacobean house. Not quite a mansion, but sufficiently looming to be impressive. It was surrounded by a high, densely packed row of Leylandii, the ones that shoot up several inches every year. They must have been eighteen feet tall at least, Goliaths protecting the interior from prying eyes. A set of solid wooden gates were just closing, shut by an unseen, electronic hand.

The air was still. No road traffic. A faint contrail. Not even a seagull. What surprised me was the topiary either side of the house. Box, if I remember my horticulture, neatly trimmed into a variety of artistic forms. A bear (rearing on hind legs), a stag (with impressive antlers) and an eagle (wings spread, diving for prey).

My car was a few yards away. A yellow lump of ancient metal and residual electronics. It was so plain I wasn't even sure of the make. All the badges had been ripped off long ago. Someone must have brought it here, which was interesting because the keys were in my pocket.

Two of the Muscle Beach contestants had gone inside, the arched front door stood open. I received a shove in the back from one of the remaining minders which forced an involuntary step forward on my behalf. I had to follow through into actual walking or fall flat on my face.

Inside was a poorly lit hallway, curtains drawn over all the windows. Once my eyes adjusted I saw stairs winding upwards out of sight, and a corridor disappearing into a shadowy void in both directions.

The geezer pointed an arm, finger extended, along the passage and into oblivion, like one of Scrooge's ghosts.

"Bit melodramatic, isn't it?"

He rolled his eyes, grunted, "Second door on the left, arsehole."

"Charming."

The door closed behind me, presumably by Mr Personality the minder. The room I'd entered was as gloomy as the corridor. After a handful of rather loud heartbeats (mine) a table lamp clicked on, throwing into relief a desk and a shape behind it. A person, seated, the features indistinct. The form shifted, more precisely rolled, until the illumination revealed a man in a wheelchair, his legs covered by a blanket of green tartan.

"Bollocks," I said.

Eric Hennessey, one-time local crime boss, didn't blink.

In case you don't know of Eric Hennessey, here's a brief resume. He had been the premier gangster on the Isle of Thanet. He didn't care what he made money from – prostitution, drugs, immigrants, gambling, bare-knuckle bouts, dog fights – it was all the same to him. He was reputed to be as tough and as cold as they came. I'd heard no end of stories in the Flag where Hennessey was idolised as a man of the people; brutal tactics to win and maintain business, to deal with snitches and the competition.

However, his activity and notoriety were all past tense. He'd disappeared before I moved to the area for good. There was talk of him being either dead or in prison; certainly not re-tired. He wasn't the type.

"You're supposed to be dead," I said.

"I am delivered, Mr Vaughan," croaked Hennessey. He raised a hand. The main lights flicked on overhead. He held a remote control. I'd seen photos of Hennessey, shots Les had published and now were archived. "There's a difference."

Hennessey looked the same but didn't. He'd appeared a big man back then, strong and powerful. But now his chest and forearms bulged, like he'd strengthened his torso while his legs wasted away. No tattoos, no jewellery – he'd not done the bling thing, but he dressed well. Still did, a tailored dress shirt stretched across his impressive frame, cravat at his throat, thick gold chain on his wrist. Hennessey's eyes, though, were still in-tense, hot coals.

"I was in a car accident," he said, "severed my spinal cord. Everything below my waist is useless. Can't even go to the toilet by myself anymore." He showed me a catheter bag from where it had been obscured beneath the arm of the wheelchair. It was full of a yellow liquid.

I didn't know what to say besides, "Sorry."

"Save it," he said with a wave of his hand. "Regret is for the Lord." Hennessey effortlessly rolled himself back to the desk, strong hands gripping and spinning the wheels. "And I deserve my incapacity after past misdeeds."

"Why am I here?"

"Relax, Mr Vaughan. It's not as if you caused my predica-ment."

"I'm sure I'd remember if I had."

"And if it were you who took my legs, I'd be embracing you as a brother and giving thanks." He raised a decanter, waved it in my direction. "Want one? Single malt, of course."

I'm not usually a whisky fan but wasn't going to admit it. Not to a maimed and seemingly ex-sociopath who'd found religious zeal. "Sure."

There was a knock at the door. Without waiting for an answer it swung open. In stepped a nurse, or at least a woman with the correct attire for me to assume that was her role. In her hand she held an empty catheter bag. The nurse knelt and began unclipping the full one. Hennessey acted as if this was all perfectly normal, which it no doubt was.

"I'll make it a large one," he said. "I suspect you're going to need it." He held out a cut crystal glass, half full of a liquid the colour of autumn leaves. I crossed the room, accepted the drink. Felt the weight in my hand. Hardly a weapon of mass destruction.

If I struck Hennessey with the glass I reckoned he would shake off the blow easily, grab me, crush me to death. Maybe run me over a few times in his wheelchair for good measure. And there was the nurse to deal with. And four geezers outside, each the size of a tow truck. I sensibly shelved the idea. The nurse, job done, departed. "You're probably wondering why you're here," said Hennessey.

Understatement of the year. "Kind of." Hennessey pointed at the wall behind me. I turned. An effigy, a nailed man on a cross, mounted above an open fire. "Jesus?" I asked.

"I was sent back to make amends, Mr Vaughan. When I was in the ambulance heading to hospital after the accident, my heart failed. I was looking down. Over myself, onto the paramedics working. It was chaos. Them pumping my chest, blowing into my lungs, hitting me with an electric pulse. Eventually, they gave up; unable to revive me or maybe they weren't interested in trying very hard.

"It was irrelevant, though. I was so calm, so at peace, so warm. I realised there was somebody beside me, a form that I couldn't resolve. A being, hazy and bathed in a bright light. I was told I was returning. I didn't want to, and I argued. But back I headed anyway.

"When I was mortal once more it was incredibly painful. In body and spirit. I felt torn into separate parts. Most of me on earth, but a small segment still on that other plane, where it remains. Then I knew I could only be whole again once I'd satisfied those above us all via penitence and sacrifice. And this is your purpose, Mr Vaughan. To be my aid."

I'm a non-believer and usually right now I'd be pointing out how stupid religion was and that "God" was a fictional construct to aid the powerful few to subvert the weak masses and had been throughout time. In this instance, though, safety first. I kept my mouth closed.

Hennessey refilled his glass, though not with alcohol but soda water from a siphon. He continued. "I spent months in hospital recovering. Being told I'd lost the use of my legs was just a confirmation of my task. I wasn't angry, how could I be?

"Once I was out I discovered much of the empire I'd built had crumbled, stolen away by opportunists. It was obviously going to happen. Any weakness is roughly exploited by players in my game, I expected nothing less. I could have fought from my bed, but I didn't have the heart for violence and suffering any more. I let go. Because that was expected."

"Why all the heavies?" I asked.

"Protection. I've plenty of enemies, plenty of people who don't believe I'm out of the game, plenty of up-and-comers who'd get kudos from taking out crippled, old, helpless Eric Hennessey."

"You don't look helpless to me."

"Meaning I'm old and crippled?" Hennessey laughed, slapped his thigh. "Last year I'd have had you tortured within an inch of your crappy life for that statement alone."

"I'm assuming I'm not here for a bible convention?" I said, putting the tumbler down on the table. Often, the zealous are also highly protective of their faith. I was interested to see if Hennessey was too.

He affixed me with a stare. "I want the person who caused the accident." Hennessey paused for meaningless effect. "The Nudge Man."

The Nudge Man Cometh

Pluck's Gutter, Kent

"Who the hell is he?" I asked.

Hennessey ignored my question, posing another instead. "Have you heard of nudge theory?"

"Don't think so, should I?" Hennessey held out a book. I stood and took it from him. An academic tome I didn't recognise, certainly hadn't read and likely never would. I didn't even bother to flick through, handed it back. "Not my kind of thing."

"Then I'll enlighten you," said Hennessey the sage. "Nudge theory is used in behavioural economics to gently push people in a certain desired direction, often without them realising. For example, politicians like Barack Obama progressed some of his domestic policy via subtle prods while he was in office."

I waved a hand, dismissing Hennessey's last point. "Anything involving politicians is bound to be bullshit."

"No arguments from me there, but Obama was trying to help people find better jobs or improve their health. Nudges are used to alter people's behaviour in a predictable way."

"I get it." I didn't.

"Here's one you'll understand. Urinals. The fly printed inside the bowl."

"What about them?"

"It's an example of your behaviour being nudged."

I laughed. "Ridiculous."

"Really? I'm guessing you aimed at the fly while peeing."

I had, many times. Hennessey smiled at the realisation on my face.

"Which," he said, "is a constructive nudge. It's about minimising the amount of urine which ends up on the toilet floor. And that's how the Nudge Man operates."

"Pisses on flies?"

Hennessey screwed up his face in irritation. "Subtly alters behaviour, Mr Vaughan. He'll find a target, give it a little shove in the direction he wants, take some money for his troubles and move on."

"Like what?"

"It could be anything," shrugged Hennessey. "We're not talking an influence on global politics here, or murder or major criminal endeavours. They're examples of a deconstructive action and hardly a nudge. No, he undertakes small stuff, things that barely reach the inside pages of the local paper. A handful have gone national, but hardly any, that's not the Nudge Man's style. I'll show you." Hennessey rolled himself forward. "Pull back the curtains."

I stood, intrigued, and did as Hennessey asked. Light flooded the room. I blinked, allowed my eyes to adjust. When I turned around Hennessey was beside a map of the UK affixed to the wall, lots of coloured pins stuck into it.

"This is his activity – what I can find anyway."

When I got close to the map I realised quite how many pins there were, each with a tiny piece of paper hanging from it with a number in minuscule script. "There's hundreds," I said, making the obvious comment.

"Occurring with increasing frequency over the last five years. And I'm constantly finding more. I've documented every single action. It took a huge amount of effort. Multiple data analysts checking news feeds, court actions, listening out for gossip on social media. Anything even vaguely matching the typical behaviour of the Nudge Man was considered and analysed. We put in months of work and I spent many tens of thousands of pounds."

I stood back, attempted to determine a pattern in the impressive array.

"It's totally random from what I can tell," said Hennessey, guessing my thinking. "And whoever it is, they're extremely clever. I've been trying to track them down for almost twelve months. Whenever I make any progress, the trail peters out and I have to start all over again. They use a Virtual Private Network, of course, for any electronic activity with multiple cut outs. Any personal interaction is via uninformed third parties, specifically engaged for the one task. Like a cell structure."

"As interesting as this is, what's it to do with me?"

"I want you to find the Nudge Man."

"That's not my game, I'm just a reporter. Hire a private detective."

"Which I've already done, Mr Vaughan. First, I had my men on it, then friendly members of the police force, then I paid for external help. They were all entirely unsuccessful. Some are in prison."

"Not massively reassuring, Eric."

He shrugged. "You might as well be aware of what you're getting into."

"I'm a serial failure too. What makes you think I'll do any better?"

"Three things." Hennessey held up a hand, ignoring my puerile attempt at self-pity. He lifted a single finger. "You'll be well paid."

"I'm used to being poor." I needed the money, as I've already said, but the idea of working for Hennessey didn't fill me with pleasure, regardless of his newfound religious fanaticism.

The second finger flicked to attention as if I hadn't spoken. "You'll approach this differently to the rest. Ultimately, this is about a story, not a hunt. The people I sent to speak with some of the victims struggled to even get an audience, never mind answers. Journalists are charmers, by and large."

There was some truth in Hennessey's belief. An investigative reporter without a degree of charisma and the ability to connect personally went hungry. If you couldn't gain people's trust, get them talking, then there wasn't copy to write and no food on the table.

Hennessey continued, "You break it, redemption follows."

"Redemption?

"A unique, untold piece of news will be yours. Totally exclusive. Your ex-colleagues from the newspapers will have to listen. There will be respect for you again." Hennessey thudded a clench fist into his open palm. "Respect from people who shunned you." Hennessey's eyes blazed. "You'll have credibility once more." Which was clearly more important to him than it was to me. I was done with that part of my life.

"You said three aspects. You've only mentioned two."

"We'll come to the third point shortly."

"You're very sure of yourself, Eric."

"Always, Mr Vaughan."

"Any questions before you sign on the dotted line?"

"Why is he so important to you?"

"He took most of my money."

"How much?"

"Several million pounds."

"Wow. He's a rich guy."

"The Nudge Man is no Robin Hood, let me tell you. My money was set to be used for good, Christian causes and now it's God knows where." Hennessey seemed to miss the irony in his last point – that an omnipotent being actually wasn't all-seeing. "But don't worry, I still have sufficient left to pay you."

"The thought had never crossed my mind."

"I'm sure."

"And this so-called Nudge Man," I said, "what will you do to him?"

"Nothing." Hennessey opened his arms wide, like a prophet. "I'm not in the revenge business anymore. I just want the money back, so it can be properly distributed. To do the good Lord's work. Now, are you in or out?"

I didn't really want this. Yes, I'd like to be solvent. However, I'd got by before and I would again. An outright refusal probably wouldn't go down very well, though. "I'll need to check this out myself," I said. At least then I had enough time to come up with a decent excuse to back away.

Hennessey grinned. "I thought you'd say that." He opened a desk drawer.

Hennessey's goon led me along the corridor, turned into the next room. A spacious library with floor-to-ceiling books, squashy chairs at intervals. And a large sash window with heavy curtains, pinched halfway down by ornate cast-iron tie backs, which faced the sculpted garden.

In the centre was a desk, laptop and chair. The arrangement seemed out of place, like it was there just for me. The thug slowly closed the door, eyeing me throughout. I heard a key turn. A rattle of the handle confirmed I was locked in. I crossed the room – tried to open the window. It wouldn't budge, either painted or screwed shut.

I went to where I was supposed to go and sat down. I recognised the scratch across the laptop lid. Somebody had retrieved it from the boot of my car. Ignoring the laptop for now, I focused on the large pile of paperwork Hennessey had handed to me, including a folder of news clippings, mostly from local papers, which I gave a cursory glance.

The contents were a litany of crimes where the Nudge Man had taken the law into his own hands. At the top of each cutting was a handwritten date. They went back about five years.

A prolific burglar who preyed on the elderly was found, bound hand and foot, in possession of some of his ill-gotten gains. Three years in prison.

A graffiti artist who'd blighted his local area. He'd handed himself in to the police.

A group of teens selling drugs on a housing estate shut down and the county line providing the supply was strangled at source.

Hennessey was right, the Nudge Man was no law-abiding citizen. But in many cases there was a strange sort of merit in his actions. Then again, the Nudge Man was apparently taking money for his efforts.

Frankly, actual data was minimal. There were whispers, rumours and suppositions in a handful of investigative articles, but nothing substantial. The big whistle blowers – Julian Assange at Wikileaks and Edward Snowden – were well publicised, of course. Were my target and these dealers in secrets related? Or was Hennessey after vapour? Making something out of nothing? It was impossible to tell and ultimately, I didn't care.

I reformed the pile, pushed it into a neat shape and crossed to the window. I stared out onto the garden for a while, burning time to make it appear I was diligently assessing the information with the objective of making Hennessey believe I'd come to an assured judgement.

When a good half-hour had crawled by, I collected everything; laptop, paper and all. I knocked on the door. The thug opened up, his bulk blocking the doorway.

"Hennessey," I said.

The guy didn't reply, picked his nose, inspected the end of his finger before stepping back and allowing me enough room to squeeze through. I headed straight into Hennessey's room without knocking. Hennessey was ten feet or so back from the entrance, directly facing it, arms resting in his lap. He appeared to have been awaiting my return.

"So?" asked Hennessey when the door was closed behind me.

I held out the paperwork for him to take. "All very interesting."

"But you don't want the job."

"Correct."

"Understandable."

A lot easier than I'd imagined. Hennessey even smiled.

"I'll be going then."

"I said there were three parts to this, we only covered two."

"Okay." I doubted anything Hennessey could tell me would alter my mindset.

"You have personal experience with the Nudge Man."

"To repeat myself, I've never heard of him." What I wanted to say was, *'That's all you have? Pathetic.'* But I held back.

"He knows you, though." Hennessey dropped the paperwork on the floor beside him. "He planted the kiddie fiddling story. I have proof." Hennessey pulled another folder from under the cover across his lap. I tentatively approached, gripped the offering between two fingers as if it was an explosive which would take my arm. In many ways that was too late.

I didn't want to go over what had happened, but Hennessey wasn't letting me off. "The evidence is in there."

My legs felt weak. I lowered myself into the nearest chair, flipped the flap and began to read. Six years ago I was an investigative reporter at one of the larger London newspapers and on the up. Until I headed down, fast, after an accusation of accessing illegal websites and possessing pornographic images of children on my computer, rather disgusting images.

It was a complete fabrication and was eventually found to be so by the police. The charges were dropped, and I was released. But not before my reputation was trashed, the relationship with my wife and kids destroyed, no job and, lowest of the lowest, existing in Thanet, the place I now called home. I'd never known who'd destroyed my name or why. To date, I'd assumed it was someone I'd dissected in an article getting their revenge.

The confirmation was laid out in black and white. Access to my work laptop, the web addresses I was supposed to have visited detailed, a payment made to one site with my credit card, a report to the police, communication to the press to leak when I was being released on bail so they'd all be outside awaiting me. Even information on the cop who'd threatened to hound me until the end of my days to bring me down.

When I was done I returned my attention to Hennessey. He wasn't smiling now. "Feels terrible, doesn't it?" he said.

"There's no indication why I was targeted."

A shrug from Hennessey. "Then you can ask him yourself, when you find him. I mentioned redemption, Vaughan. There it is. In your hands."

Hennessey had played a blinder. I wanted the gig. I wanted the Nudge Man. "When do I start?"

"It's not a when, but a where. In prison."

Spooks

South Bank, London

Fifty-seven crow-flying miles away in the capital, a phone rang. A gentle purr, which sounded closer to a roar in the silence of the office. A hand reached out, lifted the receiver as if it was the only thing that mattered in the world. Which, to Blake Midwinter, it was.

"He's bitten," said the caller, a low-life by the name of Eric Hennessey, who Midwinter had met only once, something he cared never to repeat. "Get the ball rolling your end."

Offended by the brute's audacity, Midwinter applied his stiffest tone. "I'm perfectly aware of what's required, thank you."

"Good man." Hennessey disconnected; sounding and behaving as if it was *him* in charge.

Midwinter swallowed his irritation, with a promise to deal with Hennessey in the future. He brooded for a few minutes before making another call.

Initially Midwinter had been working a back channel with the Americans. The approach had come from them first, via one of their London-based "diplomats", a man called Six. Midwinter was the obvious starting point for the Americans, given his position in the British government as US liaison, a role he was perfectly qualified for; Midwinter held an honours degree and a masters in US politics, and his mother hailed from Colorado.

The Americans were interested in a UK citizen, somebody who called themselves the Nudge Man. Apparently, he'd upset the President. When Midwinter subsequently met Six, the American handed over some documentation and Midwinter promised to take a look.

In reality, Midwinter hadn't been particularly interested. The offence sounded limited in scope and the British government was hardly disposed to help the President, following his recent state visit. So Midwinter put the file to one side. But Six kept calling until eventually, tired of the constant hassle, Midwinter actually read what he'd been given. He sat up to attention. The Nudge Man was fascinating. Midwinter immediately took everything to his boss, Lord Dennis of Wetwang.

Another meeting with Six ensued. This time involving Lord Dennis and Six's boss, via a secure conference call. Her name was Melody Blessing. They were getting everywhere these days, women. There was one in charge of the CIA, another purportedly running the UK government. But that was another matter.

The Americans possessed the interest and the resources but were adamant they didn't want to operate on English turf without sanction, because doing so would violate their relationship. The Americans had plenty more data to share – enough to track down the Nudge Man. Were the British interested in helping an old ally?

They were, until Six dropped the bombshell. The Americans wanted the Nudge Man found and extradited under international law to stand trial in the US. Dennis had called the discussion to a halt there and then. No citizen was being repatriated over a tweet. The political fallout would be huge. The President being massively unpopular in the UK wouldn't help either. Dennis reckoned the press would have a field day over it. Several field days, probably.

Afterwards, Midwinter was disappointed. Crushed would be more accurate. He believed helping the Americans was the right thing to do. What did one person matter? Midwinter – without Dennis's knowledge – met Six one more time. Six wasn't against secretly renditioning the Nudge Man, but first somebody had to track the man down. Six offered Midwinter a job – over in Washington, working at the White House – in exchange for the Nudge Man. The President would be forever in Midwinter's debt. But Midwinter didn't have the tools to operate, and his dream died.

Until Hennessey rocked up.

Hennessey wanted the Nudge Man too. Hennessey claimed to have someone qualified to find the Nudge Man. It was dicey. Should Dennis find out, Midwinter would be out of a job and maybe in jail. But if Midwinter could get to the Nudge Man and present him to the Americans, Dennis wouldn't matter anyway. Midwinter leapt at the opportunity. At the time, Midwinter was so keen he hadn't asked how Hennessey knew to approach him. Only later did the thought niggle. By then it was too late to go back.

Midwinter rattled the connection once, so a dialling tone resulted, and punched the buttons. Code 001 for the United States, followed by 202, the area code for Washington DC. The rest of the number was a secret.

"Miss Blessing's office, how may I help you today?" A man, the gatekeeper to his superior and who never gave out his name.

"May I speak with Miss Blessing, please?"

"I'm sorry, sir, but she's out of the office right now. I can pass a message along if you like?" Midwinter was used to the typically excessive politeness.

"Can you give me her number, so I can call her directly?" said Midwinter.

"I apologise, sir, but we do not give out the details of colleagues' cell phones. I will pass your message on as soon as I can, though."

"Fine." Midwinter clearly wasn't getting through this guy. "Tell Miss Blessing, Blake Midwinter would like to speak with her."

"Blake Midwinter? Like in the Christmas song? Oh, how *joyous* for you, sir."

Midwinter wasn't so enamoured with the way this conversation was progressing. "If you can just tell her."

"I surely will. You have a great day now, sir!"

"You too." Midwinter cursed his educated politeness as he disconnected. All he'd really wanted to do was tell the annoying guy to sod off. He needed some caffeine, so he got his espresso machine going. He didn't have his own personal administrator to do it for him. Not yet. He'd definitely have one in Washington, though. Everybody did.

For a while, the machine filled the room with the sound of its straining. When it was done, Midwinter caught his phone ringing, but it cut off as he reached out a hand. The number was blocked. He swore. Might have been Blessing. Midwinter sipped the strong espresso, which was decent enough. A barista-trained PA, that's what he'd get. His phone trilled again, interrupting his self-absorbed musings. He answered on the second ring.

"Mr Midwinter, I understand you were trying to reach me." It *was* Blessing. She hailed from the wrong side of the tracks – originally Kansas, Missouri, but the accent was entirely buried under a more neutral drawl. Midwinter knew because he'd read her personnel file.

"Thanks for calling me back," he said. "I wanted to confirm when you're travelling over? Then I can have you collected from the airport. Full diplomatic service, of course."

"That won't be necessary as I'm remaining Stateside now."

Midwinter was surprised. Last time they'd spoken, Six had told Midwinter that Blessing was as keen as mustard to handle the operation herself. Now she'd seemingly gone cold. As one schooled in subterfuge, suspicion reigned. "What's changed?"

"The President has other, more important issues to resolve right now."

It was a smooth response, entirely believable. The man's government was a mess, reeling from one problem to another, almost entirely self-created, often via social media. Even so, something felt off. Midwinter had spent enough time around politicians to recognise bullshit.

"Does that mean you're not interested at all?"

"My government greatly values all the benefits our unique affiliation brings, Mr Midwinter." It was a non-answer and Blessing made the connection between their two countries sound anything but singular. "However, it's all about prioritising. No point chasing a spirit if the President is out of a job, now is there?"

"I suppose not." There had been talk of impeachment pretty much from before he'd even been sworn in.

"Good, I'm glad we're in agreement. You have my administrator's number. If you would be so kind as to keep me informed via that communication channel, I'd be forever in your debt. You have a great day."

Midwinter was poised to push back but Blessing had already rung off. "Damn Americans. Think they own the bloody world."

He replaced the receiver, stood, leaned against the wall, looked out the window of his small office over the Thames. Just up the river were the Houses of Parliament. Where all the deceit took place. Men and women peddling half-truths between themselves, each other and everyone else. Which was why Blessing knew nothing of Hennessey nor of his ongoing discussions with Six.

Midwinter let his vision settle on the seat of government once more. The office bearers believed they were the power, even though they told the public otherwise. His bosses at MI6 assumed they ran the country through their secrets and lies. But Midwinter knew it was actually the Americans who called the shots. Because they did own the world.

So Midwinter wanted the Nudge Man.

Badly.

Research and Development

Wimpey Estate, Broadstairs

Before I knew it, I was pulling up on the drive outside my house, a 1970s boxy semi in a cul-de-sac on a purpose-built estate on the edge of Broadstairs. There's an industrial park one side, a cabbage field and a looming white water tower the other. Affordable was about the best that could be said of my abode. All the road names had a tree theme, mine was The Maples. Beside the house was a patch of public grass where some of the local kids congregated to play football on sunny days, the little bastards.

I couldn't remember any of the last thirty-five minutes getting home. I'd done the lot on autopilot, while my front brain analysed the discussion with Hennessey. I turned the engine off.

Before I'd departed, Hennessey had made a financial offer. He handed me a credit card, black rather than gold, for expenses. There would be a six-figure bonus at the end, when I found him.

The Nudge Man.

He might be the key to my life achieving a balance again. My family back. Getting off Thanet forever.

I was in, regardless of the financial benefits, and we'd shaken hands. Finally, Hennessey assured me there would be no problem accessing the prison to see whoever I was supposed to, that he'd make a few calls "to make it happen".

I removed everything from the passenger seat – my laptop along with the ream of documentation Hennessey had on the Nudge Man and his activities – and went inside, not bothering to lock the car. Inside, I dumped my mobile and the paperwork on the dining table where nobody actually ate and plugged in the laptop. The charge was low. I grabbed a beer from the fridge, didn't bother with a glass.

My mobile rang. Hennessey already.

"10am tomorrow morning," he told me when I answered. "HMP Swaleside."

"Who am I seeing?"

"Pomfrey Lavender."

I burst out laughing. It was one of the most ridiculous names I'd ever heard. "You're taking the piss, right?"

"I don't joke about such matters, Mr Vaughan. Remember, this is the Lord's work."

"Of course, sorry." I wasn't.

"Keep in touch."

"Sure."

A thought occurred to me. "Do you know Aaron Conn?"

Hennessey sounded puzzled. "I'm not familiar with the name. Who is he?"

"Nobody. It doesn't matter."

"Frequent contact remember?"

"I will."

Hennessey cut the call. So, if Conn wasn't down to Hennessey, who the hell was he working for? Assuming Hennessey, once a criminal of the first order, was telling the truth, of course. I should have asked him face-to-face, so I could read his expression. Anyway, for now it didn't matter. HMP Swaleside and Pomfrey Lavender were first.

The address for the prison was easy to find, a matter of seconds via a popular map website. I spent a little longer reviewing the facility itself. An HMP page helpfully told me Swaleside was a grouping of three facilities. Overall it was classified as "Category B" – for inmates who did not require the highest level of security but would pose "a large risk to the local population should they escape". Half the prisoners were lifers. I felt sorry for the neighbours. I bet the prison was a major drag on local house prices.

Swaleside's notoriety was because of its past internees – Michael Bettany, a convicted spy; and the recently released Kenneth Noye, an infamous crook convicted of killing a man in a road rage incident, yet previously acquitted of the murder of a policeman he stabbed to death. Noye was also involved in the ill-famed Brink's-Mat robbery as a fence. I felt sorry for myself now because I'd be entering the lion's den.

Enough of that. Focus on Pomfrey Lavender.

There couldn't be many people in the world with that name. As part of the information pack, Hennessey had supplied his bio. Joined the army at sixteen, Coldstream Guards, reached the rank of sergeant. Served in a number of war-torn regions – Afghanistan and the like. He'd resigned his commission, moved back to the UK and ... disappeared. Not just out of the army, but off the grid. No explanation, his service terminated, and fallen from sight.

Until a couple of months ago, when he'd been detained by the police in a café on a back street in Gravesend. His crimes

were many – armed robbery, affray, actual bodily harm, assault
with a deadly weapon and so on. Violent and aggressive. Lavender pleaded guilty in court and the judgement was swift – a
minimum of fifteen years. There was nothing on where Lavender had lived between leaving the army and his arrest – what
he'd been up to beside his life of crime.

Next in the file were some photographs of Lavender. One
from his soldiering days – a head and shoulders shot. High
cheekbones, shaven head and diamond-hard eyes. Then his
mug shot from when he was arrested. He had a full head of
long, wavy hair and a beard. Tattoos were obvious where there
hadn't been any previously. I put the file to one side, hit the
world wide web.

Lavender appeared not to have a social media presence,
not even one before his incarceration. Expected for a drop-out.
Why disappear, then throw updates all over Facebook or self-
ies on Instagram? I searched the news outlets around the time
of Lavender's arrest. There was virtually nothing. A splash on
the front page of the local rag, *The Gravesend Reporter*, a smaller story on the inside of the wider distributed *Kent Messenger*
but little else. Lavender hadn't merited much. A brief interview
from the arresting officer said the police had received an anonymous tip about Lavender and they'd swooped. Had he been
targeted by the Nudge Man too?

Now I understood why Hennessey had arranged for the
visit. It was the only route to getting the detail. From the man
himself.

I had one more task I wanted to get sorted. I'd taken a shot
of Hennessey's map of the Nudge Man's activity on my phone.
The image was far too small to be useful, so I needed a larg-

er copy. I emailed it to my laptop and opened up the file on screen. Although larger, the detail was hard to properly focus upon. I'd have to take the analogue approach.

I owned an inkjet printer, buried somewhere in a cupboard. Once I'd tracked the machine down, I hooked it up to the laptop, installed and updated the drivers and tried to run off a page. But I was short of two vital ingredients – ink and actual paper.

After a twenty-five-minute return trip to the Westwood Cross shopping centre to get what I needed, I was back up and running. I got to work. There was a lot to do before tomorrow.

Lavender's Ills

Isle of Sheppey, Kent

Her Majesty's Prison Swaleside was located just outside Sheerness, the largest town on the Isle of Sheppey, a small, flat and marshy land mass of around forty-six square miles, joined to the United Kingdom by a road bridge just off the M2, and home to some 37,000 people. Go back a couple of thousand years and the island was called *Sceapig*, which meant "Sheep Pig". This was a farmer's atoll of poor soil suitable for livestock and not much else. It would have been an economically deprived area then and it remained so today.

The drive from my home took just over an hour. First approximately due west towards the capital, then a turn onto the Sheppey Crossing. Next, north-east for Sheerness, nestled on the northernmost tip of the island. The island's capital overlooked the Thames Estuary, along which massive boats navigated to reach the port of London from all over the world. I checked my rear view several times in case someone was following me.

The rain started when I began the crossing onto Sheppey, a heavy downpour. The windscreen wipers struggled to keep the glass clear. There wasn't much to halt the weather's assault, just the wide-open river for the elements to sweep along until it smacked into the coast.

The approach road to HMP Swaleside was inevitably long and straight. Maximum visibility for the guards. I drove slowly, turned onto the edge of the facility proper, halted by a red and white striped barrier. The gatehouse was a low, brick building. A man slid back a window – steamed-up interior, rain-dappled exterior. All I could see of him was a stern face and the standard uniform – white shirt, black tie and blue jumper. A badge, which I struggled to read, was pinned to his chest. He seemed oblivious to the rain which lashed down in gusts.

"Name?" he said.

"Harrison Vaughan. Here to see Pomfrey Lavender."

He maintained a poker face. He glanced down, presumably to check a visitor list. "I need to see some identification," he said. I passed over my driver's licence, retrieved from my wallet. He squinted at the photo, compared it to me, handed it back. "E wing, general and induction."

"Where do I park?"

"Just follow your nose, sir." He slid the window closed and disappeared from view behind the glass. The barrier rose silently. I drove through. The visitor spaces were close by the prison entrance, though not near enough to prevent me getting soaked between there and the entrance.

I was allowed into the prison building by another guard in identical garb, who pointed me to a desk in an otherwise open reception area. A third guard said, "ID again please, sir." I gave him my licence and a bank statement to confirm my address. He copied the documents, returned them.

"I need to take a photo and get a fingerprint scan," he said.

"No problem."

On the desk was a machine, with a lens on a rigid umbilical cord. He told me to look into the camera and not smile. I complied. Then I had to hold my thumb down on a backlit scanner the size of a credit card.

When we were done, the guard said, "No recording devices, cigarettes, lighters or e-cigarettes are allowed in the prison. Do you have any of these items?"

"A phone."

He held his hand out. I gave my mobile to him. "Thank you, sir. We'll keep this securely for you until you return."

Then a fourth and final guard took over. I had to pass through a metal detector, arranged like an open doorway, before being subjected to a pat down. It was like being at an airport.

Finally, after jumping through all the security hoops, I was led along corridors and through secured gates (unlocking them first, of course). The guard didn't speak a word – wasn't interested in conversation. His eyes were wary, his head constantly shifting. He walked at pace, forcing me to keep up.

As we progressed, a smell grew in my nostrils. A mix of body odour, fried food, sweaty feet. And a constant series of sounds. Metal banging, shouts, the occasional scream, doors slamming. In just a few short minutes the auditory and olfactory assaults became wearing and took me back to my own unpleasant incarceration.

Suddenly the guard stopped dead in his tracks, caught me by surprise. I almost ran into the back of him. He pushed open a door with his left hand, remaining in the corridor. Clearly, I was meant to go inside. So, I did. He didn't.

Inside was a blank room painted white. There were marks and scuffs on the walls. High windows coursed with rain, barred on the outside. A table and a couple of chairs. The door closed behind me, followed by the snap of a key. I tried the handle, locked in.

I was imprisoned; in prison with a woman.

Hutch

Interview Room B, HMP Swaleside

She stood with her back to me, head tilted to stare at the downpour. Cropped short grey hair, dressed in a conservative suit-like arrangement that's always puzzled me. Why do women think they should dress like men? Maybe it was a power thing. Or wanting to belong in a world they felt wasn't theirs. I'd always told my daughter, when she still lived with me, that she could be whatever she wanted, however she wanted. None of this imitate the male of the species bullshit, please. We're not exactly good role models.

"Why are you here?" she asked, still regarding the mizzled glass. "The real reason, not some fabricated answer."

"Research. For a book I'm writing."

She turned around, revealed a make-up-free expression of disbelief. Her chin was dimpled in the centre, freckles across her cheeks. "Really."

I shrugged. It was partially true. All reporters, good and bad, hanker to find *the* story. Therefore, it was a natural approach to cook up. And one Hennessey had fed me, after all.

"It seems everybody wants to be a writer these days," she said. "Sit." She pointed. This was someone used to being in charge. Trouble is, I've always railed against authority.

"I'll remain standing, thanks."

The woman smiled at me with bared teeth, the smile not reaching her deep green eyes. Reminded me of Bonzo. "As you wish."

"I assume you're the governor?" The prison website had only listed a name, no photograph. Although it didn't take a genius to work it out.

"That I am, Mr Vaughan, Jemima Hutch." She didn't offer to shake hands, which pleased me. It's one of those awkward acts which often never quite works. Too soft or too firm a grip or, worst of all, sweaty palms. "All these dangerous people are under my supervision. And you want to see one of them."

"I can't imagine this is the first time this prison has had a visitor."

"Of course not, but you're the only person who's requested to see Mr Lavender. And I received a phone call to arrange it, from London, of all places."

"Not a popular man, then?"

"Convicted criminals with a violent history are on many people's party invite list, Mr Vaughan. Look at Peter Sutcliffe the Yorkshire Ripper, or Ian Brady the Moors Murderer. There's been a multitude after those two their whole time inside. From pen pals to marriage proposals." Hutch shook her head, as if it was lunacy. "Mind you, Brady's dead now, good riddance. No, in this case Mr Lavender is more of an invisible man. No next of kin, no friends, no enemies."

"Why are you asking me all of this? As far as I understood the visit was all arranged."

"This is about you, not Lavender."

"Nothing's ever about me. I'm not that kind of person, I'm not particularly intriguing."

"I wouldn't say that, Mr Vaughan. I've read your police file."

"See anything interesting?"

"99% of the prison population protests innocence. It's only the hard core that don't. Lavender is in the 1%. You, though, are of the former."

"Because the charges were cooked up."

"Are you aware what you're getting yourself into? With Mr Lavender, I mean."

"I'm just a man working on a story, Governor Hutch."

"That's what I'm concerned about. Mr Lavender is a highly intelligent and extremely dangerous individual. He can be charming –your best friend. Equally he can be cold and distant. It all depends on whether he perceives you as a threat or an opportunity."

"Which do you see in me?"

"You're a risk to no-one other than yourself."

I felt like I should be insulted at Hutch's slight, but she was correct.

"I'll be careful, governor."

"Mr Lavender is prone to bursts of violence. He's been kept in solitary confinement since the first week he arrived."

"I understand."

"I hope you do, Mr Vaughan." Hutch stared at me for a long time before crossing the room, banging once on the door. Over her shoulder she said, "For both our sakes."

"Promise, cross my heart." I held back at "hope to die". Not until I knew who the Nudge Man was.

The door opened, Hutch departed, the door closed. I was awaiting Pomfrey Lavender, psychopath.

The Not So Private Dick

Interview Room B, HMP Swaleside

Pomfrey Lavender, when he arrived with Hutch and a prison guard either side of him, was entirely true to his record. Lavender stood regarding me across the table. He was shorter than me, a few inches beneath six feet. Not big, but muscly in a taut sinewy way – lean. His head was shaved to the bone, the long hair and beard from his arrest photos gone.

He wore loose-fitting trousers, a vest and tattoos. Lots of them. Vivid colours, complex designs. Sleeve tats. Chest tats. Neck tats. The most obvious of all was a very large crucifix, the top of which poked above the vest. The horizontal bar appeared to run between his nipples, so the vertical would probably end at his belly button.

His face, though, was an expression of zen-like calm, as if in a state of half meditation, alpha brain waves predominant. He appeared happy to see me, content with his lot, perhaps. Lavender lifted the chair away from the table, rather than dragging it, and lowered himself slowly like he was taking up the lotus position.

"Hands," said one of the guards. Lavender raised his arms in front of him, revealed cuffs. The nearest guard pulled out a set of keys from his pocket and got within reaching distance. The other guard stood opposite. Edgy, ready.

Scared.

An air of restrained tension arose from them, the opposite of that emanating from Lavender. The first guard unlocked the shackle around Lavender's left hand, swiftly looped it under a bar fixed to the table, before fastening the padlock again. The internal pressure dropped a notch and the guards shifted to either side of the room, both still tightly focused on Lavender. Hutch took a chair, sat ten feet away but in Lavender's eyeline. I'd been watching her. She wasn't bothered by Lavender at all.

"What's she doing here?" asked Lavender in a Northern English brogue, flat vowels, eyeing me like a lizard regards a fly. All narrow and focused.

Hutch answered on my behalf. "*She* insisted."

"Amazing. Your lips didn't even move," said Lavender to me. He rose to his feet, as far as he could while held with the chain which he yanked on, like a dog straining on a leash. The guards took a couple of steps forward, primed. "Interview over," said Lavender.

"We've not even begun," I protested.

"I talk to no-one in front of her."

I turned to Hutch, implored her with my best puppy-dog look. She beckoned me over. Lavender remained standing, hunched.

"I am *not* leaving you with him," she whispered.

"Clearly no discussion is going to happen unless you go."

Hutch grunted, not liking it. She said, "I don't like it."

"There's two guards here, he's handcuffed to the table, what can go wrong?" Hutch pursed her lips, appearing as if she was about to decline my request. "Anything happens, it'll be on my head."

Hutch glanced past me towards Lavender, eventually nodded. "I'll be outside, and the door will be ajar," she said. "If I hear one comment I don't like, I'll stop the interview immediately. Okay?"

"Deal."

Hutch crossed to the table, leant down to Lavender, but spoke to me. "He's a dangerous man, Mr Vaughan. Trust nothing Mr Lavender says. Do not get drawn in."

"Thank you for the compliment, governor," said Lavender.

"I'll be outside."

I regained my seat. Lavender shifted his attention back. He tilted his head slightly, spent a few moments regarding me. It was like being caressed with a snake's breath. He licked his lips, grinned slightly, showing teeth yellowed from tobacco. I returned Lavender's gaze with my own.

"I'm Harry," I said.

"Yes," he replied.

"You've seen some stuff over the years, Mr Lavender. Afghanistan in particular."

Lavender's eyes narrowed. "I'd say extremely unpleasant, all of which I don't care to remember, Mr Vaughan."

"Nice ink."

"I enjoy the pain, it helps me forget. You came at a good time. They're moving me soon. Somewhere higher security, even further away from people. Where nobody can get to me. Which means you clearly have friends in high places. The governor was very upset when she was told she had to let you in." Lavender grinned. Like Hutch before him, the humour was absent. "Let's cut to the chase. I assume you're here for The Nudge

Man. I'm of little consequence otherwise. What's your interest?"

"I'm pulling together a book."

His eyes dug in, chipped away at the illusion. "It's more than that though, isn't it?"

"I'm just a writer."

"Tell me." Lavender flickered out his tongue, licked his lips.

"There's nothing to say."

"There's always something to say. Share your story and you'll receive a reward in return. That's a promise."

I remembered Governor Hutch's very recent warning, not to trust a word Lavender uttered.

"Who sent you?"

"I'm freelance."

"Because nobody will employ you anymore. I read all about why."

I blinked. "None of it's true."

"So, who are you working on behalf of?"

"I'm doing this for me."

Lavender regarded me for a long moment. "I believe you. But this is one to walk away from, Mr Vaughan. Even if you think the prize is worth it."

"Why?"

"Sometimes the bodies just have to stay buried."

He was beginning to seriously irritate me. Time to push back. "I'll track The Nudge Man down, Pomfrey. Whether you help me or not."

"Rest assured, you won't succeed. I tried, see where she got me." Lavender indicated each of the four walls, one after the other. It was very theatrical. "I strongly advise you to give up your quest, right here and now."

I frowned. "You said 'she.'"

"Just a turn of phrase. I strongly urge you to follow my recommendation, and never even think of the Nudge Man again. You'll be better off."

"You're shackled to the table, what are you going to do?"

Lavender slowly raised his hands, so I could see them. The cuffs dangled from one wrist. Me and my big mouth.

The guards, realising Lavender was free, froze like rabbits in headlights. Lavender reacted first. He roared and threw himself across the table as I rose to make my escape. His momentum bowled me over as I was halfway to my feet. The chair, with me still in it, went backwards. I hit the deck hard, knocking the wind out of my lungs. I could have done with the oxygen as Lavender wound wiry fingers around my neck and applied pressure. His thumbs pressed hard into my windpipe.

"Leave them alone." A shout which turned into a shriek. "Leave them alone!"

As dark spots began to play across my eyes, the guards appeared in what was left of my vision. They tugged at Lavender. He released his grip briefly to knock one of the guards spinning. I dragged air into my lungs. Then Lavender was back on me, squeezing harder.

The last thing I saw before I blacked out was Lavender's manic snarling face inches away.

Heaven's Gate

HMP Swaleside Infirmary

When I came to, everything was white light. Was I in heaven at last? Had I finally left the cruel, heartless world behind? Had Hennessey been telling the truth about another worldly plane? Could I see my children from above rather than via social media?

The illumination dimmed as an approximation of a face swam into my blurred view. "He's awake." A male voice, not one I knew, tarred, gravelly. Did angels smoke? The head withdrew, replaced by another.

"I don't suppose I should say, *I told you so*, Mr Vaughan?" asked Governor Hutch.

I sighed. I wasn't dead after all. "Bollocks."

It was a further quarter of an hour before my vision settled. My throat, however, was another matter entirely. It was sore, bruised. I sounded like a worn-out toad when I spoke. Governor Hutch remained in the prison infirmary the whole time, although she paid me no attention until the doctor confirmed I was healthy enough for a stinging verbal interrogation.

"What the hell did you say to Lavender that got him so riled up?"

"Nothing much." I took a sip of water, barbed wire in my gullet. "I thought you were listening in?"

"I had a phone call. Stupidly, I took it. Repeat your conversation. Word for word. What you think is nothing may be the opposite to a man like Lavender."

So, I told Hutch. She listened with an increasingly irritated expression until, at the conclusion, she threw her arms up in the air with so much vigour I thought her shoulders were going to dislocate.

"He mentioned bodies?" said Hutch. I nodded. "I knew I should have stayed! I was such an idiot to believe everything would work out for the best."

"Sorry."

"I should bloody well think so."

"Why do you think he attacked me?"

"You threatened to out the Nudge Man, which was like waving a big red flag in front of his face. According to his psychological report, Lavender is suffering from London Syndrome and Cotard Delusion."

"What are they? I'm no medical expert."

"I assume you've heard of Stockholm Syndrome, Mr Vaughan?"

"King Kong."

"Excuse me?"

"The woman taken by the gorilla suffers Stockholm Syndrome. It's when captors develop a psychological alliance with their captors as a survival mechanism."

"You're brighter than I thought."

"Pleased to have confounded your expectations."

"Don't be. Lavender is beholden to the Nudge Man. He'll do anything to protect whoever they are. Your menacing crossed a line."

"What's the other condition? Cotard Delusion?"

"It's when the person believes they're already dead."

"Jesus."

"Jesus was dead, Mr Vaughan, then apparently came back to life. Maybe he was the first person to suffer Cotard Delusion?" I couldn't answer that one. Hutch continued, "Lavender's analyst concluded the condition results from his army days in the Middle East. He spent some time holed up in a house hiding from the opposition army. He shared the space with a murdered family."

"Poor bastard."

"I don't disagree. But it makes Lavender a very damaged man. If he considers himself dead already then he has nothing to lose."

"He said he was being transferred soon, is that why?"

"Lavender has to be located where his conditions can be better handled. We don't have the facilities here."

"Why now?"

"His issues have only just been diagnosed and verified."

I stared at the ceiling for a few moments, wondering and failing to understand what Lavender must have gone through. "Please thank whoever stopped him."

"That would be me."

"Oh, thanks then."

"Just be glad he's locked up."

"I am." And I was.

"Good, because he threatened to kill you, should you ever meet again. Men like Lavender don't issue warnings lightly. But rest assured, he'll be inside for many years to come."

I think I was supposed to show gratitude to Hutch once more at that point.

"One more question," I croaked.

"Fire away."

"You mentioned a phone call from London. When did you receive it?"

"Yesterday morning, why?"

I didn't answer because I was too busy thinking: that was before I'd even met Les in the Flag.

Lavender Plans

Cell 37, HMP Swaleside

Pomfrey Lavender lay on his cot, ignoring the guards as they backed out. The slam of his cell door echoed briefly along the corridor. Ordinarily, Hutch would be deciding right this minute what his penalty for attacking Vaughan would be. Lavender was already in solitary – had been within days of arriving, as was the plan – so removing further human contact wasn't really possible.

From past experience, the punishment would be the denial of exercise and any form of entertainment. However, tomorrow Lavender should be moved north so recrimination for his actions would be short-lived.

He considered how events had unfolded with the idiot reporter – of course Lavender had known who Vaughan was and what he wanted. On reflection, Lavender couldn't be sure whether his words and actions had got through to Vaughan, only time would tell. If not, then maybe he'd have to take Vaughan down. For all their safety.

Lavender went to the hiding place behind the toilet, withdrew the Samsung smartphone that had been smuggled in for him. He switched it on, checked the charge. Plenty left. Lavender possessed a store of SIM cards which he rotated periodically, flushing the old one down the toilet when he was literally done.

The signal dropped in. Every time Lavender expected to obtain a message stating 'No signal' when the prison authorities finally saw sense and implemented a blocking system. That day had not yet arrived and after this message it wouldn't matter anyway. Two bars, plenty of reception for what he needed. He texted: "2morrow still a go?"

The response was immediate. "Yes." A pause, then another text came in. "What about Vaughan?"

Lavender tapped out a carefully worded reply. "May need further persuasion."

"In hand."

Lavender switched off the mobile, hid it again and lay down on his bed. He had always known this day would come. That forces would mass in opposition. It was why he'd gone to prison in the first place. A concerted effort to track the Nudge Man down was inevitable. The Nudge Man, able to act in ways Lavender could only dream of, using technology where Lavender relied on his quick fists and considerable guile. But now, Lavender needed to be back on the outside. To stop anyone and everyone, he had to be. His final mission, possibly.

Soon he'd be on the other side of the wall and fully effective once more.

An Obscene Offer

Old Town, Margate

After Hutch's revelation I'd wanted to get away from her, HMP Swaleside and Lavender as fast as possible, no matter how crap I felt. I dressed, waved off the prison doctor's concerns and drove back to Margate.

En route I thought over everything that had happened in the last twenty-four hours. Hennessey's money had never been the clincher and I was starting to wonder whether clearing my name was relevant if I ended up dead before I could do so. I needed a solution.

Beer.

I found a spot to park the car in a bay at the foot of the cliffs beneath the Winter Gardens, before walking around the rear of the Turner Centre art gallery to the Old Town.

Inside, the Flag was unusually empty. It was that lull before lunch. Soon people would have an hour off from work and pop down for a top-up. My only compatriots were Tiny Al (he's huge, by the way), who was feeding coins into the slot machine over in the corner, and a northerner by the name of Thwaite, stood at the bar cracking the shells of monkey nuts. Thwaite liked to spread the detritus around to annoy the landlord, Dick, who was too nervous to do anything about the mess. Thwaite was like that. Controlled aggression just beneath the surface of his voluminous moustache.

"Has Les been in?" I asked Dick.

Dick carried on spit-polishing a glass with a rag that was more grime than textile. He possessed a dishwasher, although it had probably never been turned on because cold water in a sink with a bit of soap was cheaper. Dick held the glass up to the mote-filled light and regarded it carefully, the backdrop the huge George Cross nailed up on the wall, the clearest statement of patriotic xenophobia possible.

"I can't say unless silver crosses my palm," said Dick. He leant on a wooden barrel into which Thwaite stuck an arm, withdrew more monkey nuts. This was Dick's most recent commercial venture, designed to appeal to new customers. It failed, but Dick didn't like change or people he didn't already know, so it was always a puzzle when he attempted these periodic ventures.

"I'm all out of every metal you can think of." I didn't tell Dick I possessed a couple of notes. He wasn't getting what little money I owned. I needed to eat. However, it was one of those circular things. I was expected to cough up cash to find Les, cash I wouldn't have until I found Les, who owed me. Another one of life's ironies.

"Then I can't help," shrugged Dick and wandered off to serve Tiny Al; a simple man who had simple desires. He was waving his glass to get Dick's attention like he was holding a banner at a parade.

I needed the bathroom, a sudden urge. The nearest public toilets were in the New Town, or over on the harbour arm. Both were an unwelcome walk. Dick's bogs were significantly nearer, but distinctly more unpleasant.

I headed past Dick, ignored his stare, using the facilities without buying something was a red line for the landlord. Down a short corridor to the bathroom. There was only one. For men. There wasn't a Ladies that I knew of. Women weren't even allowed over the threshold. That had happened once in my memory and had been a disaster. She'd thrown Tiny Al out of a window. So, add sexism to the racism charge against Dick.

Within the bathroom were floor-to-ceiling tiles and a large drain at the centre. It was basically a wet room. Reputedly, Dick entered once a year and sluiced away the assorted bodily fluids. I shuddered before pushing tentatively at the door, knowing what was coming. It was dim within, the bulb broken and just a grime-covered small window, the glass inset with wire, high up in the wall. There was a drip, drip sound and a scurry of urgent feet. By the stench, it had clearly been a while since Dick's last annual hosing down of the place.

I should turn around, take the long walk elsewhere, but the pressure from my bladder was too great. I shut my eyes, held my nose and felt my way in. The door slammed behind me like a coffin lid.

After moving along two walls I discovered a pipe running vertically. Success, one of the two urinals. Trying exceptionally hard not to look or breathe through my nose, I focused solely on the task at hand. Like being faced with Medusa, I had an almost overwhelming urge to open my eyes, which I fought against with every fibre of my irrelevant being. As a result, I was completely unaware of the presence beside me until I heard a cough. It was impossible to close my ears with both hands engaged. The door must have been opened and closed silently. That was a mean feat in itself.

"I'm just here for a piss," I said, "nothing else."

"Good," said Thwaite. "I'd hate to break your arm for getting the wrong idea."

"I'm relieved." I actually was. I zipped up, kept my other hand over the bits of my face that allow air in an out of my body. Opened my eyes. Thwaite loomed over me. He's a big guy. All was in shadow. The moustache entirely covered his mouth. It was the eyes, though. Intense, restless. Like Lavender's.

"You wanted Les," he said.

"He owes me money."

"What's new?" Thwaite snorted in an approximation of amusement. "He's not been in since yesterday, left just after you did. In a hurry."

"Any idea where he went?"

"No, but he'd just taken a phone call."

"Okay, thanks. I'm leaving now." I went back into the corridor, not washing my hands first, Thwaite following.

He said, "Someone is looking for you. Now, in the bar."

"Who?"

"Never seen him before, but I know the type." Thwaite went to the fire exit. "Which is why I'm leaving. You should too. But you won't, so be careful." Then he hit the fire door push bar. A brief slash of bright sunlight and he was gone.

Out in the pub three pairs of eyes were fixed firmly on my every move. I paused, as if caught in a spotlight. Dick tilted his head. I thought he was telling me to get out too. Or he had a twitch. He did it again. Then he rolled his eyes and pointed away from him. My sight followed the invisible path from digit to interloper.

Conn, the lawyer, stood in the middle of the carpeted floor, looking like he'd stepped in something nasty. Which was a distinct possibility. He wore a fresh suit but had ditched the tie, his collar open at the neck. He held a briefcase, soft hands crossed in front of him, both grasping the handle. Bizarrely, a long chain connected his wrist to the case.

Dick had a scowl on his mouth the width of the North Sea. The landlord disliked anyone and anything he didn't understand. Which was a significant aggregate.

"Mr Vaughan, I've been looking for you everywhere," said Conn. "I heard you were often to be found in this, uhm, establishment."

Dick turned to me. "What did he call my pub?"

"Establishment, it's a posh word for boozer."

"Oh." Dick was slightly mollified. "That's good, right?"

"Definitely." I might have bought Conn a few minutes of survival.

"Is there somewhere we can converse?" asked Conn. "Privately?"

"We can sit in the corner and whisper. Good enough?"

It clearly wasn't, however Conn seemed to be a man who dealt with compromise rather than confrontation. He nodded.

"As we're remaining, what can I get you?" Conn moved towards the bar. "We still have to celebrate your fortuitous release from the police station yesterday."

"A lager," I said.

"In a bottle?"

Dick actually huffed at that. If he possessed a fridge it too would be switched off to save on the electricity.

"A pint from the pump is fine."

"Are you from London?" asked Dick of Conn. Tiny Al took an interest in the developing conversation, pausing in stuffing the slot machine during his losing streak.

Conn nodded, apparently unaffected by the landlord's acrid glare. "How could you deduce that fact?"

"Most people round here have proper drinks. Except Londoners. Everything I serve is in a pint glass."

"What about wine?" Conn smiled.

Dick pulled the lager. "As I said mate, *everything*."

"What's the bitter like?" Conn leant down and read the handwritten sign on the pump. "Cinque Porter. Fulsome, I expect?"

"Try it later," I suggested, deferring a potential poisoning episode. It wouldn't be the first.

"Then I'll partake of the same refreshments as my friend here," decided Conn. Dick scowled at an opportunity missed. "Would you please transport said drinks to our table?"

"What do you think?" Dick held his hand out for payment, even though only one pint was half pulled. There was a distinct air of mistrust hanging around, similar to mustard gas in a First World War trench.

"Credit card?" said Conn.

"This gets worse by the second," said Dick. "You're *really* pushing it now."

"Cash is best," I told the lawyer. "I'll pay," I offered.

"Thank you" said Conn.

"With your money."

Conn didn't bat one of his perfect eyelids, pulled out a tenner. "Is that sufficient?"

"Probably not."

He shrugged, threw in an extra fiver as if it was confetti.

"Why don't you go and sit down?" I asked Conn.

"What an arse," said Dick when Conn was gone. "I'm half tempted to ban you, just for knowing him."

"This is only the second time we've met."

"He said you were friends." Suspicion was to Dick like body odour to Little Al – a permanent companion.

"Just a turn of phrase."

"Don't make a habit of it."

I carried the lagers to the table where Conn was currently inspecting his palm and picking something off it.

"The table needs a clean," he said.

"Everything needs a clean. Here." I handed over his pint. "You haven't told me what you want."

"It is not what I want, Mr Vaughan, but what I can *give*."

"Which is?"

I took a gulp of my drink then sprayed it everywhere when Conn said, "One million pounds sterling."

If I Were a Rich Man...

The English Flag, Margate
I wiped my chin, staring at Conn. "A million quid, just like that?"

"Not quite." Conn smirked. "You would have to earn it, of course."

"How?"

"By doing nothing."

"Sounds like my kind of work."

"Excellent." Conn raised his glass in a brief salute and took a draft.

I waited, assuming Conn was going to confirm what I wasn't supposed to do. Eventually he caught my look. "Oh, yes, of course. Your objective is to *not* find the Nudge Man."

My motto is "when in doubt" – and I was in plenty of that – "bullshit". So, I did. "Who?"

Conn sighed. He pushed the pints out of the way and deposited the briefcase onto the table. He rolled the combination locks, a couple of clicks and the lid was up, blocking my view of the interior. He fished around inside, withdrawing a Mac laptop and a thin cardboard sleeve. He closed the case.

Conn opened the sleeve, slid over a photo. I was the star of the glossy rectangle, all moody in black and white. Me in my car staring upwards at a barrier. Then another where I was climbing out of the vehicle, then walking along a corridor, entering a room, finally Lavender following the same path.

"This has been grabbed from a CCTV feed at HMP Swaleside," I said.

"We have some highly competent technicians," replied Conn in a droll, ultra-matter of fact tone. I wanted to punch him.

"Who's we?"

"I am simply a lawyer, Mr Vaughan."

"With a briefcase chained to your wrist and offering me a small fortune. Who's your client?"

"I can't answer. I'm bound by a fealty of non-disclosure. You've been asked not to undertake a task. The small fortune, as you put it, is to change your mind regarding the aforementioned activity. To demonstrate my seriousness on the matter I'm willing to transfer the sum to your bank account right here and now."

Conn started the laptop, which was almost as thin as the pile of photos. Eyes down, he tapped away on the keyboard. After a minute he said, "If you would care to sit adjacent to me?"

I moved around beside him. The screen had one of those diffusers on it whereby unless you were looking directly at the monitor, it appeared black.

Conn tapped at the keyboard. He turned the laptop towards me. He was in my bank account, the screen showing the balance. £1.39, which was pretty good.

"How ...?"

Conn held up a hand, palm outwards. Conn twisted the laptop slightly, the diffuser meant I couldn't see what he was doing. He tapped away briefly, then paused, had a drink.

"What's going on?" I asked.

"We're waiting."

"For?"

Conn's mobile buzzed. He checked the screen, tapped at the keyboard again. "This." He showed me my bank balance again. It now read, £1,000,001.39.

"That belongs to you," he said, "if you accede to my request and make no enquiry after the Nudge Man." Conn returned to his briefcase while I contemplated my potentially enriched life. He pushed a document at me. "This is a contract outlining your obligation and the remuneration for the accompanying lack of effort."

"Let me get you another one." I pointed at his half-drunk pint "On me." Strictly, as I was using what had been Conn's cash, this was a lie.

"Very generous, thank you."

Munificence was nothing to do with it; I just needed time to think. A million pounds? A man could do a lot with seven figures. On one hand I was being paid twice, by a God-fearing ex-gangster and some invisible benefactor. On the other I had a death threat from Lavender hanging over my head, should I go after the Nudge Man. On the third hand there was a potential opportunity to get my family back. It was a difficult choice. At the bar I paused for a moment too long.

"You all right, son?" said Dick, who was splitting monkey nuts with primate abandon. Shell shards were strewn across the bar. Nobody ate the bloody things besides Dick and Thwaite. "Because if you're going to die, best take yourself off to somewhere that gives a shit."

"I'm fine," I lied again.

"What do you want?"

"Want?"

"Jesus, son, what's up with you? This is a pub. Booze, crisps, nuts, that's what we do. Pick one, pick several, maybe. Just get on with it. I'm busy here."

As you already know, the bar was practically empty. Tiny Al, a terrible eavesdropper, sniggered.

"A pint of your finest Cinque Porter, please."

Tiny Al halted his incessant feeding of the relentlessly ravenous slot machine. Dick paused, mid-chomp. Both Al and Dick stared at me in a rancid mix of confusion and slack-jawed horror. Dick bent at the waist, leant to the side, glanced behind my back, presumably to check no-one was holding a gun to my spine.

"You're *voluntarily* requesting to drink my beer?" said Dick when upright again, blinking like it was going out of fashion.

"Your beer is your finest, isn't it?"

This placed Dick in a quandary. He couldn't admit the stuff he charged less than a couple of quid for was actually brewed by his own grubby mitts in the cellar beneath our feet and was probably solely responsible for a flow of the unwary punter to the Accident & Emergency department at the local hospital. Rumour had it that one poor sod had even gone blind.

"*You* want *my* beer?"

"No." I hiked a thumb over my shoulder. "He does."

"Oh." A serial killer grin spread across Dick's countenance. "Coming right up."

Dick pulled down his smartest, saliva-polished glass, held the throat beneath the brass nozzle and heaved on the bar pump. An overly thick, suspiciously crude oil-coloured liquid chugged out. He deposited the pint onto the bar, breathing heavily. "What about you?"

"Lager again."

I paid. Two beers, I still had money in my pocket afterwards and still more, a hell of a lot more, in my bank account. This was truly a bizarre day all round.

Back at the table I administered Conn his concoction and he handed me the contract. "Please examine the proposal in detail."

Before I could lower my eyes to what would no doubt be legal jargon, the pub's double doors bounded open. Heralded with a blast of white sunlight, someone stood in the entrance like a gunslinger in a bad spaghetti western.

"Oink, oink," said Dick.

Tiny Al, heeding the warning, headed out of the bar towards the toilets at speed. He'd be going the same way as Thwaite, via the fire exit to the back alley and the car park where no cars actually parked. Conn, demonstrating equally surprising speed, closed the laptop.

"What can I get you, Sergeant?" asked Dick. "On the house, of course."

"Nothing, thanks," said Gregory. "I'll only be here long enough to discuss a murder with Mr Vaughan."

I'll readily admit Gregory's statement was unexpected. But I kept my cool as I had two points on my side. First, Gregory didn't have any supporting uniform behind him, so he probably wasn't arresting me. Second, and most importantly, I hadn't killed anyone.

"Who's dead now?" I asked.

Conn appeared equally interested in the answer. "And will my client be requiring a lawyer?"

"Not at this juncture," said Gregory. "I just need Harry's help."

"I would advise against doing so," said Conn, "and we have not concluded our discourse, either."

Gregory, clearly tired of talking, whistled and a couple of uniforms came through the doors. I'd got that wrong then. They behaved slightly more aggressively than their superior officer and before I could protest I was bundled out of the Flag, into the rear of a police car and was travelling at a speed well above the limit, Gregory beside me and the contract still in my hand. I folded the document and pushed it into an inside pocket.

On the upside, at least my reputation would be a tick higher with the regulars. On the downside, I'd failed to finish my drink.

A Sticky Ending

Cliftonville, Margate

We left the Old Town and turned right up Fort Crescent. I'd fully expected the journey to be one of moments, curtailed by a sharp right turn into the police station before I was hustled into the same interview room as yesterday. In fact, we sailed right past. The road hugged the coastline, multi-floored terraced houses to the right, all with commanding views of the muddy sea opposite.

"Where are we going?" I asked.

"To where your erstwhile guru, Les Garrett, lives."

We raced past the Winter Gardens, an entertainment scene sunk into the chalk cliffs, same with the Lido leisure centre and the Walpole Bay Hotel. All were linked by the fact that they were witnesses to glories long past. Fading relics attempting to reinvent themselves, like the town itself. Success varied, from outright fail to minor triumph.

Within a mile or so, the crowded houses fell away, replaced by the grander, detached residences which marked Margate, evolving into the Palm Bay area of Cliftonville where the real money had been, years ago. To the left, tennis courts, bowling greens and a new-looking, low-slung, walk-in National Health Service medical surgery for the town's druggies and alcoholics.

Eventually we turned onto one of the leafy avenues. The houses were just as impressive here too. The car pulled up a few hundred yards from the main drag outside a high, red brick and flint wall. The uniform posted outside the gates crossed to a keypad set on a post and tapped in a code. The barrier silently slid back.

We drove through the entrance, hitting a gravel drive. The house was huge, possessing an imposing, double-fronted façade which looked as if it belonged in the early 1900s.

"Is this it?" I asked.

"Yes," said Gregory.

"Wow." It was an impressive asset for such a tight bastard. Which was probably how he'd acquired it. The wealthy were apparently known to be stingy. Something I couldn't appreciate having never even got as far as the "w" in wealthy. "And I freelanced for Les. He was hardly a mentor, sergeant."

Gregory shrugged. The driver bounded out of his seat and opened my door. I felt like royalty. Gregory left too and awaited me by the front entrance, which was an equally majestic iron-studded oak, weathered into a gnarly grey.

I followed him inside. The hall was spacious; floor laid with pristine black and white tiles; equally spaced antique furniture; wood half way up the walls, the space above white-painted plaster, and dotted with morose art of browns and blacks framed in gilt, mainly portraits and a few landscapes. A single staircase extended upwards and a corridor beyond stretched away into the middle distance.

Gregory, without pause to absorb the magnificence, took the stairs – which were carpet in the centre, dark polished wood at the edges. Halfway up, the steps switched back on themselves. The wall was broken up by a stained glass window, some heraldic emblem in the centre. Perhaps Les had delusions of grandeur?

At the apex, another passageway stretched in either direction. More paintings, more furniture, more doors, all closed. Except for one. Which was directly opposite where Gregory had paused.

I spied, with my little eye, the glaring white of a bathroom. Being nearly as good a detective as Gregory, I guessed that was our destination. I awarded myself the hint of a smile when I was proven correct.

"Something funny?" asked the copper.

I shook my head. Because the bathroom wasn't entirely as expected. Internally it possessed all the typical paraphernalia (although the bidet was a bit unusual). And it was incredibly clean, the stench of bleach overpowering.

"What am I looking at?" I asked.

Instead of replying, Gregory bent down and picked up a handheld strip light. When he flicked it on, the bulb emitted a calming neon blue light. Gregory shone it on the wall above the bath, revealing a patina of drops, followed a large smear which ran from shoulder to knee height. "It never ceases to amaze me how far a few pints of blood can go," he said.

I felt like throwing up. "I've seen enough."

"Good," said Gregory, "because we need to talk."

"Fresh air first."

The garden was just as neat as the house. Certainly not low maintenance. An abundance of lawn, shrubs and flowers in borders which required regular tending. The soil was well tilled, weeds non-existent. This must have been Les's third love, after the paper and the horses. I couldn't imagine him paying a gardener. It explained the ever-present crud under his finger-nails.

Gregory dragged out a wrought-iron chair from beneath a similarly constructed table – scraped the concrete patio in a fashion which put my teeth on edge. The patio extended from expansive glass doors which opened out from the living room, so even on days when the weather was bad the garden would be part of Les's experience. This was all quite shocking.

"What is?" asked Gregory.

I must have vocalised my thoughts. "I'm having to reconsider my view of Les."

"Death does that."

"Are you sure it was him?"

"It's a theory. Certainly, somebody suffered here, given the quantity of blood and the spatter marks. Either at Les's hand or someone else's. The pathologist reckons a slashed artery. Little chance of coming back from that."

"What's this got to do with me?"

"Seems you were the last person to speak to him. In your grotty local pub, yesterday."

"Les was alive when I left him."

"Who's to say you didn't follow him home?"

"Why would I do that? I didn't even know this was where he lived until you dragged me here."

"Friends of Eric Hennessey tend towards violence."

"I don't know Hennessey."

"You're working for him."

"Hardly."

"I have it on excellent authority that you were at his house only yesterday."

I decided stony silence was the best option.

Gregory leant in towards me. "People who play with fire usually get burnt. Look at Les."

"He was associated with Hennessey?"

"Who sent you to the scrap yard?"

"I was just passing by..."

Gregory cut me off. "And saw the dog, I know. I also know that's bullshit. It was Les who asked you to go, wasn't it?"

"None of this makes any sense."

"Eric Hennessey owns O'Neal's. And if Hennessey wanted to ensure you were right place, right time it makes perfect sense. My colleague who arrested you at the scene has a connection to our mutual enemy. I'm sure of it, but I have no proof."

"Hennessey said he's found God."

"I seriously doubt Hennessey will be allowed through the pearly gates when it's his time."

"Does the lawyer belong to Hennessey as well?"

"Conn? He's a mystery. I'd like to understand more about his involvement."

Me too.

Gregory's phone rang. He fished the mobile out of his inside pocket, made half an apology, and wandered off a few feet, his back to me and the device pressed to his ear. The call lasted half a minute at most. When the sergeant regained his seat he wore a grim expression on his dingy face. "It seems Les has turned up. Well, some of him anyway."

"Some of him?"

Gregory nodded. "What's left is oozing out of the compactor at O'Neal's."

"Jesus."

"It's not divine intervention," Gregory leant in, fixed me with a beady eye, "it's Hennessey. That's who you're dealing with, Harry. People who are willing to kill in a gruesome fashion to make their point, to protect their business, whether they believe in the Almighty or not." I stayed quiet. Hennessey had claimed otherwise yesterday. Gregory eventually tossed out a resigned sigh. "When you're ready to talk, here's my card."

He dropped it onto the table. He left without another word.

I contemplated the world for a few minutes. Listened to the birds sing and the seagulls screech. Watched new growth on plants emerge into the early spring sunlight, until I decided it was time to revisit Hennessey.

I found the constable at the front gate. The car Gregory had whisked me here in was absent.

"He's gone," said the PC, stating the obvious, the way cops often do.

"Can I get a lift back into town?" I asked.

"I'm here on my own. You'll have to get a taxi or walk."

I didn't have enough money to waste on a taxi. "Great."

"At least it's not raining."

"There is that."

I got shambling. Half way back, the heavens opened. Somebody up there hated me.

Smash and Grab

Somewhere in London

The crash, when it came, was even harsher than Pomfrey Lavender had anticipated. Without a watch, Lavender was forced to estimate the timing. He'd been bracing himself for a good few minutes when the transport van was thrown violently to one side. There was the sound of rending metal, car horns and a scream. Despite his preparedness, his shoulder hit the wall of his temporary cell. A tiny cubicle he'd been expected to inhabit while being shifted between prisons. A firm seat and little else.

The van came to a halt and there was a moment of brief silence before muffled shouting outside and a groan from the other prisoner being transported in the adjacent cell. Lavender hadn't told him what was coming, of course.

Then the rattle of keys as the outer door was unlocked. Sunlight streamed in. The guard, a slightly overweight man employed by independent security firm G4S, looked scared shitless. Then again, when an aggressor, face concealed by a black balaclava, was pointing a sawn-off shotgun at your balls, fear was a perfectly natural reaction.

The guard fumbled as he searched for the right key to Lavender's cell. Shotgun shoved him forward to move him faster. The keys hit the floor. Shotgun slammed the butt of his weapon into the guard's stomach and he sagged to his knees, gasping for breath. Shotgun kicked the guard in the head, stepped over his prostrate form and scooped up the keys. He tried one after the other until he found the correct one.

Lavender departed as another form blocked the doorway. A second masked man, brandishing a sledgehammer, and another G4S guard, entered the space. The latter was young, barely into his twenties, Lavender guessed. Expected an easy life, a uniform and plenty of kudos with the ladies. As the youthful guard stared down at his unconscious colleague, Lavender reckoned his illusions were being stripped away, fast.

"Come on," said Sledgehammer.

"Open the other one," said Lavender.

"There isn't time!"

"Let him out. The cops will have their hands full chasing him down, as well as looking for me."

Sledgehammer stared at Lavender, eyes unblinking, mouth open while he thought.

Shotgun stepped forward, breaking the moment. He unlocked cell two, which was barely containing a huge man with rotten teeth and breath so bad Lavender was surprised he was still alive. Lavender pointed at the exit. His fellow prisoner needed no second bidding. Within seconds he was gone.

"Inside," said Shotgun, gesticulating for the young guard to enter the cell with his weapon. The guard meekly complied, Shotgun thumped the door shut. He and Sledgehammer crammed the unconscious guard into what had been Lavender's cubicle, locked both gates, dropped the keys on the floor.

"Let's move!" shouted Sledgehammer. There were sirens, faint in the distance but nearing. Sledgehammer jerked his head towards the exit and freedom, pointing Lavender in the right direction, but he had other things on his mind. He turned to the CCTV camera fixed in the corner of the van, behind a wire cage, and blew it a kiss.

Pomfrey Lavender, convicted violent offender, was free.

A Realisation Hits

Margate Old Town
    I entered the English Flag. I needed a pint (again) and to dry off. The rain beat at the door when I closed it, as if God hadn't thrown quite enough at me yet.

"Is it wet out?" asked Dick.

"No," I said. "I just tipped a bucket of water over myself for fun."

Dick shrugged. He didn't care, never went alfresco, as his insipid skin would attest. Only the climate inside mattered.

"Lager, please."

"I want a word first." Dick didn't wait for a response; just lifted the flap to allow me access to his personal space. I frowned. Going into Dick's domain was new.

A bleep from my mobile telling me I had a notification from a news app. The sound elicited a glare from Dick over his shoulder. He stabbed a finger into a sign he had recently hammered to the wall with vastly oversized nails. It depicted a mobile with a large red X through it – the message pretty transparent.

He descended a ladder into the cellar, meaning the update would have to wait. I left the phone in my pocket. The hatch was permanently open to allow Dick a fast exit should a fight kick off. Once we were underground, he closed the trapdoor and plunged us into relative darkness. I had to bend at the

101

waist as the cellar was only about five feet high. A few rays of light entered between floorboards above my head. The cellar was musty, damp. There was a squeak from nearby. My skin crawled. The space was on a par with the men's room. It smelled a lot better, though.

"Can we turn the light on?" I asked.

"Waste of electricity," said Dick, "besides, I know this place like the back of my hand." Which meant warts and a fungal disease. "I've got a problem."

"I've got plenty of those myself, thanks."

Dick prodded me in the chest. "*You're* the problem. And I want it to stop."

"What are you on about, Dick?" I was getting fed up of being pushed around.

"People, coming in here."

"The cellar?"

"No! My pub!"

"You don't want people coming to your pub?"

"Of course! But I only want a certain type of person. You know, regulars. Ordinary Englanders. Not weirdos, foreigners, like."

"What's this got to do with me?"

"It's your fault *they* all keep coming in."

"Who?"

"A Londoner, a cop and now *him*." I didn't bother pointing out London was in England.

"Who is 'him'?"

Dick nudged up the hatch a few degrees. A beam of light groped its way in. "Over there. An American." He spoke like he had something foul in his mouth.

I followed Dick's eyeline through the open hatch to a bloke perched on one of the stools, back against the wall. A pint of Dick's homebrew beer sat on the table in front of him. He certainly wasn't a regular in the Flag. He wouldn't even be a regular in Thanet by his appearance. I stopped breathing. He seemed familiar.

Slip-on shoes, chinos with a sharp crease, a golf shirt and sports jacket. Average height, hair and jaw shaved to the bone. A nice colour to his skin for this time of year. He may have been considered good looking if it wasn't for the sneer. In the right crowd he'd be anonymous. When there's fewer people in a room than fingers on your hand it's a different matter. The American reached inside his jacket, extracted a phone and began speaking.

"Deal with him," said Dick, dropping the hatch closed once more and breaking the spell.

"What do you mean?"

"I dunno. Just get him to leave. And then make sure no more of them return. Otherwise you're barred. Forever."

Dick flung back the flap and pushed me up the ladder. But the American had disappeared, his half-finished pint the only evidence he'd really been there. I went outside. He was nowhere in sight. I headed back to the bar where Dick had my drink waiting and his hand held out for payment.

I passed over a ten pound note. My hand shook.

"You all right, son?" asked Dick. "Looks like you've had a nasty shock."

"I'm fine," I lied. Because the American seemed just like the guy who had been following me recently.

My phone bleated again, another glare from Dick. I waited for him to turn his back before fishing it from my pocket. The news app headline screamed, 'Prison Breakout'. As I read the story, my stomach sank deeper and deeper.

A ram raid on a G4S van transporting two dangerous prisoners from HMP Swaleside to an undisclosed location further north. Only one of the escapees was named, Liam Stubbings, but there was a photo taken by a witness on a mobile phone. It was from a distance and not particularly clear, but the resolution was sufficient for me to recognise the prisoner glancing over his shoulder. Pomfrey Lavender. I sat on one of the tall bar stools, the risk of my legs giving way greater than that of the chair's.

Lavender, free and on the run. I read the story again, slowly. The job sounded well organised. Neatly done and over quickly. So yesterday he must have known he was escaping, meaning his threat to come after me was real.

I needed the police. And I had just the man to help me. I asked Dick to look after my unfinished beer and got walking. Very quickly, one eye over my shoulder.

America First

US Embassy, London

Melody Blessing waited impatiently for the call to connect. She felt dizzy from jet lag. She hadn't slept well, and her body clock definitely hadn't adjusted yet. When Six finally answered, she said, "What the hell took you so long?"

"I had to get somewhere safe," replied Six, judging by his tone, unaffected by Blessing's rebuke. Six was a Californian by birth, Los Angeles, specifically. To her mind, all bullshit and façade. Perma-tan style, perfect hair, plastic surgery.

"Where are you now?"

"On site." Which meant Margate.

"And the target?" She meant Vaughan but wasn't saying so over the phone.

"Here too, of course."

"Have you made contact yet?" Blessing was becoming more exasperated. This was painful.

"No."

"Why?"

"The timing wasn't right."

"When will it be?"

"At the point I decide. You need to leave it to me to choose. I'm an expert at these things." Meaning Blessing wasn't.

Blessing squeezed the bridge of her nose between thumb and forefinger. Strictly, Six was right. This wasn't really her game. She hadn't worked in the field before. A desk jockey, no blood under her fingernails. Six knew it, which was why he was treating her with contempt. Blessing realised she needed to take control of the situation, get near to Vaughan and stay with him.

"We have to be working on this together," said Blessing.

"Right." Scepticism in Six's tone.

"The President said so."

"He did?" Interested now.

"Absolutely."

"Okay." Acquiescence.

"I'm on my way down. Where are you staying?"

"A guest house in Canterbury."

Blessing didn't know where that was. It wouldn't be next door to Margate, for sure. It was good Blessing hadn't unpacked because she'd be sleeping somewhere else tonight. She told Six she'd see him soon and ended the call.

But when she reached Canterbury she found Six had checked out and disappeared. There was only one person who could save her now.

Harrison Vaughan.

Banged to Rights

The Police Station, Margate

I seemed to be spending all my time with the law or criminals. Here I was at the station once more. A cop, a sergeant by his stripes, who hadn't introduced himself, faced me across the desk. Small moustache, large ego. Cherubic cheeks, plump lips. Bushy brows, short fingers.

"I'm here to see DS Gregory," I said.

"Is he expecting you?"

"Yes," I lied. In fact, when I'd called Gregory on the way over, it had gone straight to voicemail. I couldn't wait, not with the spectre of a murderer on my trail. I'd never been so relieved to reach a police station.

"What's your name?" asked the desk sergeant with a sigh. He picked up the phone receiver.

"Harrison Vaughan."

The cop narrowed his eyes then tapped away at the buttons, mumbled my name a few seconds later, listened and put the phone down.

"He's in a meeting." The sergeant returned his attention to the computer screen and keyboard I'd dragged him from.

"That's it?" I asked.

The sergeant gave me a "Are you still here?" glance. "Sergeant Gregory is unavailable. You can wait over there." He pointed to a row of three chairs against the wall, bolted to the floor.

"I have to see him right now. It's a matter of life and death."

The cop opened his mouth to respond, but his words would forever remain unuttered because somebody else spoke instead. "What seems to be the matter, Sergeant Morgan?"

I turned. A woman beside the counter, her arms crossed. Tall, tough, tired. Blonde with a sharp fringe, high cheekbones, arched eyebrows. She was smartly dressed in an ankle-length cream skirt and a pale blue high-necked blouse.

"DCI Hamson," said Morgan, straightening a little. He wiped a hand across his moustache. "Mr Vaughan here is demanding to see DS Gregory."

Hamson regarded me with a cool look, head to toe. "A matter of life and death, you said."

"That's right."

"Whose?"

"Mine. Because of Pomfrey Lavender."

Hamson stiffened. "I'll be with you in a moment." She threw a glance at Morgan. "Show Mr Vaughan into one of the interview rooms."

Morgan led me along several corridors until he reached a door marked with a number three. He pointed me inside. It was a plain white cube with table and chairs. Morgan closed the door on me without the offer of refreshment. I already knew the chairs would be uncomfortable, so I remained standing until Hamson arrived. Thankfully much quicker than the forty-one minutes I was kept waiting last time. She held out a manicured hand to shake. Her grip was strong and no-nonsense, matching her image thus far.

"Take a seat, Mr Vaughan. You mentioned Pomfrey Lavender. What's he got to do with you?"

I sat facing the door, which Hamson had her back to. "He threatened to kill me yesterday."

"That's a very serious allegation, sir."

"Which I took very seriously. And he assaulted me immediately afterwards."

"Did you report any of this?"

"I was in prison at the time."

"Excuse me?"

"HMP Swaleside, where Lavender was occupying a cell. The governor said she would deal with the incident through her own channels. Which I accepted."

"Why were you there?"

"Interviewing him. For a book."

"And he just attacked you?"

I nodded, then told Hamson the story. Well, most of it. Angled in a way to generate sympathy. She made notes, frowned a fair bit, chewed a pen, which made me forget my words until prompted to move on. I displayed my neck, exposed the bruises which she viewed disappointingly dispassionately.

"And now Lavender is on the loose," she said.

"I was trying to reach Sergeant Gregory to see if he could provide any protection. Perhaps you could instead?"

"What do you mean?"

"You know, put a squad car outside my house? Have someone stationed inside too?"

Hamson frowned yet again. "That's very unlikely, Mr Vaughan. We don't have the resources."

There was a knock at the door. A plain clothes cop entered – the same guy who'd arrested me outside O'Neal's yesterday.

Hamson twisted in her chair. "DC Fraser, what do you want?"

Ignoring me completely, Fraser closed the door behind him. "Sergeant Morgan said you needed me in here."

"I told him no such thing." The puzzlement was obvious in Hamson's tone.

"Are you sure?"

"I'm perfectly capable of handling this, thank you."

"Sorry, must have been a miscommunication." Fraser smiled. "I'll leave you two alone."

Hamson returned her attention to me. As she did so, Fraser's expression morphed from ambivalent to stern. He gave a small shake of his head and drew a finger across his throat before he departed.

"Is there anything else you want say?" asked Hamson. When I didn't answer she said, "Mr Vaughan?"

I mentally shook myself. "No, that's everything."

"I'll call the governor at Swaleside, see what she thinks. Until then, let us do our jobs. We'll catch Lavender." Hamson rose with a scrape of the chair. "I'll see you out."

Fraser wasn't in the corridor, nor at the front desk where Morgan ignored me while Hamson waggled my hand and told me not to worry. Like that was going to reassure me.

When I was back on the street my phone rang.

"Mr Vaughan," said Eric Hennessey. "I hear you've been to the police." I closed my eyes. "Why?"

"That lunatic Lavender has escaped. He threatened to kill me earlier."

"Perhaps you would be so kind as to give me an update."

I had an unfinished pint at the Flag, so I got walking back there while I filled Hennessey in with pretty much the same story I'd told Hamson. I was nearly at the pub by the time I was done speaking.

"You should have called me for protection," admonished Hennessey, "rather than go to the police. Now they have a connection between you and Lavender. Who knows what else they might dig up."

"I didn't think."

"Worse, Mr Vaughan, you panicked."

"Sorry."

"The Lord forgives."

But what about you? I thought.

"Where are you now?" asked Hennessey. "I'll send a couple of men over to keep watch."

"I'm heading to the Flag in the Old Town."

Hennessey laughed. "That den of sinners? How apt. Stay there for now."

I went inside the pub. Hennessey hadn't said anything about not getting drunk, so I made a good start.

"Time" in the Flag is measured in alcohol consumption rather than elapsed minutes. Hennessey's guys arrived when I was four pints down. When Hennessey's heavies entered, I was sitting on the bar stool Les had occupied just two days ago when this nightmare started, sharing monkey nuts with Dick and Thwaite. The heavies were the pair I'd been squeezed between in the rear of Hennessey's car during the kidnapping. Dick took a step backwards towards his escape hatch.

"They're with me," I said. Both Dick and Thwaite eyed me with disbelief.

"All right, dickhead?" said one of them. "Mr H says you need babysitting."

Scepticism morphed into scorn. Things were back to normal. Thwaite, however, raised an eyebrow at me. He'd help if I gave a sign, but I held fast. This was down to me.

Hennessey's other thug said, "Beer first, Jason."

Jason nodded. "Good call, Stan." Stan shifted over to the slot machine, barging Tiny Al out the way. Jason laughed, switched his attention to Dick, who stood as tall and proud as he could, which wasn't much. "Two pints of your finest. He's paying." A thumb was hiked at me.

Now, Dick was a dick, but he protected his patrons, even if he didn't like them and vice versa. "Certainly," said Dick in an obsequious tone. As Jason went to stand behind Stan at the fruit machine Dick pulled down a pint glass and placed it beneath the outlet for his home brew beer. Dick looked to me for permission. Stan and Jason were hunched over the reels, trying to work out whether to nudge up or down.

"Go for it," I said.

Dick smiled, a rare event, and began heaving on the Cinque Porter pump. A minute later, when he was hot and sweaty, he placed two pints on the bar. "Here you are, gents."

Gents, Jesus.

"Took your time," said Stan.

"All good things come to he who waits."

"Fuck off." Stan returned to the machine.

I held out a fiver to pay Dick. He held his hands up, palms out. "On the house."

Wonders never ceased.

Breakout

Wimpey Estate, Broadstairs
"Just here," I said to Jason in some sort of cross-eyed control. I was in the passenger seat. Stan was driving my car. No point being nicked for being drunk at the wheel. Hennessey's men had no such cares, however, and brought their own car, a mid-range black BMW. My house was a good fifteen-minute drive from the Flag.

As Jason neared, he clipped the wing mirror of a parked car, bumped up the kerb, drew up at an angle beneath a lamp post.

I got out. Jason wound his window down as I passed. I swear his skin had taken on a greenish tinge, but it may have just been the light. "I'm here," I said, pointed to my door.

"We're staying outside," said Jason.

"You feeling okay?" Like I cared.

"Fine." Jason belched. I backed away from the beery fug.

"Okay, sleep well."

"We won't, thanks to you."

I heard Stan call me a prick as I walked away. He was probably right.

Inside I checked all the doors and windows, upstairs and downstairs, to ensure they were firmly locked before I retrieved a beer from the fridge, went into my living room, which was furnished simply, just a rickety high-backed chair and a TV. I sank into the upholstery. I'd rescued the chair from a skip a couple of years ago. The smell it had originally possessed, a mix of mouldy cheese and rancid cat piss, was thankfully long gone. The TV's cathode ray tube took a while to warm up. I flicked on the news channel. The ticker tape at the bottom led with the story of the escaped convicts.

It wasn't long before the actual footage came up. The newsreader, a guy with slick grey hair, introduced the basic events before moving to a reporter on location, a woman in her early thirties, hair scraped back making her appear even more tired. She was wearing a raincoat and huddling under an umbrella.

In the distance, behind a police cordon of tape and uniforms, was a security van with a car mashed into the bonnet. The crash had occurred at a set of traffic lights on a dual carriageway on the edge of south-west London. Scenes of Crime Officers, resplendent in white crimplene from head to foot, moved slowly and steadily around the written-off vehicles.

"Earlier today three masked men assaulted a prison van transporting two highly dangerous inmates. The men guarding the convicts were assaulted and locked inside the cells. The BBC has managed to obtain some CCTV footage of the event."

A long shot, black and white, of the traffic lights came up on the screen. The van was approaching head on. The lights were red, and the van halted, awaiting its turn to get moving again. Without warning, a car raced in from the right. One second the van was alone, the next it had undesirable company.

The offending vehicle smacked into the driver's front wing, merging the two chassis. There wasn't any sound, but I could imagine the crunch of metal, the screech of tyres. Maybe the scream of a bystander or two.

Within seconds two people, dressed in black from head to toe and of similar build, leapt out of the car, seemingly unaffected by the impact. They rushed side by side for the dazed van driver. One balaclava-bound guy used a sledgehammer to smash the window.

Before the glass had finished cascading, his identically clad mate stuck a sawn-off shotgun under the driver's chin. The guard threw his hands up in the air, nodded violently at something he was told and eased himself out. There would be fear now. The tang of sweat merging with that of seeping oil and burnt rubber.

The trio, in perfect sync, shifted along the side of the van towards a door set halfway down. The driver, who was slightly ahead of the pair and had the shotgun wedged under his armpit, used a bunch of keys which hung from a chain at his side, unlocked it. Sledgehammer slammed the driver into the side of the van. The armed one bent inside, weapon leading.

The footage cut out briefly, a few moments of static before the picture returned, this time an interior view from a CCTV camera positioned in the corner so it stared down on the action.

The first guard was struggling to get the cell unlocked. He fumbled with the keys. Then he was knocked to the floor by Shotgun. Sledgehammer appeared with the second guard. Lavender was released. However, instead of clearing off, there was a brief altercation – Lavender remonstrating with Shotgun. Lavender seemed to win because the second cell was opened, and the other prisoner did a runner. Then the guards were bundled into the cubicles, the doors locked, and the trio exited.

Outside a car raced up, driven by another masked man. Lavender and his liberators bundled in and the car sped off.

The shot cut back to the reporter at the scene. "With me is Superintendent Marsh." The shot panned out to reveal an officer of the law, gold braid on his shoulders, and cap under his arm. His buttons positively sparkled. "This is all rather embarrassing, isn't it Superintendent Marsh?"

"The escape was a highly co-ordinated and professional job."

"Which you didn't see coming."

"We've already apprehended Stubbings. As of an hour ago he was back behind bars again."

"But the other escapee remains at large."

"I anticipate he will be caught soon. Stubbings was the more dangerous of the pair. The prisoner who remains at large is nobody to be fearful of. You can trust me on that. In fact, we are already following up on a series of positive leads and we expect to catch him within hours. Now, if you'll excuse me, I must get back to the operation."

Marsh walked away. I turned off the TV and sat in the dark for a few moments. Marsh was playing the whole episode down. He hadn't even mentioned Lavender by name.

I drained the beer can and threw the empty can into the recycling. I checked all the windows and doors once more. I returned to the kitchen, selected the sharpest dull knife I possessed, and headed up to bed. Duvet pulled tight around me, blade clasped in one hand, ears like a bat, listening intently at each and every sound. There was no way I'd be sleeping tonight.

Six

Wimpey Estate, Broadstairs

I must have fallen asleep, because I woke up. The room was as dark as an aged piece of mahogany, which is how I like it. Blackout blinds, then thick curtains drawn over those. The merest chink of light is disturbing, summer being the worst, when the days are long and the sun is a pain in the arse.

In the corner of the room, a circle of brightness rose then fell. My foggy brain took a few moments to figure out it was a watch face, one of the digital smart ones. I sat up, reached over, clicked on the lamp.

A guy sitting in the corner, staring. But not just any guy; the American who Dick had pointed out in the pub; the one I thought had been following me. And he'd got past Hennessey's men. I felt for the knife, moving my fingers slowly so he didn't notice.

"Your protection, they're in hospital," the guy drawled. He meant Jason and Stan. "Gut problems. I'm surprised you didn't see the ambulance."

"Dick's beer," I said. The blackout curtains would have done for the blue light and my room is at the back of the house.

"I don't know who Dick Spear is. Nor do I care." The American raised a glass, one of mine – had a drink. "Your vodka tastes like horse piss."

"I wouldn't know, but I apologise."

"That's all you Brits do. Complain and say you're sorry."

"Don't forget, we love a good queue too. And traffic. And the weather." I couldn't find the knife, it must have fallen on the floor.

"You looking for this?" The Yank held up the blade.

"I was using it to pick my nails."

"Right." He pulled a face, like he was irritated I considered him stupid. "My name is Six."

"Six? That's it? No first name? Or Sir Six?"

"Six is enough."

"For what?"

"Anybody."

"What do you want?"

"A word."

"Not six words?"

"That's too funny." Six didn't appear particularly amused.

"I like to think so."

"Find the Nudge Man."

"Not you too." I slumped back.

"It's important you tell me first, once you track him down."

"How do you know I will?"

"The U S of A knows all."

Six finished the vodka he apparently hated, put the glass down, stood up. He came across the room, stopped a few feet away. Held out a mobile. "Take this. It's a cell."

"Really? Thanks, I'd often wondered what they were."

"Still with the wisecracks."

"It's my armour, Six."

"Whatever. My number's in there. Call me with updates." I didn't take the phone so Six placed it on the bed, followed by the knife. He stared at me a moment, perhaps to make his point in a strong, silent way, before leaving.

I didn't hear his feet on the stairs. I waited a long, long minute before stepping onto the landing. I cocked an ear, nothing. I headed into the spare bedroom which overlooked the street. Six was walking away. Jason's car was parked where he'd left it, but I couldn't see anybody inside. I ran out onto the street, the tarmac cold on my bare feet. The car was empty, the doors unlocked, keys in the ignition.

My defence was gone. Six had entered my house despite all the locks. I wasn't safe. I needed backup. And I knew just where to get it.

Bonzo Returns

O'Neal's Scrapyard, Manston

The carpet was still in place over the barbed wire fence surrounding O'Neal's scrapyard. I legged it over with significantly more grace than the previous occasion, having had the practice.

The interior was in total darkness, the spotlights unlit. Saving energy? Or in mourning after the body discovered in the compactor? I shone my torch onto the ground immediately ahead of me, avoided the puddle I'd fallen into previously and made my way to the building in the compound's centre. I was like Bill Murray in *Groundhog Day*.

The door was still unlocked and Bonzo, my impending minder, was sitting where I'd last seen him. Slap bang in the middle of the corridor. He elicited a low growl.

"Hey, Bonzo," I said. The rumbling stopped, and he tilted his head. A small whine now. I moved slowly towards him, in case his memory failed him. As I neared he got to his feet and wagged his tail. I dropped to my knees, gave him a vigorous rub behind his ears.

"Do you want to come with me?" I asked. I repeated myself in a playful voice and Bonzo began to bound around, hopping from left to right and back again. I stood, walked back towards the door. A glance over my shoulder, Bonzo was following at my heels.

Back at the fence I was faced with a dilemma, how the hell to get him over? I hadn't figured that one out in advance. The barrier was a good eight feet high. Bonzo appeared heavy. I experimented – one brain cell believing I could lift him over – got my arms under his stomach and heaved. His feet left the floor, but only up to my chest before I had to give up and drop him back down.

But I wasn't leaving without Bonzo. I headed back into the building, spent a wasted ten minutes looking for something like bolt cutters to create a hole in the fence. No luck. I walked the perimeter, Bonzo in my tracks, seeking a way out. But the fence held firm. It was at the front entrance when I had a breakthrough. The double gates were locked, a chain looped through them and padlocked. However, someone had the key. That someone was standing outside, showing it to me. That someone was Detective Sergeant Gregory.

"You're on private property," he said.

"Bollocks."

Gregory leant against the rear wing of Jason's BMW, Bonzo inside, doors closed, the windows open a crack, while I explained why I was here.

"You want the dog for safety, from Pomfrey Lavender?" said Gregory when I'd finished.

"That's right," I said. "He threatened to kill me yesterday. I didn't take it seriously until I heard he'd broken out."

"Why did he threaten you?"

"I came into the station about all of this, instead I spoke to your much nicer colleague, Hamson."

"You're right, she is far more pleasant than me. But you're not telling me everything. For example, why are you driving one of Eric Hennessey's cars?"

"This belongs to Eric Hennessey?" I hoped my tone was sufficiently innocent.

"The registration matches a vehicle in his possession."

"It's a hire car."

Gregory ran fingers through his hair. "I don't believe you, Harry, not entirely. I think you're actually deep in the shit and don't know how to get out. You're flotsam on the raging sea, with no control over what happens to you or where you'll wash up."

"Wow, that's amazingly eloquent."

"You need help, Harry."

"And you'll provide it?"

"I will."

"Why?"

"I want Hennessey and I think you can give him to me." When I didn't answer, Gregory continued. "I'm well aware how dangerous he is, but are you? Now's the time to come back, Harry, to decide whose side you're on."

"I'm on nobody's side but my own."

"You're being used." Actually, I was being both coerced and paid, but who's splitting hairs? "Work with me and I'll do my best to get you out of all this."

God, I was tired. And not just because of being woken up at a ridiculous hour by a chillingly clinical American. But from so many people wanting something from me that I didn't know if I could or would give.

"Harry," prompted Gregory.

"Okay," I said.

"Good, but first we need to feed Bonzo."

Gregory's Game

Wimpey Estate, Broadstairs
After a pause at the twenty-four-hour Asda superstore around the corner from my house to pick up food for the dog and milk for me, I led Gregory to my very humble abode.

"Nice place," he said as we stood in my kitchen while I filled the kettle and got it boiling. I could tell Gregory was lying.

"I like it," I lied too.

Gregory got a spoon inside a can of meat, scooped the lot out into a breakfast bowl he'd helped himself to from a cupboard and placed it on the floor. Bonzo was straight in. I opened the back door, so he could access my back garden if he wanted. It was all weeds and long grass, so good luck with that, hound.

"That's all you're doing for him?" asked Gregory.

"What?"

"A bit of meat and kick him out? You didn't get him a bone or any toys?"

"He's not a pet. He's a guard dog, to guard me, Guy. Not something to be pampered, Jesus." I ignored the fact that he'd been rubbish at the guarding thing so far, I was hoping for outward intimidation from Bonzo.

"Do you even know what breed he is?" Gregory bent down and ruffled the skin on the top of Bonzo's head.

125

I shrugged. "I'm not a pet lover. Dragging animals around on a chain, picking up their crap in a bag. It feels barbaric."

"Well you need to be aware and fast because Bonzo is a Malinois."

"And that means, what?"

"They're attack dogs. The police use them. Bonzo, if angry, would take apart a German Shepherd. They're tough."

"Great! That's exactly what I wanted."

"Do you know how to handle him?"

"Just shout 'kill!' and he'll go for the jugular of whoever I'm pointing at, I assume."

Gregory rolled his eyes. "Actually, the command is 'bite'." Gregory mouthed the last word, presumably so Bonzo didn't hear and attack. "I'd advise caution, Harry. If you mess this breed around, they'll turn on you. I once saw three of them attack a handler because they didn't like his behaviour. It was like the velociraptors in Jurassic Park. And they were puppies."

"I'll be fine. It won't be for long."

"Don't say I didn't warn you." Gregory turned to Bonzo. "Sit." The dog flopped onto his backside, ears pricked. "Lie down." Gregory pressed the air down with a flat palm and Bonzo hit the floor. "Seek." Bonzo began to sniff around the kitchen. "Set." Bonzo snarled like he was going to kill, ears flattened. "He's been trained for sure, he might even be a reject from the police. You give it a try."

I sighed but attempted the sit and lie down commands. Bonzo ignored me. "What's the problem?" I asked.

"Lack of trust, maybe."

"But he responds to you."

"What can I say? I'm a likeable guy."

"And I'm not?"

Gregory just shrugged. "Keep working on him. With dogs the more you put in the more you get back."

"Very profound, I'll not remember that one." Frankly I didn't really care beyond the next few days. I just wanted a barrier between me and Six or Lavender or both of them. I had no intention of having a four-legged companion for the long term.

I retrieved two chipped mugs from the sink. One had a picture of Charles and Diana before their wedding day. An oddly matched couple, like Gregory and me. "Milk or sugar with your coffee?"

"Plenty of both," he said, leaning against the formica units. The less than impressed expression remained on Gregory's face. Whatever. I spooned two scoops, a further two when Gregory nodded to keep going. Same with the milk, an overdose. There would be no flavour left, but he was drinking it, not me. I handed him the Charlie and Di mug.

Gregory took a sip, sighed as if savouring nectar which, with the sugar overload, it pretty much was. "That's excellent." I kept my opinion to myself, which I was getting decent at. "Why did you break into O'Neal's the first time around?" he asked.

"Do you have to use phrases like 'break in'? It makes the process sound illegal."

"It was illegal." Gregory winked. "But I'm turning a blind eye."

Gregory was keen to help, and I needed it. "Les Garrett wanted a document."

"What document?"

"Something about planning permission for a load of houses on the airport."

"Do you have it still?"

"I took a photo, emailed everything to Les, then deleted the lot."

"That's a shame."

"I just did a job."

"Do you know how that sounds?" Bonzo finished his food, whined at me. We both switched our attention to the mutt. "He's probably after water," said Gregory, the animal expert. But he was right. Another of my bowls, which the animal drained before heading outside to hunt for Dr Livingstone who was lost somewhere in the jungle which began a few feet from my back door just beyond the totemic pile of fag butts and ring pulls.

"Did you use your phone for the photo and email?" asked Gregory.

"Of course." Who'd carry an actual camera these days?

"Give it to me." I handed over my mobile. Gregory swiped at the screen. "No security code, Harry? Sloppy." He tapped away for a few moments, squinting. "This?" He'd brought up a document.

"Looks about right. How did you get it?"

"From your email trash folder." Gregory fell silent while he read, frowning as he did so. Eventually he said, "There's nothing interesting here. It's all public domain. In fact, there have been protests against the plans."

I sort of remembered a march being reported on the news, but it seemed these days somebody was always going off about something. Vegans against animal transportation, xenophobes against immigration and Remainers against Brexit ... don't get me started.

Gregory continued, "What made you assume this was what Les asked for?"

"It was the only concealed document. I went through the building in depth. All else was easy accessible, whereas that was locked in a drawer and hidden away."

"I suspect Les was setting you up." Gregory handed back my phone. "Somebody wanted you there; wrong time, wrong place. For you at least."

"Who?"

"Hennessey, I'd assume. DC Fraser is suspected to be his man, remember?"

I did. "I saw him again earlier today."

"When?"

"I came into the station to see you, got a DCI Hamson instead."

" Why were you after me?"

"Pomfrey Lavender," I said.

Gregory tilted his head. "What's he to do with you?"

Too many questions from Gregory, so I told him the majority of events in my last forty-eight hours. My trip to Hennessey, his financial offer, visiting Lavender and his threats.

"Jesus, Harry," said Gregory when I'd finished. "You're in deeper than I thought."

"I wish that was all. Earlier tonight I was visited by an American, some guy called Six."

"Who's Six?"

"That's exactly what I asked. He totally creeped me out. He's why I went to get Bonzo."

"What did he look like?" I described Six. "I'll see if I can track him down." Gregory scratched his head. "I don't get why you're suddenly of interest. A washed-up reporter living at the outer edges of the UK."

"Thanks, I feel so much better now."

"No problem. What's the connection, Harry? I've a hunch."

"They all want me to find somebody called the Nudge Man. Have you heard of him?"

"I'd remember such a ridiculous nom de plume."

"I hadn't either, until two days ago."

"What about Conn, your legal representative?"

"He told me to stay away from this Nudge Man. I've no idea who Conn is, who he's working for."

Gregory pulled out his wallet, extracted a business card and waved it at me. "What about calling his office?"

"I'd meant to do that but hadn't got around to it." I took the card from Gregory's fingers. "Glad you reminded me." I wasn't even sure where I'd put the card I'd picked up in the interview room. "Still too early, I'll ring later when the office opens." I drank some coffee. My mouth was getting dry with all the talking.

Bonzo came in from the outside, his fur covered in bits of green. The sticky plants we used to throw at each other when we were kids. The dog flopped to the floor, rested his head between his paws and closed his eyes.

I asked, "What's the status of the investigation to find Lavender?"

"Thanet police aren't involved specifically. There's an APB out, but no sightings as yet. Seems he's gone to ground. The other guy, Stubbings, was found at his mother's house in Tilbury."

"That's just great."

Gregory ruffled his hair, grimacing. "There's too much going on here to make sense of."

"Tell me about it."

"We need to write this down, mind map everything, see what connects and what doesn't."

"Wait here a minute." I headed out to my car, the crap one, not Hennessey's, retrieved my laptop and the information the gangster had given me. I keep anything of value in the car. It's a wreck, who's going to steal it? When I returned, I led Gregory into the living room.

"What the hell is that?" he asked, pointing at the wall. I'd printed out a stack of paper, going through several ink cartridges, to faithfully reproduce the map of the Nudge Man's activity and it was stuck up beside the table, the sheets overlapping.

I handed over the folders. "Perhaps it's better if you read some stuff first."

Saviour of the Universe

Flash, Staffordshire

Pomfrey Lavender was in his fourth vehicle since his escape, not including the G4S security van. The current transportation was a battered old Land Rover; a rust-pitted, powder-blue four-seater, perfect for the steep inclines and tight corners of the Peak District byways. The driver, a bald man who'd been hired to stay silent, changed down into second gear as he took the tight turn. Rain lashed at the car, a typical welcome to the highest village in the United Kingdom.

The conurbation was small: a scattering of houses, a pub called the New Inn, which wasn't new anymore, and a Methodist church just off the A53 Leek to Buxton road on the south side of Oliver Hill. The houses were built low and long back in the day, to deal with the weather. And to shelter the farmer's family and livestock, which would have shared the accommodation at opposite ends.

Lavender loved the remote moorland, where often winter arrived early, and spring broke late. It wasn't unusual for Flash to be cut off by snow for days, or even weeks, at a time. And there was the village's association with a dubious past. The name Flash came from the trading of counterfeit money in the nineteenth century at nearby Three Shires Head, the confluence of the counties of Derbyshire, Staffordshire and Cheshire.

Flash had been a wild place, where illegal practices like prize fighting continued long after they were banned elsewhere. The ring was set up in one of the three counties. If the district police arrived, there was plenty of warning. The windswept land here was largely free of trees and cover. The ring was simply picked up and moved a few feet over the boundary line into a different jurisdiction, meaning the police could do nothing but watch, maybe even place a bet themselves.

The driver headed through the village and, just as the road began to descend, paused at the entrance to a track. A hand-painted plaque read, *Quarnford Farm*. A CCTV camera on a pole eyeballed the entrance. After a moment, the gate blocking their way silently opened.

The vehicle bumped through the ruts, splashing muddy water onto the verge as it descended the slope. The driver stopped outside the whitewashed single-storey building, allowing enough time for Lavender to disembark before turning around and returning the way he'd come. There wasn't a suitcase for Lavender to collect from the boot. He only owned whatever he was wearing. Lavender had no other material possessions in the world.

Lavender knew the old workhorse was on its final journey. Later it would be torched, like the other three cars, to destroy any evidence of the escaped convict's presence.

He didn't need to knock on the front door. Like the pugilists of old, the property owner was forewarned of his arrival. The woman who opened up hadn't changed much since he'd last seen her. Maybe a touch more grey hair at the temples, but that was all.

Elizabeth Vaughan, now Elizabeth Eckersall, dragged Lavender inside, threw her arms out and pulled him tight, kissing him long and deep. He felt her strong body, one that had become used to her new life and surroundings. Elizabeth had gone through several identities, moving from safe house to safe house, but had never discarded her first name, which was her grandmother's. She'd stated several times when Shaw had told her to make a complete change that it was all she had left of the past. Likewise, for the children who remained Maddie and Jack, though with the surname Eckersall.

Eventually Elizabeth released Lavender. "I've missed you."

"Same here." And he had. For years, it had been difficult for Lavender to express the depth of his feelings because of his army experiences. Not all in the profile the Nudge Man created prior to his stint in prison had been fabricated. Elizabeth, thankfully, understood.

"Do you want something to eat or drink?"

"Water will be fine, thanks." Lavender hadn't taken any form of narcotics for a long time either.

They entered the kitchen, a simple affair dominated by a wooden table in the centre and an Aga kicking out plenty of radiant warmth. The windows, overlooking rolling moorland, were small, the walls thick, all designed to retain heat. She took a glass from a cupboard, drew him some water from the tap and handed it over.

"The whole village should know you're here by now," said Elizabeth.

Lavender was well aware how small places operated. "Nothing will be said." People knew your business, though they didn't intrude. Mistrust of the authorities went back generations. And there were only a few tourists, walkers typically, this far off the beaten track. It had been the perfect choice for the Vaughans once Lavender realised the witness protection scheme was compromised. "Where are the kids?"

"Jack's at school. Maddie went back to university." Jack was in his first year of sixth form in Buxton, a once-grand spa town the Romans colonised for the healing effects of a spring that issued from the ground. Much later, the Victorians obsessed over the same source but subsequently the town fell on hard times.

"How's she doing?" Lavender was well aware that Elizabeth had struggled with the idea of Maddie leaving home – of not being able to protect her daughter any more. But she had to let go one day.

"Really good. Great actually."

Maddie was studying computer science and politics in Lancaster, a quiet student town further north-west, just above Blackpool, near the coast. She'd wanted to join the Navy, to specialise in cyber warfare. Enlisting would suit her sense of duty too, but Elizabeth drew the line at the armed forces. Maddie would be in the system then. It was too much of a risk.

"I told you she would."

"But she's struggling to act like your average student." Elizabeth grinned. Maddie was bright and very experienced. "She has to go a bit slower than she'd like." Not sticking out again.

"Better safe than sorry."

"That's what I told her." Elizabeth took Lavender's hand. Her grip was firm and dry. "I'll show you to your room."

A corridor cut along the length of the longhouse. The kitchen at one end, bedrooms the other, living quarters in the middle. Elizabeth lifted a heavy looking latch and pushed open a door made of ancient, warped planks. "This is yours." Elizabeth gave Lavender a coy look. "I'm directly opposite."

The space was furnished with a wrought-iron double bed and a wardrobe of dark wood. Another open door exposed an en-suite bathroom. A floor-to-ceiling window was a more recent addition to frame the view over the farmland to the front. The arrow-straight driveway rose upwards at an angle to the road.

"The locals thought I was mad when I took the drystone walls down," said Elizabeth.

"Makes sense," said Lavender. There weren't any hedges and no major cover within hundreds of yards. It would be impossible for anyone to reach the house unseen. The CCTV added another layer of security.

"I got you some things." Elizabeth opened the wardrobe where plain shirts and trousers hung neatly.

Lavender flicked through the clothes. "This is perfect, thanks." He heard the latch fall into place. He turned.

"Jack won't be home for a while. We have the place to ourselves." Elizabeth began to unbutton Lavender's top.

Monkey Nuts

Wimpey Estate, Broadstairs

The ringing of a mobile awoke me. I glanced around, trying to locate the phone. I was sitting in my shabby chair in the living room, sunlight streaming through the windows. Gregory was slumped over the table, head on his forearms. He jerked upright, bleary eyed, hair askew, a Post-It note stuck to his cheek. There was more paper heading towards my feet from my lap in a cascade. We must have fallen asleep while working.

The phone was buried beneath documents somewhere on the floor. I scrabbled around, located the mobile, focused on the numbers.

"Hennessey," I told Gregory who was suddenly alert and watchful. I answered. "Morning, Eric."

"You're supposed to be contacting me with regular progress updates, Mr Vaughan." No platitudes from Hennessey then. But he sounded calm, collected.

"I will." I was equally as blunt. "When I make progress."

"So, you've got nowhere?"

"I didn't say that. I've made a start. Investigations often begin slowly. It's the latter stages when they speed up."

"What are you doing then?"

"Investigating." I swear I heard Hennessey's teeth grinding. "*Specifically*."

"I'm attempting to find a place to start. I think I need to speak with some of the people who've been clipped by the Nudge Man to get an idea how he works."

"Seems sensible." A degree of mollification now.

"Trust me, Eric. I know what I'm doing." Gregory rolled his eyes at that.

"I understand my two idiots were taken ill. Poisoned, they said. Any idea how?"

"Maybe it was the nuts."

"What nuts?"

"Monkey nuts. The pub sells them."

"They stayed in the pub?"

"Oh yes, for quite a while."

"They were supposed to leave with you immediately. Alcohol is a sin."

"Sorry, you didn't know?"

There was a long silence on the other end. "I do now."

"I hope I haven't got them into trouble, Eric." I did. Gregory grinned.

"There is forgiveness in my heart, Mr Vaughan. I'll send some more of my people around later."

"No need. I picked up some protection overnight." By the expression on Gregory's face he clearly thought I meant him. I let him have his dream.

"Only if you're sure."

"I am, and you have a gap to fill. Two men down."

"Very true, Mr Vaughan. Let's do as you suggest. One other thing. Keep the BMW. It sounds like you'll be doing plenty of miles and your car is a death trap."

I'd have comfortable transport with actual suspension, air conditioning, maybe even a medium wave radio! "It's a deal."

"When do you think you'll have something useful to report?"

"Difficult to say. At least a couple of days. I'll call when I do."

"Then God be with you." Hennessey disconnected.

"You're a vicious bastard, Harry," said Gregory.

"Coming from you, that's a compliment. I need a coffee. Want one?"

Gregory nodded. I made a brew, fed and watered Bonzo, took a cup of sugary caffeine to Gregory. He was flipping through the data again.

"I think we made some progress," he said.

"That's not what you said last night."

"Sometimes it's good to sleep on it." Literally, in Gregory's case. "I reckon we could do with help, though. A lot of this stuff... it's dark web. Well beyond my capabilities. There's someone I can trust."

"Who?"

"Let me talk to her first?"

"DCI Hamson?" I was hopeful.

"Not a chance. The person I'm thinking of is ex-CEOP."

"Child Exploitation?"

"That's right. Unfortunately, she knows her way around the deeper recesses of the internet."

"In the meantime, I'll phone Conn's office," I said. "We may be able to add to the information pile."

"Good idea. Where's your bathroom?"

"Top of the stairs."

As Gregory left I tapped Conn's number from his business card into my mobile. It rang once before being answered. "Challinor, Lockheed and Conn," said a woman in a very precise and clipped tone.

"Mr Conn, please."

"Who's calling?"

"Harrison Vaughan, one of his clients."

"Putting you through now, sir."

The line went quiet for a few moments. "This is Challinor, Mr Vaughan." A deep, bass tone of a voice. "How can I help you?"

"Oh, I was expecting to speak with Aaron."

"I am afraid *Mr* Conn is on an extended leave of absence and is uncontactable."

Now, I'm no fan of privilege; though I wasn't so stupid as to think the British class system was anything other than alive and well, just a little more underground than it used to be. However, what I loathed was when people openly demonstrated their belief that they were better than me. Usually they were right, but I didn't need it rammed down my throat.

Last night I'd surfed the web and found the lawyer's website. The partners were listed on a separate page with a photo and bio. Challinor appeared to be another stuffed suit. Stiff, with a full head of grey hair and pursed lips. I'd immediately taken a dislike to him and the start of the call reinforced my initial perception.

"Do you know when he'll be back, *Alex*?"

"It's *Mr* Challinor, if you wouldn't mind."

"Sure, no problem, Alex." There was an intake of breath. Like I'd told Challinor an inappropriate joke laced with profanities. Good. "You were going to tell me about Aaron's availability?"

"As I said, Mr Conn is on a leave of absence and I really do not know when he'll return."

"What's he doing?"

"I'm not aware of the details."

"You're partners, though."

"Only in the business sense, Mr Vaughan. People are allowed to take time away from the company. Even Directors." He laughed. "Really, that's all I can say, I am truly sorry." Another falsehood. And I clearly wasn't going to get any more from Challinor.

"Thanks for your help, Alex." I rang off to a choked splutter.

"Well?" asked Gregory. He was standing in the doorway, appearing slightly more refreshed.

"Conn is on extended leave. I'm sure there's more, but the bloke I spoke to wouldn't give anything up. I thought you, as a fine upstanding officer of the law, might be able to apply some influence."

"Possibly." Gregory grinned. "But later. Let the guy think he's in the clear. I spoke to my colleague. She'll be here in half an hour or so. I could do with a shower first and a change of clothes. Is thirty minutes enough?"

I wasn't going to admit my ablutions would need twenty-seven minutes fewer than his suggestion, so I said, "Sure."

Gregory's helper duly arrived, bang on time, whereas Gregory did not. Perhaps he'd fallen asleep in the shower.

"Emily Wyatt," she said, standing in the doorway. Her pale skin was in contrast to her long, dark hair which was cut into straight lines. A sharp, horizontal fringe sat immediately above her eyes. "Where can I get set up?"

I showed Wyatt through to the living room. To her credit she didn't blink at the paucity of my accommodation and just got on with her work. I considered how long it had been since there was a woman in my house.

Not counting Gregory, of course.

The End is a Start

Wimpey Estate, Broadstairs

"My head hurts," said Gregory.

"Want another coffee?" I asked.

"Christ, no. I feel like I'm swimming in the stuff."

"Emily?" I had to wave because she was wearing headphones and listening to something.

"I'm fine." She held up a mug, my cleanest and least cracked. Turmeric tea, of all things. She'd brought her own supply. I didn't stretch beyond caffeine. Nobody sensible would.

We'd been working in the living room for a couple of hours. Gregory sat at the table, painstakingly entering all the information into Excel and Access to better analyse the data. Me hunting down any news reports online, of which there were very few. Wyatt surfing the upper reaches of the internet and the murky levels of the dark web. She returned to whatever was holding her attention.

"We're missing something," said Gregory.

"Alcohol," I replied.

"No."

"A curry then. That'll get the synapses firing."

"Be serious, Harry."

"I am."

Wyatt chose that moment to scuff the headphones off. She said, "I've got something. Might be a lot, actually."

I moved next to Wyatt, bent over. "Shoot."

Gregory rolled his eyes.

"This Nudge Man has an underground fan base. I found a couple of forums buried deep, where anonymous contributors chat about what they perceive to be actions by the Nudge Man. There's even a section for people to raise issues for him to resolve."

Wyatt tapped the screen. Poisoned cats: could the Nudge Man track down the perpetrator? A house fire: the arsonist was known, but the cops didn't have enough evidence. Could the Nudge Man sort it out? Gangs of kids on an estate that the requester wanted "put down like vermin".

"This is great," I said.

"That's not all. I found an audio clip. The person who posted it claims to be your man." Wyatt shifted to a pop-up window, a media player. She clicked the triangle and a bar along the bottom began to move. The file was only a minute or so long. Initially nothing issued from the speakers. I leaned closer. "Wait," said Wyatt.

There was the sound of weather. Of a gusting wind. The bleat of a sheep in the distance between the peaks and troughs of gusts which carried the mangled caw of a crow.

The voice, when it came, was unnatural. A machine used to alter the tone and inflection to make identification impossible. Nevertheless, it was compelling. Could be male, could be female. Impossible to tell.

"Let's start at the end," said the Nudge Man. "With death. If you want someone murdered there are plenty of people to choose from. From the subtle to the blunt. From the lone wolf contract killer to the mercenary band. Some cheap, some not.

A few even the average person on the street has heard of. But there's only one of me. I make a difference.

"Up for a job but got competition? I'll ensure the rival doesn't arrive for the interview. A contender in love? They'll be discredited, leaving you without competition. A suspected paedophile down your street? Time for them to move on.

"You may not even realise you need me until I've been and gone. Cleared that blockage in the u-bend and taken a contribution from your bank balance for my efforts. Here's the rub.

"I don't kill. I don't need to. I ... persuade. Maybe break a few bones in a hit and run. Plant some drugs or some photos where they shouldn't be, visit some websites that are off limits but leave a backwards trace. Redistribute stolen money from crooks to more worthy causes.

"I'm not a hitman. I'm unique. One of a kind. I'm the Nudge Man."

Wyatt hit stop. "It's simply a statement of intent," she said. "I could have the background noises analysed, but I suspect nothing would come of it."

"Doesn't give us much then," said Gregory.

"What Emily's found is pretty bloody brilliant as far as I'm concerned." I threw Wyatt a grin. She remained impervious.

Gregory crossed to the map. "There's still a gap." From what I could see, the layout was a melange of dots, like a Damien Hirst on a bad day. We knew the colours were subscribed to types of crime. Blue for financial offences like embezzlement or bribery, red for theft, orange for revenge porn and so on.

"This is Hennessey's." I tapped the red marker on Pluck's Gutter, the several million pounds the Nudge Man was supposed to have stolen. "How does a serial crime start, Guy?"

"Small. If they get away with it, they get a little buzz. As time goes on, the trivial stuff isn't enough anymore so they escalate. Bigger risk, bigger buzz. A vicious circle."

The Nudge Man's list of misdemeanours had certainly climbed, though each attack seemed to be to right a wrong. And there were none of the category A felonies such as murder or drug dealing. "It's like they're handling the stuff the police can't be bothered with."

"I think 'lack the manpower for' is a better phrase," chipped in Wyatt.

"Tomato, tomayto."

"It could be they haven't taken the next step up," said Gregory. "And we just haven't seen it."

"There's hundreds of incidents, though. Surely if he was going to intensify his actions he would have by now."

"Maybe."

Wyatt was frowning. "What did you say earlier, Harry?"

"Something crap, probably," I said.

"Seriously."

"Beer? Curry?"

"After that."

I thought for a moment. "I asked Guy how this stuff starts."

Wyatt grinned at me, generating a little frisson of excitement in my soul. "You could be right, that might be it."

"Makes a change."

She took Gregory's laptop, tapped at a few keys, waited briefly. "I've sorted your data by time." Wyatt clicked her fingers. "Bingo."

"What?"

"Have you got anything to mark the map with? Pins, for example?"

"Actually, I do."

I'd bought them when I was picking up the paper and ink to reproduce the map but couldn't be arsed sticking them all in. I located the pins in a drawer and handed them to Wyatt. Gregory stood back, as bemused as me.

Switching between laptop and map she stuck one pin after another into the wall. After a few minutes she stepped back. What resulted was five bunches of markers, coloured by location, rather than the category of crime. One group was very tight around an area, others a little wider, just by a few miles. And differing numbers. Three here, eleven there, seven more elsewhere.

"Each set of incidents occurred over the period of a few weeks to a month. Then they stop for a couple of weeks before beginning again somewhere else," said Wyatt.

I thought the implications through, took in how crammed together the "incidents", as Wyatt had called them, were. "Localised and time specific."

"Exactly."

"As if they're moving around," said Gregory.

"Correct."

"Getting used to a new place, scoping out what's happening and taking action."

"That's what I think," said Wyatt.

"We'll make a cop out of you yet," said Gregory to me.

"God, no." I pulled a face. "I'd like to retain what little credibility I have. What about the most recent data?"

"Give me a moment."

Wyatt started once more with the pins. Thankfully I'd bought several boxes. It took her considerably longer because there were far more of them and the spread much greater. All over the country, in fact.

"The pattern's gone again." I was disappointed. I'd hoped for a clear indicator. Life was never that simple, though.

Wyatt consulted the laptop again. "There's another trend. The events become more electronic over time."

"What does that mean?" asked Gregory.

"At the outset the activity was physical in nature. Behaviour deemed bad by the Nudge Man was dealt with by brute force. A beating here, a broken bone or a threat of violence there. Four years later and all the physical stuff stops. Nobody is beaten up any more. All the recriminations become electronic. Email blackmail, an exposé dumped onto the internet, etc. That's why the markers are spread out now."

"A population unrestricted by mere geography," I said.

"Correct."

"So, we've just got no choice but to start at the beginning and physically follow the trail," said Gregory. "Somebody has to go to some or all of these places."

I looked at the map – saw where Wyatt had ended. "But that's ..." I couldn't say it.

"Up north," said Gregory, amused.

"It'll be freezing. And they speak funny."

"Pack some jumpers and a phrasebook and you'll be fine."

"You're full of great suggestions."

"I know."

"You're coming with me, right?"

"I can't, I've a job to do. I'll keep you up to date with the investigation into this Nudge Man and an eye on the hunt for Lavender from here." I'd briefly forgotten about him. "Don't worry, there will probably be miles between you and Lavender."

"If he's still in London." I looked again at the map. There were two different methods I could undertake to follow the route. Going chronologically would zig zag me across the country, back and forth, meaning a hell of a lot of travelling. Or I could be selective, driving steadily north, and pick off what appeared to be the prime locations.

Because I'm lazy, and it's no fun driving in the UK anymore due to the volume of traffic, I chose the latter. Which meant the first destination was another island called Mersea.

The only thing left to do was get packing. Which wouldn't take long. I wasn't sure I even owned a suitcase these days. I soon discovered I didn't. All I had was a carrier bag from a local supermarket.

Classy ...

It's Bleak for Blake

Euston Road, London
Blake Midwinter took the Northern Line to Euston.
It was 11am, before the official lunch break, but the pubs were
open, and he had to get out, to think. Euston had the benefit of
being far from the office.

Between the station and the intensely busy thoroughfare of
the same name stood the watering hole, the Euston Tap. Actually, the Tap was two ornate, small buildings called the East and
West Lodge, serving cask beers and ciders. Inside, Midwinter
ordered a pint of stout, strong and dark, brewed somewhere in
the depths of Dorset near to where he'd grown up.

Midwinter knew the pub because he used to go to Barry's
Bootcamp across the road. A so-called gym, where they'd bul-
lied and battered him into some sort of shape and emptied his
wallet in the process. If only Barry could see him now, knocking back the calories. But Barry was somewhere in the US. The
exercise facility was a global brand, with locations from Milan
to Dubai to Copenhagen and the Americas. So, Barry wouldn't
care about Blake Midwinter's waistline. Instead he'd be counting his dollars.

Standing at the bar, Midwinter downed the first pint in a
matter of minutes and ordered a second. By the time he was on
his third, he decided he needed to sit down. He took his definitely half-empty glass upstairs.

He had the space to himself. A low ceiling, a scattering of mismatched tables and chairs and a small window overlooking the gap between this and the other lodge. Midwinter sat, beginning to feel drunk, and it wasn't even noon. However, maybe it wasn't the booze making his head spin. Maybe it was the stress.

He'd screwed up big time. Lavender's transfer had turned into a complete disaster. He was on the loose, God knew where. Then again, Midwinter didn't believe in God. He wondered if he could keep this from the boss – Lord Dennis no less. The man was an arsehole. Because Midwinter had gone too far. If Dennis knew Midwinter had carried on the operation after being told to close it down, Midwinter would be in big trouble.

Midwinter was absently studying the tiny head of foam on his beer, wondering what to do next, when he felt the bench lurch as somebody sat beside him. When there were six other tables free, for fu ... Midwinter held back before he swore. His mother wouldn't like it.

"Terrible weather, as always." An English accent, well spoken, educated. And one Midwinter knew well. He closed his eyes. Allowed himself to swear this time.

Lord Malcolm Dennis of Wetwang – wearing a Savile Row pinstripe suit, old school tie in a Windsor knot, and holding a cane – sat a couple of feet away. "You're a bloody idiot, do you know that, Midwinter?"

"I don't know what you mean, sir."

Dennis sighed heavily. "Do you think I wasn't aware you and Six remained in communication?"

Midwinter had taken precautions, of course. Then again, Dennis was a veteran of British secret services. Midwinter stayed silent.

"You underestimated my abilities," said Dennis. "And, as always, overestimated your own."

"Yes, sir."

"What did I tell you on your first day, Midwinter?" But Midwinter wasn't given a chance to reply. Lord Dennis ploughed on. "That you are just a junior rank-and file in diplomatic services. A fetch-and-carry type who I use periodically to, well, fetch stuff and carry it where I tell you."

Midwinter knew damn well the process Lord Dennis was referring to was termed plausible deniability. Let a lackey make the running. If all went belly up, then the minion took the tumble. However, if by some miracle the assistant succeeded then they'd get a pat on the back and Dennis would step out of the shadows to receive the applause. On this occasion, Midwinter had actually tripped and fallen badly.

"Consorting with a foreign government, my boy," said Dennis. "That's treason in my book."

Midwinter quaked. He was finished. Maybe he and Lavender would be trading places.

Small Time Crimes

Mersea Island, Essex

I parked the BMW on Victoria Esplanade in West Mersea, a small seaside village in Essex, the adjacent county to Kent. I'd driven from Broadstairs towards London along the A2, hit the M25 which circled the capital, traversed the Dartford Bridge, paying the French company who now owned it for the pleasure, before turning off the motorway and heading north-east. In all, it had taken almost two and a half hours, guided by the well-spoken sat nav. Throughout the journey, Bonzo had lain quiet and asleep on the back seat.

I switched off the engine, stepped out into the salt-laden air feeling calm and relaxed. The ride had been smooth, considerably better than if I'd have taken my own car. If it had even been capable of getting this far. Hennessey had made a smart suggestion. I opened the back door for Bonzo. He drifted away to sniff lamp posts, or something.

Unlike Thanet, the five-by-two-mile stretch of Mersea which overlooked the Blackwater Estuary was an actual island. At each high tide the causeway was fully submerged, and I'd had to cross when the water was low enough to expose the road. The nearest major conurbation was Colchester, just nine miles to the north and once a major Roman city. The island itself was unofficially divided in two. The eastern side was sparsely populated and mainly farmland. The west was a mix of commerce, leisure and residential.

I'd parked in front of a single row of beach huts that stretched in both directions as far as I could see. They were painted various pretty pastel colours. Clearly their owners cared deeply for them. Beyond the huts was a narrow strip of stony sand and the waters themselves, calm and receding. A few miles across the estuary was another land mass, dominated by a blocky construction which I knew was a nuclear power station because of the design. There was an obsolete facility just along the coast from Thanet at Dungeness. They were always located in out-of-the-way places where a disaster would affect comparatively few people.

Behind me was my objective: an apartment block, four storeys high. I pressed a button on the key, which automatically locked the car, a novel experience for me. The indicators flashed a couple of times to say, job done. I whistled hoarsely for Bonzo, but he ignored me, engrossed in some focused smelling. He could look after himself, then.

I crossed the piece of grass separating housing from street and checked the address. Flat 3B was the one I wanted. The name, Mourtice, was written roughly on a piece of paper above the bell. But I was hungry. My target could wait for now.

Nearby was a sign pointing towards the aptly named Seaside Café. One hundred yards away, apparently.

The establishment was a low, white-weather boarded construction. Next door was a closed sweet shop with a 'For Sale' sign in the window. If I had the money I could swap one backwater for another. I didn't, so I wouldn't.

Around the front of the building were several neatly arranged picnic tables bolted to the floor and a rack of beach-going items available for purchase – windbreaks, footballs, flip flops. Further along was the Seaview Holiday Park, marked by a large, welcoming sign, and more beach huts.

Inside, the café was quiet. Two of the tables were occupied, by a retired couple and a white-haired woman with her back to the door.

"Take a seat, menus are on the table," said a young guy, who was placing a coffee in front of the couple. I pulled out a chair, red of all colours, sat down. A laminated piece of card was propped up between salt and pepper shakers.

The young man came over. His lip was pierced by a black ring. His long dark hair was tied in a top knot, the sides of his head shaved to the skin. "First time visiting us?" A name badge said, "Will".

"First time on Mersea."

"It's a great place if you like to sail. Specials are on the board." Will hiked a thumb over his shoulder. "Can I get you a drink?"

"Flat white."

"Great choice. I'll come back to take a food order in a few minutes."

I glanced over the options while I waited. When Will returned with a large coffee in a white china mug I said, "All day breakfast, please."

"Coming right up, my man."

"Can I take it outside? I've a dog I'd better keep an eye on."

"Sure, whatever you want."

I took a table out front. Bonzo was gambolling on the beach with another mutt half his size. It seemed like they were having fun. I had a sip of the coffee which was good, strong enough to be interesting.

Will brought the breakfast not long after. "Brown sauce or ketchup?" he asked as he placed a large plate in front of me.

I stared at him like he was mad. Who had ketchup with bacon and sausage? "Brown sauce, of course." He gave me a thumbs up and a bottle of HP. "And another flat white, please."

"No worries, my man."

I switched off from everything while I ate. Lavender, Hennessey, Conn, Gregory, they all were forgotten for a few minutes while I inhaled the bacon, sausage, egg, hash brown and beans. Bonzo returned when his playmate was dragged away by the owner. He collapsed at my feet. I fed him some bacon rind from my otherwise empty plate which he happily accepted. While I nursed my coffee, Will cleared up. There was only him and me nearby.

"How was your food?" asked Will.

"Very good, thanks."

"Glad to hear it."

"Quiet today."

Will shrugged. "Quiet most days except the summer. We make enough then to tick over for the rest of the year." Largely, all coastal towns were the same. Not much work, little money for the residents, besieged by visitors for a few months.

"Are you a local?"

"Born and bred." He grinned. "I love it, so close to the sea." He wiped a rag over the table surface. "Are you here for long?"

"Depends."

"Well, if you want any advice, come see me. I know most people around and the best places to go."

"Thanks." I handed over Hennessey's credit card. Will popped inside to get the machine. When he reappeared and was feeding the card in I asked, "What about Adrian Mourtice?"

Will tried hard not to pull a face and failed. "Went to school with him."

"What's he like?"

"Why?"

"I'm about to meet him."

"Are you some sort of detective?"

"Reporter."

"I guess you're here about the ghost then?"

"Ghost?"

Will snorted. "Talk of the town a few years back. Go see Adrian first, then come back and we'll compare stories. Just don't laugh. The last guy did and Mourtice beat him half to death."

Thoroughly puzzled by Will's obtuse comments I headed over to Mourtice's flat with Bonzo on my heels. I pressed the intercom buzzer.

"Hello?" The tone was gnarled, suspicious.

"Mr Mourtice? I'm Harry Vaughan, I'd like to speak with you."

"I don't talk to nobody. Piss off." The was a squelch over the speaker when Mourtice released the button.

I tried again. "I want to know about the ghost." I let go, waited for a long moment.

"What did you say?" asked Mourtice eventually.

"The ghost. I believe you."

There was a loud metallic click as the lock dropped. "Come on up."

The door to flat 3B was ajar. I pushed it wider and stepped slowly forward, half in, half out. "Mr Mourtice?"

"Here," he said from along the corridor. "Close the door behind you."

Mourtice occupied a high-backed chair in the living room. It was dark, the curtains closed, blocking off the view over the bay and all the light. The only illumination came from a lamp in the corner. I stood within the entrance, Bonzo at my side.

If Will, who appeared no older than early twenties, hadn't told me he and Mourtice had gone to school together I'd have thought him middle-aged. His clothes, a T-shirt and tracksuit bottoms, were loose on his frame. There was several days' stubble on his chin and, by the smell, it had been many more days since he'd showered. I wished I still smoked, maybe that would mask the smell. I was desperate to open a window but felt I couldn't ask.

"Are you here to take the piss?" he asked, leaning forward, elbows on thighs.

"I want to learn," I said. "About the ghost."

"The others – they took the piss." Mourtice peered at me to see how I'd react.

"I wouldn't do that. Be sure to ask me to leave if you don't like me."

"I won't ask," said Mourtice. "And it'll be through the window."

"Okay." I patted Bonzo's head, Mourtice seemed to notice the dog for the first time. His eyes narrowed. "Can I take a look?" I asked.

"At what?"

"At how high we are."

Mourtice raised an eyebrow but nodded. I crossed to the curtains, opened them slightly. The light was piercing after the gloom. The drop was a good twenty feet into some bushes. I shut out the brightness.

"That'll hurt," I said.

"Hopefully." Mourtice sounded less certain now. He watched Bonzo who gave a low growl.

The room was even more austerely furnished than my own. There was only Mourtice's chair, no television, no sideboard, nothing else. "Do you mind?" I pointed to the floor.

"Be my guest." Mourtice waved as if he was allowing me to park my arse on a Louis the XIVth chaise longue. "Where do you want me to start?"

"Tell me something about yourself." Let's have familiar ground first. Bonzo settled down beside me, put his head between his paws but kept his glare on Mourtice.

Mourtice shifted in his chair. "Me? I'm nobody. Born in Mersea. I'll die here."

"That can't be entirely true. Ordinary people don't see ghosts."

"You're right." He nodded, as if only just realising his special status.

"When was your first time?"

"Four years, six months and three days ago."

"That's precise."

"I can tell you to the hour as well." Mourtice leant over the side of his chair, picked up a mug, waved it at me. "Impossible to forget. I was minding my own business when out of nowhere this mist surrounded me. I woke up in hospital with a broken arm."

"What were you doing?"

"Standing on the corner by the café, as you do."

"What else did you see? Besides the mist?"

"Nothing really, only a vague outline before I went under." Mourtice stuck the cigarette in his mouth.

"Of what?"

"A large shape, sort of human but not. Indistinct."

"Did you see it again?"

"Oh yes, several times. A shadow, before everything went dark and I'd be back in hospital. The ghost is why I don't go out any more. Because the ghost has it in for me. My mum brings food around. That's all really." He took a gulp from the mug. "Do you believe me?"

"One hundred and ten per cent," I lied.

Mourtice stared at me for a long moment. "Wait here." He stood, passed by me. He was back half a minute later. "Look at this." He held out a phone then pulled it back. "I'm not sure I believe you."

"I promise nothing bad will be printed about you, Adrian." That much was true. "In fact, if you prefer, this can be entirely off the record. Your name won't be used."

Mourtice thought for a moment, then offered me the mobile again, his hand shaking. I took it. "Press play." He loomed over my shoulder. The footage was shaky and shifted fast. It was at night, shadows of buildings, clearly near the café. A sweep to one side, a few seconds of twitching facing one direction, then the sweep again and so on. "It's coming," he said. "There!" Mourtice stabbed at the phone, paused the footage.

"I can't see anything."

Using two fingers Mourtice zoomed in. There was an indefinable shape on the edge of an alley between some houses. "That's the ghost. See?"

No, I thought. "Yes," I said.

"I bloody knew it! I've never shown this to anyone. Nobody has been like you before. They all thought I was mad."

"I don't understand why." I did.

Mourtice went back to his chair. He flopped down. "Thank you," he said. "This means a lot."

I didn't think Mourtice could tell me anything more. "You should get out of here, Adrian. See the world. Get your life back."

"Really?"

"When did the ghost visit you?"

Mourtice thought. "At night."

"Always?"

"Yes."

"Then be outside during the day. I don't think the ghost will harm you again."

"Maybe."

"I'll see myself out." But Mourtice was in his shell, possibly thinking about what I'd said. "Come on, Bonzo." I closed the door quietly behind me.

"Well?" said Will when I got back to the café. He was behind the counter, stacking mugs.

"I felt sorry for him."

"Take a seat, I'll make us a coffee and tell you all about the real Adrian Mourtice."

The Ghost

West Mersea, Essex

Will sipped his drink before he began, as if gathering his thoughts.

"You said you went to school together," I prompted.

"Everybody goes to school together round here." Will grinned. He did that a lot. "But, yeah, there's a good place to start. Adrian lived on a farm in East Mersea. He was a decent kid at first, nice parents, pleasant sister. We were good mates, best mates really. I used to spend time on the farm helping, he'd come over to mine and play football. Up until he was about sixteen."

"What happened?"

"Nothing, that was the problem. If you're not into boats or fishing, there's not a great deal to do. Adrian got bored. I'd joined the sailing club and was competing a lot. I tried to get him involved but after one try out when he fell overboard he wouldn't come back. Eventually, he got in with a couple of older kids from off the island, Chichester lads. They hung around the beach causing a bit of trouble. Adrian started doing drugs; a bit of weed, eventually a lot of speed. His school attendance and grades crashed, he dropped out of sixth form. His parents struggled to cope. We stopped spending time together once he began pushing."

"It's a familiar story where I live too," I said. Seaside towns, they look idyllic but scratch a little beneath the surface ... "What was he selling?"

"Anything he could get his hands on. He became a conduit for his Chichester '*friends*'." Will made air quotes.

"What about the police?"

Will snorted. "I'm sure you've had the same experience. They mean well but cutbacks force them to focus on the larger towns, cleaning up after Saturday night raves and the like. The rural problem spots get much less attention."

I nodded, very familiar circumstances. "What about this ghost?"

Will shifted in his seat. "That was when everything got weird." He sank some more of the coffee. Mine sat untouched. "Life round here was becoming out of hand. There were burglaries, muggings, stuff like that. Adrian was the influencer, people were scared of him. It was the tourists he liked the least, incomers invading his space. Everything changed once this family moved in. They were the usual mum, dad, daughter, son. Kept themselves to themselves. Mostly it was just the father who I saw around, occasionally the four of them together. I can't even remember their names now. Neither of the kids went to the local school. It was strange, they were strange. Adrian hated them immediately.

"Me too. Adrian was off his head most of the time. He swore something spoke to him, warned him off, wanted him to stop dealing and leave people alone."

"Did it work?"

"Not a chance. We all laughed, behind his back, of course. Until one night when somehow, he managed to catch the boy.

It was assumed he'd left the house and gone for a walk by himself. Adrian and his mates starting pushing him. Thankfully nothing happened because the dad arrived and got in the way, but by all accounts, the kid was shaken. Within twenty-four hours Adrian was in hospital." Will pointed at my cup. "Want a fresh one?"

"I'm good, thanks."

Will crossed to the machine, began making himself another brew. "We often get sea mists here, occasionally they're heavy. Visibility drops down to next to nothing inland, because it's so flat. There was one the day Adrian was taken out. Him and his mates were pissing around on the sea front when the fog came. When it rolled back they were all gone. Adrian was found in one of the beach huts. He'd been systematically assaulted, though if you saw him in the street it would be hard to tell. All the bruising was on his torso, not a mark on his face, no broken bones. He only spent a night in the hospital. Somebody was careful."

Steam hissed from the machine, cutting Will off briefly. "When he came home he was exactly the same, like nothing had happened, still dealing, still full of bravado. But he was beaten again, several times. After maybe the fourth occasion he morphed into a different character entirely. Scared of his own shadow. He didn't deal anymore. His townie mates stayed in Chichester. At least we never saw them again.

"Adrian moved into a flat here and he never leaves it now. His mum, poor cow, does all the shopping for him. I went around to see him on a couple of occasions. He only let me in once. He was as twitchy as hell. Swore the ghost had got him, that it was watching all the time. I stopped visiting in the end because after that he never answered the door." Will brought over more coffee.

"What happened to the boy and his family?"

Will shrugged. "They left a few weeks later. It's weird, though. The house they stayed in seems to be for transients. Sometimes it's a couple, another time two guys or three women. They never mix, and nobody stays for long." He laughed. "Perhaps the place is haunted. Ultimately, everyone was just pleased Adrian stopped, whatever the reason."

"Mersea is small, though. Surely everyone knows the next person's business?"

"How many people live where you're from?"

"Broadstairs? I don't know, at a guess 7000 or so."

"And are you aware of everything your neighbours in the next house are up to?"

"No, of course not."

"And that's my point. West Mersea isn't any different."

He made sense. "Thanks, Will. I appreciate you telling me all of this."

"I was hoping if somebody spoke to Adrian it might help. I was really angry at the time, now I'm just sad for him."

"You never know, he might be again."

"Maybe." Will shook himself out of his melancholy. "Anyway, how long are you staying in town?"

"Just overnight."

"Have you got anywhere to sleep?"

"I thought I'd book myself into one of the B&Bs." I'd seen several vacancy signs hanging outside houses on the way to the sea front.

"Go next door to the holiday park and tell them I sent you. There's caravans spare at this time of year. They'll sort you out."

"That's good of you, thanks."

"My parents own it." Will grinned. "Got to make money somehow."

Hennessey was paying, so what did I care? "One last question, Will."

"Shoot."

"What's the address of the place where that family were staying?"

The house was a decent detached construction a few hundred yards up the road. PVC windows, basic front garden, a driveway with a large wrought-iron gate across its span. It was unremarkable except for one aspect. The security.

CCTV cameras were discretely located on each corner of the building. And the gates, when I tried them, didn't open. They were sealed tight with a magnetic lock. There was an intercom on the brick-built support post. I pressed the button, but nobody answered. I gave up on the third attempt and began the walk back to the BMW. The nearby properties were built from the same plans but were subtly different. Better tended and easier to access – no bolted entrances.

When I was inside my car I called Gregory to update him.

"High security you say?"

"Compared to the other houses, absolutely."

"And transients who never stay long."

"Seemingly. What are you thinking?"

"I've an idea but let me check into it some more."

I said goodbye, made my way to the caravan site as Will suggested. As Bonzo and I neared, I saw movement at the block of flats. Mourtice was standing in the doorway, an arm across his blinking eyes.

He took a hesitant step outside.

The Purcell Problem

E dgeware, North London
The flat was above an opticians on the Burnt Oak Broadway, also known as the A5, which stretched between Elstree, adjacent to the M1 motorway, all the way into central London, near Hyde Park. For city access this was a prime spot, with a nearby underground station and an over ground rail link also.

The surrounding area was made up of strips of stores along the busy thoroughfares – betting shops, charity shops, fast food joints, regional restaurants, Halal butchers, Polish supermarkets – perfectly reflecting the culturally diverse nature of London. House prices, like most of the capital, were sky high. The kind of place I owned in Broadstairs would cost me three times as much here. The UK property market was, frankly, crazy.

"This is a really good area," said the estate agent who was letting the flat; a short Asian man, with glasses and a beard thick enough to scrub barbecues clean, called Mr Aziz. He'd shaken hands vigorously just after I'd entered his showroom and enquired about the two-bedroom apartment advertised in the window. He met me here within fifteen minutes. Aziz was keen. I was pretending to be. Bonzo sat beside me, bored. Aziz eyed the hound. He'd already told me he was sure he could persuade the owners to allow a pet, if it sealed the deal.

169

Access to the flat was gained by a set of wooden stairs out the back of the shops above the A5. A walkway ran along the exterior, providing access to each accommodation. We were standing on the balcony now while Aziz searched for the right key on a spectacularly crowded chain. The residence I really wanted was two doors along. I'd knocked earlier, but nobody answered. I felt it would be helpful to get a look inside, just to get an impression of the location.

The agent finally found the key. With an expansive grin, Aziz twisted the lock. The door stuck part-way open. He put his head around to see what the problem was before sliding through the gap. A moment later, he pulled the door wide, a pile of paper an inch or two thick in his hand.

"Takeaway menus," he said by way of explanation. We were in a corridor which appeared to run the length of the interior. The flat smelled damp. And it was dingy. The wallpaper, with a swirly, psychedelic pattern, was peeling off here and there. "Lovely accommodation," he said. I didn't agree.

Aziz walked ahead of me, pointing into each unfurnished room as we progressed. Kitchen, bathroom, two bedrooms, living room. The latter space possessed two sash windows. The buzz of traffic was constant. The throaty roar of a punchy motorbike, a lorry, a siren in the distance. At least in here the exhaust smell was barely detectable.

I parted the grey net curtain which hung across one of the grimy windows and was rewarded with a view of the street; a queue of vehicles and the top of people's heads as they walked the pavement below. I turned, took in the rectangular room. Aziz beamed at me from the doorway.

"How much?" I asked.

"£525 per week. A bargain!" Again, I didn't share his enthusiasm. It was depressing. And expensive. If the flat two doors down was equivalent, and, according to Hennessey's analysis, the Nudge Man had been an inhabitant for any length of time, he must have been desperate. "So, shall we sign the contract? You can move in straight away!"

"I'll be honest," I said, "it's not quite what I was looking for."

Aziz's smile slipped slightly, but he kept fighting for the sale. "You'll need to be quick, there's not much available around here."

"I'll take my chances."

"Okay." Aziz shrugged like I was some sort of fool. "If you're sure." He showed me out of the flat and shook my hand at the bottom of the stairs before he stalked off. I trailed behind, slowly. I'd parked half a mile away or so on a residential side street, though I had no intention of returning to my car yet.

When Aziz was out of sight I headed back up, bypassed the flat I'd just viewed and knocked at the one I wanted. Again, no response. Previously I'd looked through the letterbox, but the view was blocked by a dark fabric, perhaps to catch the mail. A window next to the door was for the kitchen but it was frosted for privacy. All the other flats had normal glass. Someone standing at the window could be in front of the sink, maybe washing up, and I wouldn't have a clue as to their identity. I paused for a moment wondering what to do next. I wasn't ready to give up. According to Wyatt there had been quite a lot of electronic traffic from this property, to do with petty crime.

I went to the neighbouring flat, knocked on the door. It was opened by a young black woman, her hair hidden by a scarf. She glared at me through the crack, a chain across the gap, flicked her eyes down to Bonzo and back up to me. She said nothing.

"Excuse me, do you know who lives next door?"

"No." The door was slammed shut. I knocked once more, but I was ignored. A drop of rain hit my shoulder. The sky was darkening.

I shifted to the flat on the other side, rapped on the glass of the white PVC door. There was movement; the rattle of locks. An old boy pulled the door wide. He had neatly combed and greased silver hair and a moustache. He was dressed in a suit and wore a tie in a style harking back to the formality of the forties and fifties before the age of the hippy.

"How can I help you, young man?" he asked.

"It's been a while since anyone has called me that."

"Everything is relative." He smiled. "I'm Godfrey Purcell."

"Harry Vaughan." We shook hands.

"What a magnificent beast." Purcell knelt so he was level with Bonzo and rubbed his side over his ribs. Bonzo rolled on-to his back and showed his stomach to the old man. After half a minute of Purcell asking whether Bonzo was a good boy and not getting a word back in response, he stood with a creak. The rain began to fall properly. "Why don't you come in out of the blasted weather?"

"I'd be happy to."

Purcell's flat couldn't have been more different to Aziz's. It was bright, clean and full of furniture from the seventies that would cost a fortune in a retro shop. Purcell turned immediately into the kitchen. "Cup of tea?"

"That would be great, thanks."

Purcell filled the kettle then took a bowl out of a cupboard, splashed water into that too and placed it on the floor before Bonzo. "How can I help you, son?" Bonzo lapped noisily away.

"I'm trying to track down the people who lived next door about four years ago."

He frowned. "Are you a private detective?"

Again, with the assumptions. I said, "Freelance reporter."

"Why do you want to find them?"

"To help."

Purcell peered at me, eyes narrowed. "I've spent years around liars, Mr Vaughan. I think we can talk." The water was boiling. "But over a hot drink, shall we? Life always seems less complicated with a cuppa. Will Earl Grey do you?"

Purcell made his tea the old fashioned way. With a pot, leaves and a strainer. I waited in his living room while he brewed. Bonzo had flopped down and promptly gone to sleep. Atop a mantle surrounding a log-effect gas fire were many framed photos and a bank of medals mounted on a wood block.

Several of the images were recognisable as Purcell himself, sitting on a tank, a Sherman maybe, in one black-and-white shot. His sleeves were rolled up. It appeared bright and hot. Then Purcell in what seemed to be a police uniform. Another in front of a church, happy with his wife. Finally, children and grandchildren as he and his partner steadily aged.

"Lesley died six and a half years ago," said Purcell as he entered carrying a tray. "Not a day goes by when I don't think of her." He placed the tray on a table between two wing-backed chairs which faced the fire.

"How long were you married?"

"Nearly forty years." Purcell straightened.

"That can't have been easy."

"You have no idea, Mr Vaughan." Purcell waved at one of the seats. "If you'd like to rest your weary self?"

I settled in the left hand of the pair, which, I assumed, had been Lesley's. Purcell poured. "I got out the good stuff. It's not often I have visitors." He poured tea of a light brown colour into a cup, catching the leaves in a sieve. "Milk?"

"Should I?"

Purcell shrugged. "Up to you. I'm too old to care about etiquette."

"Then I will."

Purcell added a splash, handed me the cup and saucer. He sat waiting expectantly so I took a sip. It was hot, fresh and floral. "That's good."

He chuckled. "It bloody should be, given how much I paid for it."

Once Purcell held his own cup I said, "You used to be in the police?"

"On the beat for most of my career. Not round here, though. Never piss on your patch, my old sergeant used to tell me. That's how I knew about them next door. That they were cops and they were concealing someone."

"You're sure?"

"Oh, yes."

"Who were they hiding?"

"I've no idea. It doesn't pay to get involved in other people's business these days. And I'm not as handy as I used to be."

"What did they look like?"

"I never saw them. It was very strange. But the walls are thin. I could hear a couple of females and two or three males – even though they tried to keep their voices down. They arrived late one night and were gone within a month."

"You seem to remember it well."

"It's not every day there's a raid on your neighbour."

"A raid?"

"That's right, and not by the authorities." Purcell took another sip, seemed to be gathering his thoughts. "But that's not the beginning of the story. Wait here a moment." Purcell stood, left the room. When he returned he was holding a scrap book, which he passed to me as he sat back down. His thumb was in between two pages. It was a newspaper article about Purcell. A photograph of him in this very living room. He was wearing a uniform and nursing a black eye. The headline blared, "War Hero's Medals Stolen".

"I was on my way to the Cenotaph for Armistice Day when I was jumped from behind by a couple of lads," said Purcell. "They took my medals; gave me a bit of a kicking. I was so ashamed. The day after the story came out there was a man on my doorstep. I didn't know him. He was asking questions about the incident. He told me my property would be returned. He was very certain about it. And he was true to his word. Within twenty-four hours he was back. He handed over my medals in a paper bag. I tried to thank him, but he was gone.

"He made me realise I'd become too cut off from the world, that I'd forgotten the reason I joined the army and the police in the first place. For other people, not myself. I could help, even at my age. And the obvious place was to start with whoever was hiding next door. I didn't go around and knock, they were clearly staying out of the way for a reason, but I kept watch, made sure they were all right.

"It was late one night, a Sunday, just a couple of weeks later when I heard a lot of noise through the wall. I was sitting right here. I'd dozed off in front of the fire. I didn't sleep in my bed much at the time, just in case they ever needed me in a hurry."

"What was going on?"

"They were leaving and quickly. Two men, a woman and two others. Not little ones, teenagers. The men were in charge, directing the family. I watched through the kitchen window. I kept the light off, so they didn't see me. Within minutes they were out the door with a couple of bags, down the stairs and into cars which had their engines running. Then they were driven away at speed. It fell silent. Seemingly I was the only person who noticed their departure." Purcell shook his head. "Nobody cares anymore."

"Did you go round?"

"It didn't seem wise. They were gone so fast I assumed someone was coming. So, I stayed at the window. And arrive they did. It felt like forever, standing and watching. My hip began to ache. But eventually a van reversed into the car park, its lights off, blocking the entrance.

"Somebody got out of the passenger side and opened up the rear of the van. Three people exited. The way they moved they were well trained. Silent, crouched. I reckon they were armed but concealed. They made barely a sound as they came up the stairs. I stepped further back into the shadows, barely daring to breathe. I was as scared as I'd ever been. My legs felt like they were going to give way.

"One remained at the front door while the other two entered. They weren't inside long and came out much less cautiously. They weren't happy, there was quite a bit of swearing. They went back down the stairs. That's when I noticed there was somebody else in the car park because they spoke to him."

"Do you know who he was?"

"No." Purcell finished his tea. "But he was in a wheelchair."

Hennessey's Game

Pluck's Gutter, Kent

Eric Hennessey poured himself a stiff whisky, leaning on the cabinet for support as he drank. He kept the wheelchair beside him, the blanket to hand, just in case he needed to be seated in a hurry. Only the nurse knew he had the full use of his legs, and she was operating under a powerful non-disclosure agreement – the savage death of her girlfriend and entire family should anybody uncover the truth.

Hennessey had watched his father, a miner back when there were still accessible coal seams in Kent, metaphorically crushed underfoot by the ruthless Thatcher government and betrayed by the incompetent left-wing union leadership of the time. Hennessey had decided there and then that he was going to be rich, independent and vote Conservative.

These days, Hennessey was an admirer of the latest US President. He liked the disruptive rhetoric, the sabre rattling threats to the old order, the devil-may-care decision making. Hennessey too was anti-immigration, anti-abortion and anti-free speech. Pro-guns, pro-profit and pro-self. He wished the UK would shift further to the right. Brexit was helping, though not fast enough. And that woman Prime Minister. He didn't believe she really wanted to break from Europe.

So, when the American administration had come calling, requesting his help, Hennessey had answered. The man he'd met was called Six, a dead-eyed murderer possessing a total conviction in his beliefs which aligned thoroughly with Hennessey's. Six said he needed local help, that there was only so much he could achieve by himself. Hennessey had the people, the wherewithal and, eventually, the incentive.

It was Six who'd shown Hennessey it was the Nudge Man who'd stiffed him. Six who'd given Hennessey a contact in the UK government. Six who'd provided all the data on the Nudge Man which Vaughan now had. The number crunching and analysis of the Nudge Man's activities was something Hennessey could never have done by himself.

However, the UK representative the government sent (Blake Midwinter, for God's sake) had proven to be a fop, hardly characteristic of Hennessey's ideals. And now he was off the board, along with Lavender, free and gone to ground somewhere.

Then there was Vaughan, who was proving near useless, so far turning up nothing. Maybe he'd employed another ball of fluff. But Six seemed pleased enough.

Hennessey was literally tracking Vaughan as he moved about the country. The BMW's sat nav in constant communication with Hennessey's laptop. He monitored all his cars, in case any of his men took the piss, therefore it had been a stroke of immense fortune when the two idiots had been hospitalised. It was an easy way to keep an eye on Vaughan. In the old days his men would have suffered several broken bones as a lesson for being so stupid. But he needed the numbers right now.

Hennessey's mobile rang. He dug the unit out of his pocket and glanced at the screen. Blocked. He didn't have voicemail activated; he wouldn't commit anything to any form of recording, written or verbal, because of the chance it could be used against him. This investigation against the US President right now so many emails being bandied around. Were they all so stupid to think they were utterly untouchable?

Therefore, very few people had Hennessey's number. He answered. Six spoke and Hennessey listened.

Vaughan Gets Suspicious

M 25, Essex

I dialled Gregory from the car. The call immediately dropped into voicemail, so I left a brief message asking him to ring me right back.

I'd stayed with Purcell for another half an hour or so, just talking. He was a fascinating man with plenty of stories he delivered in an engaging, understated fashion. And we were both lonely. It was only when Bonzo began to complain that Purcell ushered me out to give the dog a walk. I left my phone number with Purcell and the promise that I'd pick up if he rang.

A sharp, loud bell sounded over the car speakers. It was Gregory, according to the screen. I pressed the green button on the dashboard, said hello. Then swerved to get myself back on the right side of the road accompanied by the sound of a truck horn as it blew by.

"I met one of the neighbours," I said, "and he told me the flat was raided by a couple of gunmen minutes after a group escaped. He reckoned it was two men, a woman and two teens staying there."

"Jesus."

"That's not all. One of the group was a large man in a wheelchair." There was a long silence over the speakers.

"Hennessey."

"Could be somebody else."

"It *has* to be him. Too much of a coincidence otherwise."

"Plenty of other people in the UK are wheelchair users."

"But how many have a direct connection to the Nudge Man?" He had me there. "I told you he couldn't be trusted."

"I never disagreed with you. And now we know he definitely has a less than benevolent lean towards the Nudge Man, we can act accordingly."

"Maybe."

"What else do I do? Give up?"

"It's an option."

"Not happening. I'm on the way to Norfolk as we speak."

"Can I give you one word of advice?"

"Of course."

"Use cash for all your future expenses. Take as much as you can out of the bank. Keep Hennessey on a short leash. Make the man think you're still working for him, but do not tell him anything of value."

"That was a lot more than one word of advice."

"Sorry."

"No need to apologise. It's valuable." I pulled up to a roundabout, pausing before crossing. "Any developments at your end? Has Lavender been caught?"

"He's gone to ground, no sightings since he escaped. And, in terms of progress, I've been speaking with a couple of colleagues. Wyatt put me onto a DI called Pennance in the Sapphire Unit at the Met. Between Wyatt and Pennance they're checking out these addresses you're going to. I don't have the right access. I'm still waiting to hear back."

"Why is it taking so long?"

"They have to be careful. None of us can just log onto the Police National Computer and dig this stuff up, you know."

"I feel like I'm up against a ticking clock here."

"I get it, Harry. Really, I do. I'm doing my best."

"Sorry, I didn't mean to be a wanker."

"You can't help how you were born." I could hear the grin over the speakers.

"What about that American – Six – anything on him?"

"Nobody in the database matches his description. I've hit a brick wall there. Look, I'd better get back. I'll call when I have something."

"Cheers," I said, but Gregory had already gone. It was just me and the tarmac now.

Paper Ghosts

Hockwold cum Wilton, Norfolk
     The detached house was on the left-hand side of a narrow track bordered by high hedges outside the village of Hockwold cum Wilton. To the east was the expansive Thetford Forest, to the south RAF Lakenheath, to the west the cathedral city of Ely in Cambridgeshire. The surrounding area was flat, reclaimed marshland as far as the eye could see.

I drove past slowly. A middle-aged woman, her hair under a patterned red scarf or handkerchief, was working in the garden, pulling up weeds, jerking the plants hard to get them out of the ground. A few yards along was the entrance to a field, the mud deeply rutted by heavy tractor tyres. I swung around, being careful not to ground the BMW's bumper on the ridges. This car was hardly suited for the location. On the way back, the woman glanced up, pausing with a gloved hand full of nettles. I mounted the narrow verge, wound down my window. Bonzo sat up when the engine was turned off.

"I'm a little lost," I lied.

The woman dropped the nettles onto a large pile of vegetation, came forward a few yards. Her face was flushed, presumably from the effort of weeding. We were separated by the line of laurel bushes running along the border of the property. The house itself appeared to be early 20th century, brick-built, sash windows, tiled roof. The setting sun reflected off the glass in the upper storey.

"God, a proper bloody accent!" she said, her own clearly London as she pushed a lock of black hair from across her eyes. "Where are you from?"

"Kent."

"Then what the hell are you doing in this Godforsaken place?"

"Just visiting. I was told there's a good walk around here. For my dog."

"Ha, so you'll be escaping soon then. Lucky bugger. Unfortunately, I can't be much help. I'm pretty recent here myself. Gordon, my husband, fancied the idea of living in the middle of bloody nowhere. He gets the train into London on a Monday from Thetford, isn't back till Friday and then he pisses off and plays golf most of the weekend. He says it's idyllic. Try being stuck out here seven days a week!"

"It doesn't sound fun," I said. In her own way she was as lonely as Purcell.

The woman shook her head. "Sorry, listen to me complaining." She glanced over my shoulder. "Your dog looks thirsty. Will he want some water? And what about a cup of coffee for you? To make up for my whining?"

I grinned. "Sounds great."

"I'm Amanda, by the way. And you'd better bring your car onto the drive. Farmer Giles isn't happy if he can't get his tractor along here at all hours to spray his crops. And the muck spreading, ugh." She paused. "He's not actually called Giles, but that's how I think of him."

"Whatever works."

"My sentiments exactly. I'll leave the door open."

I reversed a few feet and drove onto Amanda's property. There was a skip full of rubble, household junk, tiles, bricks and the like out front, which I parked beside. Bonzo wouldn't leave the car, stubbornly settling down on the back seat, so I opened a window and let him be. The front door stood wide. I entered and closed the door behind me.

"I'm in here," she shouted. Her face showed briefly at the end of the corridor. "Be careful where you step. Just don't break a bloody leg. Gordon would kill me!" It appeared Amanda was part-way through a renovation. Some floorboards were up, wallpaper pulled down, taking plaster away in places. I passed a room where a wall was in the process of being removed, knocking one space into another.

"Sorry it's such a bloody mess. Something else for me to deal with while he's gallivanting around. Do you know how unreliable tradesmen are?" I had an opinion, but Amanda didn't give me chance to vocalise before she answered her own question. "Awful! They're next to impossible to get hold of, when they do commit to a date it slips and when they finally arrive they keep pissing off to do other stuff! If they had real jobs they'd get fired!"

"That's why they're builders."

"True. Where's your dog?"

"Sleeping in the car."

"They're lazy buggers." She handed me a mug of instant coffee, leant on a kitchen counter. "Almost as bad as cats. And builders."

"How long have you lived here?"

"Just a few months. Long enough to fall out with half the local population – country bumpkins most of them. That accent, ugh!" She picked up a glass full of ice, saluted me with it. "Never too early for a G&T. I'm assuming you don't want one, as you're driving."

"Saving myself for later."

"Very sensible. Whereabouts in Kent are you?"

"Broadstairs."

"I know it well, used to go there as a child."

"It hasn't changed much."

"Why are you all the way out here?"

"I'm a reporter following a story."

"About bastard bankers making too much money, by any chance?"

"Sorry, no."

Amanda sighed. "Pity, I could have given you plenty of inside information."

"Nice house."

"It's a bloody millstone."

"Do you know much about the previous occupants?"

"That's your story?"

"Kind of."

"Unfortunately, I don't. As I said, I'm not from the area. Gordon just landed it on me one day." She pulled herself up straight, puffed out her chest and spoke with a deeper tone. "Amanda, we are moving to the countryside. It will be good for you." She relaxed, drank the rest of her gin and tonic, the ice rattling in the glass. "Lying bastard. It was just another of his deals." Amanda turned away from me and began to mix another drink.

"How?"

"Like always," she said over her shoulder. "Bought on the cheap from one of his golfing buddies."

"Who used to own it?"

Amanda faced me again, elbow resting on one folded arm, glass pressed against a still bright cheek. "You won't put this in your article?"

"Probably nobody will publish it anyway, but sure."

"I'll hold you to that." Amanda downed some gin. "The police, that's what Gordon told me. They weren't on the deeds though, some solicitor handled it all. But I've wondered ever since, why would the cops own a place right out here? In the middle of bloody nowhere." Again, Amanda answered before I could. "I'll tell you why, to hide people."

"What makes you say that?"

Amanda put her glass down. "Wait here a minute."

When she left the kitchen, I poured most of the coffee down the plug hole – I'm not a fan of instant – leaving a dribble in the bottom so it appeared I'd actually drunk the stuff. Then Amanda was back, a pile of envelopes in her hand. "Read these," she said, and pushed them at me.

The envelopes were blank and all the same size, the letterbox-shaped ones you can buy in bulk cheaply from any supermarket. They'd all been sealed and someone, presumably Amanda, had torn them open.

I took the first in the pile, put the rest on the side for the moment. Within was a sheet of lined paper, torn out of a notebook by the jagged edges. It was dated, almost five years ago. The text was a handwritten scribble, as if written in a rush.

"Are you all right?" asked Amanda. "You look as if you've seen a ghost."

I ignored her, pulled one letter after the other from the envelope. I recognised the handwriting.

It belonged to my son.

Letters from the Edge

Weeting, Norfolk

I was staying at a small bed and breakfast just off the main street in the nearby village of Weeting, a few miles due east of Amanda's house. After checking in (essentially taking the keys to the room and throwing my carrier bag of clothes on the bed) I headed to a nearby pub, called the Saxon, ordered a pie, a pint for me and a steak for the dog. I took a seat at a table as far away from everyone as possible with Bonzo at my feet.

As usual the animal drew all the attention from the humans, the pub's patrons stopping by to pat his head and talk to me about him. Bonzo accepted the former with good grace, even rolling over onto his side for one woman to rub his ribs. The latter I rejected. I wasn't interested in talking about the hound, he was just there to ensure I was safe. We weren't "friends" and never would be. When this was all over he'd be back at O'Neal's and on his boring guard duty. I was sick of picking up his crap, fed up of the hairs on my clothes and worn out with the snoring. And don't get me onto the farts.

Instead of canine conversations I wanted to focus on the letters. I pulled the sheaf out of my pocket and organised them by date, oldest uppermost. There were twelve in all, spread randomly over a six-month period and going back five years –

around the time I lost contact with my family. Each one started with the line, "Dear Dad".

The food I'd ordered arrived quickly, interrupting my evaluation. Reluctantly I put them to one side while I ate mechanically and swiftly, not tasting anything which passed my lips. A process just to consume some calories. On the other hand, Bonzo vacuumed up his meat with relish, if the sounds from below were anything to go by. When I was done I pushed my plate to one side, ordered another pint from the bar, though my first wasn't drained, and began reading at last.

Dear Dad,

I'm not supposed to be writing this, but I have to. There's nobody else I can speak with, just you.

When Mum told me we had ten minutes to pack whatever we wanted before leaving, I freaked out. Mum said Shaw, the cop, told her we could go back home one day, that the stuff we left behind would be safe. I didn't believe him, neither did Mum. We couldn't contact anyone we knew to say where we were going or why we'd left. Not even my friends or you.

Do you know how hard it is to choose just a few things in a couple of minutes? Everything seemed valuable. Of course, I picked up paper and pens, whereas Maddie had her laptop and iPod.

At least Noah is with us. DS Maddox we're supposed to call him, but we only do when Shaw is around. Maddox is nice, we all like him and he's good to Mum.

This is all my fault, I feel terrible. I'm the one who brought this on us. It's because of me we might never go home again. It's because of what I saw and who I told.

I'm so, so sorry, Dad.

Jack.

Jack, the youngest of my two kids, was the thoughtful one, spent a lot of time on his own. He liked to draw a lot and write – not with a computer like his IT-savvy sister, but with a paper and pen. He had crazy ideas, that he wanted a career in journalism, to follow me, no matter how hard I tried to put him off. He'd have been twelve, coming up to thirteen at the time, and Maddie fourteen. It was hard to believe they'd be seventeen and nineteen respectively now. I'd missed so much.

Compared to Jack, Maddie was a social animal, always on platforms such as Facebook or Twitter chatting with somebody. She usually had her hands on either her laptop or phone. Like many children these days she knew her way around technology far better than the older generation. I'd looked for Maddie multiple times over recent years online, but never found her. At first, I'd assumed she'd taken on a pseudonym, but I knew her friends and there was no reference to her on their timelines.

I drank some beer, moved onto the next in the pile.

Dear Dad,

I'm sorry I haven't been able to write since my last letter, but we've been shifting around a lot. I think we're in our fourth place now. I'm not even sure where we are. We get moved at night, usually we have to sit in the back of a van with no windows. When we're in the house or flat the curtains stay closed. We unpack one day, then put it all away again a few weeks later. What's the point? It's like being in prison. But Mum and Maddie are just bystanders, I'm only a witness. Why is this happening to us? Why are we being kept out of sight when the crooks roam free?

We hardly see Shaw, it's just Noah now and one of his col-
leagues. Noah has been brilliant. He goes out shopping for us. The
police don't give us much money. Mum says it's hard to make it
stretch. I'd always thought people in witness protection got new
names and were well looked after. Well, we do have new surnames
(which I can't tell you!) but it's lonely. I'm so desperate to talk with
my friends. We're not allowed on social media or anything. Our
phones have been taken off us. At some point I'll sneak out and
post this to you, but I mustn't get caught. Mum would go mad if
she knew.

Jack.

Typical Jack, breaking the rules. Witness protection, that
was a shock, but why were they in the process? What had Jack
seen?

The next three letters were in a similar vein with Jack talking about where he thought they were, how boring it was, how
little there was to do, how Maddie was going mad being unable
to speak with anyone and Elizabeth clearly worried though
pretending not to be. They reflected how little stimulation Jack
was getting. It was four walls and a window to stare out of. And
Jack blaming himself. Through these letters I was his shoulder
to cry on, though I hadn't known it at the time.

Dear Dad,

They almost found out about me writing to you! I'm some-
where called West Mersea now which is in Essex. It's quiet round
here and it's been several months since we left London. As there
haven't been any problems since, Noah lets us out every now and
again, but only under strict supervision. We must pick our times
though, when the streets are empty. We're in a nice house just near
the sea, so I've been down to the beach and paddled several times.

It reminds me of Broadstairs, where we used to go on holiday. Do you remember?

So, I've been able to get a little familiar with the area. Two days ago, I managed to sneak away late one night. I'd been able to get hold of some envelopes and one stamp. The envelopes had been left by somebody else at the back of a drawer and the stamp was unfranked on some old post.

When I was outside it felt amazing being free and on my own in fresh air! I was walking to the post box when a group of lads stopped me. One of them, I don't know his name, began pushing me around. He was obviously on something. I got very scared and tried to walk away, but they surrounded me and wouldn't let me go. They were asking me who I was, whether I was a tourist or even a foreigner.

Then Noah appeared. Somehow, he knew I was out. The lads backed off, but I was freaked. Worse, we're moving again now and from a place I was beginning to like, where I thought we could stay for a while. God, I keep messing everything up!

Noah has been organising somewhere new for us. Neither Mum nor Noah are happy about it. The weird thing is the lad who pushed me around ended up in hospital, I heard Noah telling Mum. I think Noah did it. He's a really nice guy, though every now and again his eyes go hard and he's quite scary. But I don't think he'd ever hurt us.

Anyway, miss you.

Jack.

So, this Maddox guy who was protecting my family must have been the one who beat up Mourtice. However, Jack's next note was truly electrifying.

Dear Dad,

It's been nearly six months since we left Battersea and away from Hennessey.

We've been in a dingy flat in London, the worst place so far, but it was all Noah could find at such short notice after leaving Mersea in a rush. The traffic noise from the main road below is constant, though it's interesting looking at all the different people out on the street. There's something going on all the time and none of them know I'm watching. I wish I could be down there with them.

We haven't seen Shaw for ages. Noah was shouting at him over the phone yesterday. He said he was really pissed off. I wonder if Noah has a family of his own, because he's always with us. Him and Mum never seem to be apart. Maddie reckons Mum likes Noah, but I told her to shut up.

There's a nice old man next door. I didn't know his name at the time (that's the trouble, I never know anybody's *name!). I saw him down on the street. He had a black eye, somebody must have punched him, it was horrible. He looked sad, I wanted to speak with him, to see if I could help, but we're not allowed.*

I told Noah about him. He said the man was called Purcell and somebody had stolen his war medals when he was on the way to an event. I was so angry! So was Maddie when I told her, she said something had to be done about it. Noah said everything would be all right though, that there were people who would look after Mr Purcell and get back what was his.

I don't know what happened or if Noah was right because we had to move once more! Part of me was glad and at least this time it wasn't my fault. Noah woke us all up late one night. It was like Battersea all over again, but less stuff to choose from and we only had five minutes to shove everything in a case. Noah wouldn't say why, he was just urging us to get a move on. Mum was as white as a sheet.

I never got chance to say hello or goodbye to Mr Purcell, which I'm disappointed about. I think he would have been an interesting man to speak with.

Jack.

I finished the rest of the letters; mundane stuff really. The last note was written from a place called Flash. It was a location on Hennessey's map and came up in Wyatt's analysis. Jack's writing just gave me the other side of the story. My heart went out to him.

My family stuck away God knows where with criminals after them and seemingly little police protection. I was furious with Elizabeth. How could she have not got word to me somehow? I headed to the bar, ordered a double vodka and the bill. I sank the fiery liquid while the bartender rang up. I threw Hennessey's card at him, decided to have another couple of shots as the double-crossing bastard was paying, for now ignoring Gregory's advice to go cash only. I'd rectify that tomorrow when I found an ATM.

Speaking of Gregory, my phone bleeped, a text from the cop asking if I could talk? I replied to tell him ten minutes. I downed the vodka fast, ignoring the slam of alcohol into my gut.

I headed back to the B&B, Bonzo in my wake, and rang Gregory while sitting on my bed, said, "You won't believe what I've discovered today."

"Go on, surprise me."

"Letters from the people I've been following. They were written by my son. It's my family that Hennessey wants me to find. Because he's been after them too."

"Jesus."

"I had rather stronger words in mind. But who better to track them down than me? They've been in witness protection."

"Which brings us to my news. The places you've visited are safe houses."

"Makes sense. The owner of the property the letters were found in understood it had been bought from the police."

"What are you going to do?"

"Carry on, I need to get to them before Hennessey does." I lay back on the bed, feeling drained. "There's a couple of names in Jack's letters. A Shaw and Noah Maddox, a DS. Seemed like Maddox was the one on permanent guard duty."

"I've never heard of either of them."

"Maddox is the key."

Then Gregory asked, "What's next for you?"

"Jack's last letter was from Flash. I'm heading there tomorrow."

"I remember that place. Emily's data analysis threw it up."

"That's right." I paused before asking a difficult question of Gregory. "One more thing, Guy. Can you send me Maddox's personnel file?"

Gregory choked down the line as I'd expected. "Of course I can't!"

"I need something, I have to know who he is. You know this could be important."

After a long wait Gregory replied, "I'll see what I can do, but I can't promise."

"Thanks." I rang off.

I dug my wallet out and rummaged in the section where notes were supposed to go, if I had any. There was a creased photo of me, Maddie and Jack taken years ago. It was all I had of them now. Kids then, a late teenager and an adult now.

Bonzo jumped onto the bed. He pushed himself up to me. But I wasn't in the mood. I shoved him back on the floor, that's where animals were supposed to go, right? Bonzo gave me a mournful look, yet I went unmoved. Dogs don't have the same emotions as humans, how can they? Bonzo settled down, his back turned to me. I stared at the photo for an age until my phone bleeped. Again, it was from Gregory. A WhatsApp message which said, "Check mail."

I slid off the bed, booted up my laptop, entered email. There was a note from Gregory awaiting me. I clicked on the attached file. A couple of pages about Detective Sergeant Noah Maddox. Interestingly his birthplace was listed as Flash in the county of Staffordshire. At the back was a copy of his photograph, blurry and in black and white, though clear enough.

I knew him. But not as Noah Maddox.

As Pomfrey Lavender.

Locals Only

Flash, Staffordshire

The hamlet of Flash was laid out in a triangle. New Road, as it was called, formed the horizontal and vertical of the shape and encompassed the centre of the habitation, what little there was (though it included a pub, a major positive). An unnamed road running at a roughly forty-five-degree angle, off which a couple of farms stood, made the connection.

The BMW struggled with the steep hills where Flash was perched. The village itself was in the Peak District, a beautiful but bleak area in the north-west of England. I'd driven up the M1, turning off near Nottingham before climbing into the Peaks via Ashbourne. Prior to Buxton I'd climbed higher still.

The region was rolling hills, clutches of bent trees, fields marked by drystone walls and sheep, sheep everywhere. Which meant poor soil. The sky was an overcast grey, the sun hidden. Kent, the garden of England, was the opposite. Low-lying, often barely a cloud in the sky and rich, loamy earth.

Reaching Flash had been even more interesting. Wind whipped at the car. The vegetation was heather and gorse. Here and there were pockets of water, natural ponds of various sizes filled by what would be regular rain this high up. A readout on the car dash said 1,500 feet. There was a drizzle right now, like I'd steered into a cloud. That fine vapour which hung in the air, steadily soaking everything and reducing visibility.

The three-litre engine had plenty of power, but the car was front-wheel drive so the grip on anything slippery, mud for example, became a problem. Because of the tractors and proper off-road vehicles, there was plenty of dirt on the road and the rain made the tarmac slick. I decided a single loop around the area was enough. I didn't want to end up in a steep gulley, out of sight and injured.

This was where Pomfrey Lavender had grown up. I corrected myself, *Noah Maddox*. A soldier, then a cop. A man who lived by routine and followed orders, who'd been looking after my family, keeping them safe from Eric Hennessey. Until Lavender had gone to prison.

I parked outside the village pub, the New Inn, which looked old. There was a sign in the window which said, 'No Vacancies'. A second notice read, 'Muddy Boots and Muddier Dogs Welcome'. The door stood open.

I dug out my phone to see if there was anywhere I could stay locally, but I hadn't got any reception. We were probably miles away from any masts. Actually, we were probably miles away from anything.

I got out of the BMW and stretched. I'd risen early, packed, grabbed a fast shower, dragged a reluctant Bonzo away from his spot in front of a radiator, and driven to Flash without stopping. A decent journey of a hundred and seventy-five miles over three and a half hours.

I headed inside. There were a couple of locals at tables, a barman with greying rock-a-billy, slicked-back hair, sideburns and an earring, leaning against a post, reading the newspaper. He looked up when I came in, smiled. "Morning, sir." His accent was hard on my ears, I rarely heard such strong northern dialects.

However, via his grin he came over as genuinely friendly, not displaying the modicum of distrust that accompanies most first-time interactions with southerners. Bonzo stuck his nose into a large bowl of water on the floor just inside the entrance.

I scanned the pumps. "Pint of Best, please," I said. Locally brewed, by the look of it.

"Certainly." The barman lifted down a jug glass from a shelf above his head. I took one of the stools and watched him draw on the pump. The beer was dark and foamy. He allowed the bubbles to settle before topping up, leaving a thick head. "That'll be £3."

"Is the restaurant open yet?"

"Not till twelve. I've got crisps."

I ordered plain for Bonzo, salt and vinegar for me, handed over some cash. Bonzo shambled over and flopped at my feet. I tore open the packet of crisps and placed it on the stone floor beside his nose. He pushed the bag around and got eating, eyed by the barman and locals.

"Do you know if anywhere around here has a room available for the night?"

"I can give you a couple of numbers."

I waved my phone at the barman. "No reception."

"That's okay, I'll call for you. Just stick some money in the collection box." The barman tapped a child's plastic bucket beside him, the kind you'd find at the seaside. There was a lid across the top, a crude slot cut for the coins. "For the air ambulance. Bloody walkers are always getting themselves into trouble round here."

"Happy to." I dropped a couple of pounds in. They clunked onto some existing change inside.

One of the regulars came over carrying a pewter tankard. The barman began pulling a pint without needing to be asked. The old guy, wearing a tweed jacket and flat cap, stroked Bonzo's head. "What breed is he?" Bonzo paid him no attention while he licked the empty crisp packet clean, holding it down under one massive paw.

"I've no idea. He's a rescue dog." Which strictly wasn't true, but it was close enough. And I couldn't remember what Gregory told me as I hadn't been interested at the time.

"There you go, Sid." The barman passed over the pint. Sid removed his attention from Bonzo, who still didn't care, and straightened. "Good of you, Jerry."

I felt like now was as good a time as any. "Do any of you know this man?" I pulled out the copy of Lavender's photo and laid it on the bar. "Noah Maddox. He grew up round here." Suddenly the air of casual bonhomie evaporated. The old guys immediately ceased their mumbled conversation. Jerry's expression switched from friendly and engaged to surly.

"No," said Jerry.

"Never heard of him," said Sid. He snatched his drink and sat back down. I glanced over my shoulder. Sid was whispering to his companion.

"Are you sure?" I asked.

"Definitely," said Jerry.

I got up, walked over to the other regular, showed him the photo. "What about you?" The man wouldn't even look at the image, pretending I wasn't there.

"I'll see you later, Sid." The regular drained his beer, stood and left with a nod at Jerry.

I gave up, folded the paper into a small square and put it back in my pocket before returning to my stool.

"I'll call those guest houses now for you," said Jerry. "What's your name? In case I can get a reservation."

"Harry Vaughan."

"Okay." He disappeared out the back.

I drank some of my pint. I glanced over at Sid. He was staring at me, but as soon as I turned he switched his attention away, seemingly staring into space.

Jerry returned within a couple of minutes. "Sorry, they're all full."

"Nowhere's available?"

"As I said, they're taken."

"What do you suggest?"

"There's hotels in Buxton, about twenty minutes away."

"Okay. I'll have another for the road, then."

"Better not. The police are hot on drink driving round here." The barman peeled the lid off the bucket, fished out my two pounds and placed them on the counter in front of me.

"So that's how it is?"

"I can't serve alcohol to people when they're going to be driving. I'd lose my licence." Jerry went out the back again, leaving me alone with Bonzo and Sid. Then Sid departed too.

Looked like the locals were drawing together. Which meant they did know Lavender. I nursed what remained of my pint, deciding what was next.

The Lavender Dilemma

Flash, Staffordshire

Pomfrey Lavender was hammering a fence post into the spongy ground out the back of the farmhouse when Elizabeth found him. He was soaked through, his clothes sticking to his skin because of the mist, but he didn't care. It was fantastic to be outside again. The rhythmic nature of the work, the pounding of his muscles as mallet struck wood was satisfying too.

The expression on Elizabeth's face stopped him dead. She was angry, furious even. "Jerry's just called. Somebody's at the pub, asking after you. It's Harry."

For a moment Lavender couldn't figure out who Elizabeth meant. "Your husband?"

"Ex-husband, yes."

"How the hell did he find me?"

"Who cares? He's here!" Elizabeth ran her fingers through her hair. "I can't pick Jack up and move him again or take Maddie out of university. We're happy and I'm sick of running."

"You won't have to," said Lavender. "Ring Jerry back and tell him I'm on my way over."

Elizabeth placed a hand on Lavender's forearm. "Don't do anything reckless. Despite everything, Harry's a decent man. He's never done anything wrong."

"I'm not going to let him risk your safety, though. Whatever happens is down to him."

Elizabeth gave a sharp nod and released her grip. "I trust you."

Lavender collected the keys to Elizabeth's old Land Rover from inside the house while Elizabeth dialled the pub's number. Within a couple of minutes he was rolling up to the New Inn.

There were only two cars parked out front, a BMW and a Jeep. He knew who owned the latter, so the ostentatious black saloon must be Vaughan's. Leaving the Land Rover in the middle of the road with the engine running, Lavender got out and checked over the BMW. Behind cupped hands he looked through the tinted windows. Nothing on view, which was smart. He tried the door handles, locked. Lavender had a crowbar, but short of smashing windows to access the boot, which would activate the alarm and bring Vaughan running, there was nothing he could do for now.

Jerry was out the back waiting for him. "He's sat at the bar," whispered Jerry. "He showed us a photo, asked if we knew you."

"Who else was there? Sid, I guess." Sid was in the pub from opening to closing time pretty much every day.

"Yes, and Arthur. We didn't say anything, of course."

Lavender expected no less. This was a community which held together and looked after its own. Even Lavender, who'd moved away long ago, only to come back from a war in the Middle East with post-traumatic stress disorder and a drug dependency.

"What's he doing now?"

"Finishing his pint. I told him to find a hotel in Buxton and refused to serve him another beer – said it would be drink driving and I'd lose my licence." On an ordinary day Lavender would have laughed. Jerry held regular lock-ins, well past "official" closing time. Out here, who was going to check? There weren't enough cops to go around for the big stuff, never mind monitoring rural pub opening hours.

"Have you got a cordless drill?"

Jerry frowned. "Yes. Why?"

"No time to explain. Grab it for me then do me a favour, will you? Head back in and keep him talking for as long as you can."

"About anything in particular?"

"The price of sheep dip, Jerry, *anything*. I don't care."

"Okay."

"Get the drill, please. Quickly." Jerry nodded. "And some pliers." The barman ran off and was back within a minute. He handed the tools over. There was a bit already attached.

"I'll blow my horn when I'm done."

Jerry stuck up a thumb, slipped away.

Lavender headed back to the BMW. He picked a spot in the centre of the boot just beneath the licence plate and got the drill working. The metal was thin, and it took only half a minute to get through. Behind the plate, a steel rod ran vertically. However, it was offset. Lavender couldn't reach it with the pliers. He drilled again, this time exposing the rod fully. Lavender got a grip and tugged. The boot popped open.

Inside was a carrier bag stuffed with clothes and a smaller shoulder case. Lavender grabbed the latter and quietly closed the boot. The hole was obvious if you looked closely, but by the time Vaughan spotted the vandalism it wouldn't matter.

He slung the strap of the smaller bag over his shoulder and ran back the way he'd come, carrying pliers and drill. At his car, Lavender took a moment to glance through the bag. It contained a laptop and a sheaf of paper, all related to the Nudge Man. Lavender frowned. Whatever Elizabeth had said it was clear Vaughan *was* a threat to their survival. The case went into the rear of the Land Rover beneath a blanket.

Lavender clambered into the 4x4, blew his horn and started the engine. He trundled the few yards onto the road but lurked far enough away to just see around the pub and waited. Rain dappled the windscreen.

Vaughan was out as fast as it had taken Lavender to drill the hole first time around. He had a dog with him, a Malinois. A beast too. The ex-reporter unlocked the BMW and coaxed the dog inside. Vaughan closed the rear passenger door before getting behind the wheel. He bent over, fiddling with something. Maybe the sat nav, if he wasn't familiar with the area. Eventually Vaughan started the engine. Vaughan was already facing in the right direction for Buxton. Lavender followed, allowing a good few hundred yards gap. There was only one route Vaughan could take off the hill, and Lavender expected he would drive slowly. Lavender had time, and the last thing he wanted was to be seen in Vaughan's rear view.

Not until it was too late.

Vaughan is Dead

Flash, Staffordshire

I'd clearly overstayed my welcome but, being an awkward bastard, I stretched out the last dregs of my pint. Clearly, I was hitting the pub's takings. Boo hoo.

The way Jerry and Sid had responded to my question about Lavender said all it needed to. They knew something. I'd come across this sort of behaviour plenty times previously when working on stories. People often think silence communicates nothing. Instead the defensive, awkward body language speaks volumes.

Eventually I decided enough was enough. I stood, drained the last few millilitres of beer and put the glass down. "Thanks, Jerry," I shouted, expecting nothing in response. "Come on Bonzo." The dog raised his head.

"Leaving us already?" It was Jerry, back behind the bar. And smiling.

"The atmosphere," I said, "it's a bit damp."

"Damp, good one." Jerry laughed. "Because of the rain."

"Right, I'll be off then."

"Hang on. I realise I've been rude and I wanted to apologise."

"I had heard Northerners were supposed to be friendly."

"We are, so there's a pint on the house if you want it."

I was never one to turn down free beer. Free anything, actually. "Okay, if you insist." I sat back on the stool, watched Jerry slowly work the pump and the brown liquid splash into the bottom of the glass. It was as painful as watching Dick, the Flag's landlord, in operation.

Jerry placed the glass on the bar, three quarters filled, said, "Just got to let the head build." He leant on the bar, fixated on the settling amber liquid. God, this was agonising.

"Have you always lived here?" I asked.

"No, I just work in the pub."

"I meant in Flash."

"Oh, sorry. Yes, born and bred."

"So, you'd know Noah Maddox then."

Ignoring me, Jerry picked up the glass and focused on the pump, gradually drawing the beer out. Eventually it was full. He put a mat down in front of me, squared it off, then the glass itself, the handle at forty-five degrees. The foamy top was thick and dense. "Enjoy," he said.

I picked up the beer, had a drink. "Great." It tasted exactly like the last one. "I was asking you about Noah Maddox."

"Sheep dip prices have plummeted, did you know?"

"That fact had passed me by. We grow stuff like cauliflowers, apples and hops where I live. I'd guess sheep dip isn't really that important to the Kent economy."

"There's sheep everywhere here."

"I'd noticed."

"And lambs in the spring and summer."

"I'll have to come back and see them."

"They're very noisy, they bleat a lot. Particularly when the young are separated from the ewes."

"Probably because they know they're going to be eaten."

"I don't think they're that smart."

And neither was Jerry. "You were going to tell me about Noah Maddox."

Jerry glanced around the empty pub as if he was being observed. He leant forward conspiratorially. "Haven't seen or heard of him for years. He left under a heavy cloud."

"Why?"

"Nobody talks about him anymore."

"We are now, Jerry. What happened?" I lifted the glass up to my lips. Outside a horn blew. Jerry's features hardened immediately. He snatched the glass from my grip, poured the remaining beer into a sink.

"That's just how it is, Mr Vaughan. We're closed now," he said, and went to the front door. He stood by it, waiting for me.

"Come on, Bonzo," I said and clicked my fingers. The dog lifted his head at my command. He lumbered slowly to his feet and followed me outside. The door slammed behind me. It was still raining.

Somewhat stunned by events, I stood on the pavement for a few seconds wondering what the hell had happened. Jerry's demeanour had shifted with the car horn. I glanced around. Nobody was in sight. The road was empty in both directions. Mist hung across the hills all around. The street was silent. It was as if we were the last survivors of an apocalypse.

I unlocked the car. The dog took his usual place on the rear seat and I got in myself, behind the steering wheel. I was fiddling with the sat nav to find my way to Buxton when the phone rang. It was Hennessey. My hackles rose immediately.

"Mr Vaughan, how are you?" he asked, sounding cheerful.

"Doing fine thanks, Eric." I forced myself to be friendly and forced was exactly how it came over.

"Are you sure?"

"Just tired. I've been driving a lot."

"I'm enquiring about the search for our target. I haven't heard from you for a few days."

"Slow progress is the best I can say."

"But you have forward momentum, nevertheless?"

"I do."

"Then God be praised. Where are you now?"

"Heading to Newcastle." No way was I telling Hennessey my location.

"Not Norfolk anymore?"

"Too flat for my liking." I assumed Hennessey was monitoring my credit card spend to determine my location. Well that wouldn't be happening from now on. I'd withdrawn two hundred and fifty pounds from Hennesey's bank account, the maximum allowable per day, and filled the petrol tank up to the brim. "Look, I need to get going, Eric."

"Carry on, Mr Vaughan. Keep up the good work. The Lord be with you."

I disconnected, stuck two fingers up to the speaker. As if Hennessey would know I'd sworn at him.

Returning my attention to the sat nav, I checked out the local area using the miniature joystick to whizz around. From here it was back to the A53 which ran between Leek and Buxton. A few miles along the route appeared to be a turning which might give me a way back across the hills on foot, but there was no topography on the two-dimensional display.

My short-term plan was to head into town, find a cheap bed and breakfast, rather than the hotel Jerry had recommended, as I was running on cash only now. Then I'd buy some cheap boots and return. I was assuming I could park somewhere nearby before approaching Flash via a footpath. I didn't know what I'd find, but there was definitely something here that needed tracking down. I put the car in gear and set off.

I was out of Flash in, well, a flash. Past the local primary school, which occupied a wind-blown site on the village boundary. A few hundred yards along, I hit the A53, which primarily consisted of caravans, motorbikes and lorries carrying quarried stone. I swept past a weather-beaten store at a junction before starting a long climb. I slowed as the turning I wanted came into sight. It was a tight left. The road was steeper still and there was a sharp switchback which I took at a snail's pace when I felt the tyres lose a little grip. The drop beside me was brutal – sharp and rock-lined.

Then I was in the middle of nowhere. I glanced out both sides of the car. It was rolling moorland again, though visibility remained poor. Cloud hung like a shroud. I decided I was wasting my time without having a detailed map to review and I might as well head into Buxton. But the road was too narrow to carry out a three-point turn. A steep incline to the right, a sharper drop to the left. I carried on, hunting for somewhere suitable. Rounded another switchback corner.

I heard the revving of an engine close behind. I glanced in my rear-view and caught sight of a looming vehicle before it smashed into the BMW. Bonzo barked in surprise, a low, deep huff. I felt him hit the back of my seat. My belt locked, kept me from striking the steering wheel. I slammed on the brakes in reflex. However, what little grip the tyres had was gone and the car was sliding. Incredibly, I came to a halt, teetering on the verge of the precipice. Over my shoulder I saw the car, a Land Rover, backing up. I breathed a sigh of relief. Just an accident and they were coming to help.

But I was wrong. Because the Land Rover darted forward and smashed into my bumper again. The BMW went over the edge and everything turned dark.

When I came to, my neck was at an angle. My head was pounding. Most of me ached. Particularly my right shoulder, cheekbone and both legs. And there was a tightness across my chest. I was finding it hard to breathe.

After a few moments my vision cleared. I was surrounded on all sides by scrub and in some sort of dip, the sky a circle above me. The roof was pushed in, so the car must have rolled on the way down. And water was entering the footwell. Actually, water surrounded me – lapping against the doors. The dip must be a low point where the rain was collecting. In the summer it was probably bone dry. I unclipped my seat belt and turned around, my ribs flaring in pain, probably from being restrained by the belt during the crash. Bonzo was on the back seat, up out of the water. But I could only twist so far. My ankle was trapped. I pulled, but it didn't move, and a shooting pain raced up my leg.

"Bonzo!" I shouted, but he didn't move. I reached over and stroked his head. He raised it slightly, his eyes unfocused, before flopping back down once more.

I pushed at the door, but it was shut tight. I rammed my shoulder into the fascia, but to no avail. The car shifted a little, settling down further. The water rose outside, up to the windows. The level in the footwell was increasing too, as the liquid found its way in through gaps and nooks in the bodywork.

Panic welled in my throat. How was I going to escape? And with the bleary-eyed, dead weight of the dog to deal with also. I was out of sight of the road and unless anybody happened to pass by nobody knew I was here except for the driver of the car that'd struck me.

Something moved across my eyeline. The silhouette of a person up on the ridge, standing there. I couldn't see their features but, by the shape, it appeared to be a man. Relief surged within me. I banged on the window to get his attention. Finally, the person began to descend, and I recognised him.

Pomfrey Lavender.

I was doomed.

Vaughan Lives

A **Bog, Somewhere in Staffordshire**

Lavender paused when he reached the edge of the bog, before squatting to bring his eyeline closer to mine. His hair had begun to grow out since the last time I'd seen him. He stared at me through the windscreen. I had nowhere to go. The water was still rising, reaching the car seat now. The BMW settled a few inches deeper, pulled down by its increased weight, no doubt, in a vicious cycle.

His expression was flat, dead, zero emotion on his face. I could have been a piece of flotsam for all he cared. I unconsciously rubbed at my neck, where his fingers had encircled my throat last week, his thumbs pressing into my larynx. Lavender straightened, stepped into the water, sinking straight down to his knees. He waded over, the level reaching his waist as he progressed slowly, his feet probably were being sucked down into oozing mud.

We eyeballed each other through the glass. "Having a nice day?" asked Lavender.

"There's been better."

"I said what would happen if you didn't leave the Nudge Man alone."

"What can I say? I'm tenacious."

"I'd suggest stupid." Lavender shrugged. "I can make it happen fast, or I can leave you here. Could take days."

I doubted that. The water had stopped flowing quite so fast now, but it was at my waist and it was lapping well above that level outside. I was beginning to shiver, the heat draining out of my body fast. I probably only had hours. I'd slip into unconsciousness first. With a bit of luck my face might end up under the surface and I'd drown without waking.

"What about Bonzo?" I hiked a thumb over my shoulder.

Lavender glanced into the rear, frowned. "You're more concerned about the dog than yourself?"

"I couldn't give a shit about me. Never have. Compared to everybody else, I'm nothing."

Lavender returned his gaze to me for a long moment before he let a crowbar slide from out of his sleeve. He raised it – swung. The rear window shattered, spraying the pair of us with glass. Bonzo snarled. Water sluiced in now, to my chest and approaching my neck. What a way to go. Drowning in a muddy puddle, albeit a deep one.

Lavender used the cleft end of the bar to scrape away any shards before reaching inside and effortlessly heaving Bonzo up. But the dog would not fit through the gap, he was far too large. Lavender regarded me again, weighing the three-foot long piece of metal. It began to rain once more.

"What are we going to do with you, Vaughan?" he asked.

"I don't care, just get on with it. And thank you for watching over my family, Sergeant Maddox."

Lavender stood totally still, maybe considering his options. Eventually he shook his head. He tugged on the rear door handle. He had to pull hard because of the weight of the water but soon had it open. He dipped inside, picked up Bonzo, carried him onto the bank and carefully laid him down.

He stared over his shoulder. "Come on, Vaughan."

"I can't. My leg's trapped."

"Jesus."

Lavender hit the water again, tried my door handle but it wouldn't budge. He shifted around to the passenger side, tried there too. No movement. He slid the bar into the gap between door and car body and heaved, creating a gap. He leant on the metal with the weight of his body until it stood wide.

"Give me your hand," he said.

I put out my arms and we gripped each other just beneath the elbow. Lavender strained until the sockets felt like they were going to pop.

"It's no good," I said. "Leave me."

"Don't be suicidal." The rain was coming down harder now and I was sure the level was rising faster. "Which leg?"

"The left."

Lavender took a deep breath and ducked below the water's pitch black surface. I felt him clasp my ankle, moving upwards. Half a minute later he re-emerged, sucked in several lungfuls of air and disappeared again. This time he was down for longer. There was tugging and pulling, but I couldn't see what was going on.

Lavender resurfaced, breathing deeply, water running off him in streams. "Looks like you've had it," said Lavender, hands on hips. "Unless you're willing to let me saw through your ankle."

"Oh my God!"

Lavender laughed hard. Eventually he said, "Move your leg."

I did, and it was free. I pulled myself out of the car.

"Should have seen your face, Vaughan."

"Taking the piss at a time like this." I waded to the bank, Lavender at my heels.

"Comes from serving in the forces."

I knelt next to Bonzo and rubbed his fur. He opened his eyes and stared sidelong at me.

"Come on, let's get Bonzo somewhere warm," said Lavender. "We'll decide what to do with you after."

The Dog Comes First

New Inn, Flash, Staffordshire

I stood on the lip of the dip. The bog was steadily swallowing the car. The BMW's roof was barely visible now. I could still be inside, breathing my last then swallowing sludgy water. I'd lost everything – my clothes didn't matter too much, but the laptop and all the paperwork on the Nudge Man were submerged and irredeemable. I felt like throwing up.

"Come on," said Lavender. Dragging my feet, I followed as he carried Bonzo to the Land Rover. Lavender gently placed the dog on the rear bench and covered him with a blanket before getting behind the wheel. I slid into the passenger side. It felt bizarre, sitting next to someone who'd tried to kill me twice then saved me.

"Seat belt," said Lavender as he started the engine. "Just in case we have an accident."

If it was a joke I didn't feel like laughing. I shivered as I clipped in the restraint. My clothes were clammy against my skin, my shoes full of mud, hair plastered across my head. Lavender kicked on the heater, opened the vents and had the fans on maximum before performing a three-point turn and heading back the way we'd come, down the steep hill and switchbacks to the A53. I cupped my palms over the nearest outlet.

The "somewhere warm" Lavender had referred to turned out to be the village pub. Lavender parked at the back of the New Inn, lifted Bonzo and entered through the rear door which led into a passage. Immediately to the right was the kitchen. A few yards further along was a set of stairs and the entrance into the bar area. Lavender took the steps upwards, which opened into a narrow corridor with an angled roof and ran the length of the building.

He kicked back the door to room number four at the far end. In the centre was a double bed with a view over the road and into the hills. The walls were a pastel blue, where several tasteful black and white photos of rocky outcrops and moody distance shots of a lake hung. Another door, standing ajar, led into an en-suite bathroom.

"Pass a towel, would you?" asked Lavender. There were two on the end of the bed. I gave him the biggest. He shrouded Bonzo, briskly rubbed him dry. "Pull back the blankets." That I did too. Lavender carefully laid Bonzo down, drew the duvet over him. He flicked on a wall-mounted electric heater, spun the dial to the highest setting. "Get yourself a shower. I'll fetch you some clothes to change into. Then we'll talk." After patting Bonzo's head, Lavender left us alone.

My teeth began to chatter. Lavender's advice was sound. The small bathroom consisted of a shower stall, toilet and sink. A small window obscured by curtains was recessed into the wall above the cistern. I got the power shower running and stripped, kicking the ragged heap into a corner. My mobile was in a trouser pocket. I pressed a button. The screen lit up, so it seemed to still be working.

The blast of heat from the spray felt like sharp pinpricks on my icy skin. It was a pleasurable pain, though. Because I was still alive. Which was surprising, because for a long time I've really not been bothered about the prospect of death. In fact, sometimes I've gone out of my way to put myself in harm's way. I stood with my hands on the wall, head bowed while the droplets played on my back.

Eventually I stepped out of the cubicle. Steam filled the tiny room. A voluminous white Egyptian cotton towel hung over a radiator. I briskly rubbed myself dry, then wrapped it around my waist. I opened the window to let out the steam.

On the bed lay a neatly folded pile of clothes. Bonzo was asleep, his head on the pillow, facing away from me. I leant over, rubbed the flat of his nose. He growled and farted. I left him alone. The jeans fitted fairly well, a little loose around the waist. I tightened the belt. The collarless shirt was grey, the fisherman's jumper thick and warm. There were walking boots which were a tight fit. I wondered what to do with myself and decided to leave the room.

In the corridor, Lavender was leaning against the wall. "How's Bonzo?"

"Seems fine."

"That's good."

"As am I."

Lavender gave a shrug. "There's a pint waiting for you."

"Just the one?"

Lavender rolled his eyes before heading for the stairs. The regulars, Sid and his friend, were back in their same spots, Jerry behind the bar. All three ignored me when I entered. Lavender had snagged a table in the corner, nearest the blaze. Two beers there already. Lavender slid in first, facing the room. I took the seat opposite. Lavender picked up his drink, didn't bother saying anything like, "Cheers", even though we'd shared my near-death experience.

Twice.

Lavender put his glass down once he'd sunk half the contents.

"Here we are, telling stories over the camp fire," I said.

Lavender reached down beside him, dropped a sheaf of papers onto the table between us. I recognised them immediately. My Nudge Man documents. The laptop would hopefully be somewhere nearby too and the mobile Six had given me.

"What about my clothes?"

"There were some rags in a carrier bag."

"That's them."

"Still in the boot. I thought they were for a charity shop."

"Great." I had a drink. "How?"

"I drilled a hole to reach the lock, while Jerry was distracting you inside."

"More like boring the arse off me about sheep dip."

"It's a talent."

"What the hell do I call you? Pomfrey? Noah?"

"Lavender is just a pseudonym."

"A ridiculous one."

"Noah is fine."

"It's kind of ridiculous too. But anyway. Do you really believe you're dead?"

"What?"

"Hutch, she told me you had Cotard Delusion."

"And London Syndrome, right?"

"Correct."

"Pomfrey Lavender is a construct. Everything about that person exists on a computer only. Including my psychological profile and criminal record. The Nudge Man built Pomfrey Lavender, gave him a history and told the cops all about him. Suddenly there was a record, but who checks whether it's real? An arrest is an arrest. Anything to help nudge the statistics in the right direction.

"The Nudge Man told the cops where to find Lavender, then I was inside the system. I pleaded guilty to being a highly dangerous man, meaning I went into isolation, limiting contact with other prisoners. When it came to getting out we just reversed the process. Gave Lavender some psychoses which meant Swaleside was the wrong place to house him and he needed to move. Employ a couple of handy guys and hey presto, Lavender is out."

"Why?"

"We'll come to that." He sat back, tapped the paperwork. "You've been busy. There's a lot of information in here."

"I'm a reporter. I have connections. And I'm smart." One fact, two fallacies. "Therefore, I know you were working in witness protection looking after my wife and children."

"I'm impressed."

"All in a day's work. Where are my family?"

"Somewhere safe, a long way from here."

"That's not good enough."

"It's all you're getting."

"They're my kids."

"I'm mindful of that fact. But I need to be able to trust you first, Harry. I've spent five years of my life keeping them from harm. I've even been to prison for them. That duty doesn't disappear overnight."

"Okay." I was reluctant, but what could I do? Without Lavender I wasn't going to just trip over them somewhere in the countryside. He was in control and knew it. "What did Jack get himself involved in? His letters said he was wrong place, wrong time."

"Jack wrote letters?"

"Yes."

"I'd no idea."

"What happened, with Jack?"

"The aftermath of a murder."

"Jesus." I passed a hand over my face. I wasn't there for him. What the hell had he been through?

"Ordered by Eric Hennessey. He was a significant player in the London and Kent underworld and somebody we'd been after for a long time. Ironically it was another witness who Jack saw taken out. Down an alley, not far from your old house. Jack was passing by, but they didn't clock him.

"He went home in a state, unsurprisingly, told Elizabeth and, all credit to them, they headed straight to the police. Jack gave a statement and identified three men from mugshots. When one of them turned out to be Hennessey an already major case went up another couple of notches. We took your family straight into protective custody. However, before the trial was due to go ahead, Hennessey learned of Jack's identity and we had to move them, fast."

"What happened with the trial? Did Jack testify?"

"The trial collapsed just prior to commencement. Not enough evidence. All three walked free."

"And Jack's eye witness account?"

"Wasn't enough for the CPS. But Hennessey still wanted Jack – a loose end which had to be tied off. We spent three years running. Your son is a brave kid. You should be proud of him."

"I always have been. Even more so now. I could do with another beer."

Lavender snagged Jerry's attention before holding up two fingers. He continued, "The witness protection programme was compromised. Hennessey must have bought some people. He almost got us a couple of times. So we cut all contact with the authorities and disappeared. It worked. Nobody has tracked us down. Until now."

Jerry appeared with a pint in each hand and a couple of bags of crisps between his teeth. "Salt and vinegar, wasn't it?"

"You have a good memory, Jerry."

"Goes with the job," he said.

Jerry retreated, and Lavender popped open both crisp bags, laid them out between us.

"Why did you come back to Flash?" I asked. "It's the obvious place for the cops to look for you."

"There's nothing official tying Pomfrey Lavender to Flash. Noah Maddox joined the army and never returned to his birthplace, as far as anyone from outside the area knows. The residents here have never had a good relationship with authority. We're isolated, the village can be cut off for months in the winter if it snows heavily, and it does most years. I've got a place out on the moors. I'd be well aware of any visitors long before anybody actually arrived."

"Really?"

"I knew about you, didn't I?"

That was true. "Why did they lock you away, Noah?"

"We learned of various parties trying to track us down. I wanted to take the focus off your family. Ultimately it was me they were after, not Elizabeth, Jack or Maddie."

"Why would anyone want you?"

Lavender picked up a crisp, bit into it. "How did you get involved with all of this?" I noted Lavender ignored my question.

"I was employed to find the Nudge Man."

"You ignored my warning. To leave him alone."

"I had no choice. The Nudge Man gave me a problem once. Utterly destroyed my reputation and ultimately cost me my marriage. I never knew who or why. I've been trying to find out ever since. I'd always assumed it was somebody taking revenge for a damaging story I'd previously broken. I'd like to clear my name then face my children with some dignity returned. How could I turn down the opportunity to do so?"

"I might be able to help you," said Lavender. He stared at me for a long time. I returned the favour – didn't feel like I could break eye contact. "They were looking for me because I'm the Nudge Man."

The Nudge Man Revealed

New Inn, Flash, Staffordshire

It was my turn to pause, to consider. It was plausible. The person who'd beaten up the junkie, Mourtice, in West Mersea had been a man. Lavender was certainly capable and willing. The Nudge Man was also an IT expert. Wyatt's analysis had shown there had been a gradual shift in activity from the physical to the electronic, with the latter taking precedent about the time Lavender went into prison.

But how could Lavender be the Nudge Man if he was locked up? Then again, there were plenty of stories where criminals ran their empires from inside. Frankly, I wasn't sure either way. There was enough for Lavender's claim to be believable, and enough for doubt also. I decided to go with it for now while retaining a healthy dose of scepticism.

"Why did you destroy my reputation?" I asked. "I've looked at all the Nudge Man's activities and generally it's for the positive. There's a brutal efficiency, but those who come off worst typically deserve it. I'm one of the few exceptions."

"I was paid to go after you."

"By who?"

"I don't know. Everything was anonymous."

I banged my fist on the table. The glasses jumped.

"Calm down," said Lavender.

"Don't tell me how to behave. I lost everything because of you. Job, friends, my family."

"Interesting what comes last in that list."

"Elizabeth left for a reason. She was too ashamed to be with me – an apparent paedophile. I can't blame her."

I shifted in my seat, uncomfortable we were discussing my ex-wife like this. And in the past tense. Which was interesting. There was still another other issue which needed teasing out. "I was employed by Eric Hennessey to find the Nudge Man."

"Christ," said Lavender, rubbing the bridge of his nose, eyes squeezed shut.

"Don't worry, he doesn't know I'm here. I'd already figured out his intentions were less than honourable. I've been operating independently. And now I'm going to tell him I'm giving up – that it's impossible to find you. Wouldn't be the first time somebody he employed has failed in the task."

"Hennessey will just pay another mug to track me down. He'll never stop."

"I've no idea what to do about that."

"This must end here. Hennessey has to be dealt with, permanently."

"In other words, Hennessey is a loose end to be tied off."

"Well said."

"How?"

"We're going to give him what he wants. You're going to hand me over to him."

The Plan

New Inn, Flash, Staffordshire

"What's the plan, then?" I asked. "Something like, I call the bad man, tell him where to come and find the Nudge Man, he shoots you, we all go home happy?"

Lavender eyeballed me. "Nearly, but not quite, Harry. Yes, you contact Hennessey and we meet, but not in Flash. And ideally, I'd quite like not to die if, I can help it."

"Okay, we can forget the bereavement part. But why not here? It's perfect, you said so yourself. Miles from anywhere, not easy to access, we'd know well in advance of his arrival."

"Too close to home. Someone I know might get hurt. I've got another place in mind."

"Where?"

"Do you like the seaside?"

"I live by the bloody sea, Noah."

"Good, because we'll be going to St Anne's."

"Never heard of the place."

"It's a small resort near Blackpool."

"Why there?"

"For the pier. Just trust me."

"It's your funeral."

"Could be both of us, Harry. If we're not careful. Whatever happens, somebody from one side or the other is going to meet their maker."

"I'm fine with that." Not quite true.

"Get in touch with Hennessey. Say you'll hand me over tomorrow at midnight on the pier."

"I left my mobile upstairs. It was wet."

"Ring him from your room, then." Lavender raised his glass. "In the meantime, I'll get another round."

Bonzo was flat out. I patted his head. He didn't stir. The mobile was still in the bathroom. I checked the signal. I had one bar where previously I'd had none. Maybe it was because I was elevated now. Whatever. I found Hennessey's number, pressed the green key.

He answered immediately. "God bless, Mr Vaughan, how are you?"

"I've found him. I've found the Nudge Man."

There was a pause. "Are you sure?" There was a suppressed elation in his voice.

"One hundred per cent, Eric."

"Praise the Lord!"

"You can do that for yourself when you have him in your grasp."

"When? Where?"

"St Anne's pier. Tomorrow at midnight, so you've plenty of time to drive up. I'll be there too."

"Well done, Mr Vaughan!" The restraint Hennessey had displayed at the beginning of the call broke, his words a torrent. "I'll admit, I had my doubts, but you've proved me wrong."

"I don't really care either way. I just want my reputation back."

"And you'll have it, Mr Vaughan. I'll see you tomorrow. God be with you." Hennessey disconnected.

In the bar Lavender asked, "Well?"

"We're on."

"Congratulations. Let's eat and I'll tell you the plot."

I was pretty drunk by the time I headed up to my room. I can't say it was my kind of fun evening, but it had certainly been enlightening.

I unlocked the door and felt around for the light switch. When I flicked it on Bonzo raised his head from the bed and growled. "Okay." I turned the light off.

I entered the bathroom, closed the door. Under the illumination from a bulb above the shaving mirror I found a toothbrush, paste and other cosmetics. I cleaned my teeth, threw off my borrowed clothes, retaining the T-shirt and pants, and crawled under the duvet. There were a few inches between me and the dog. I considered pushing him out, he was an animal after all, but ultimately, I didn't have the heart.

I went to sleep dreaming of my family. The trouble was, something was wrong with their faces. They were a blur.

A Trip to the Seaside

New Inn, Flash

I was awoken the next morning by a thumping on the door. I felt a weight on my ribs. I cracked an eye. Bonzo had rolled over during the night and a front leg was stretched across my chest.

"How sweet." It was Lavender, framed in the doorway, leaning against the jamb. Bonzo leapt off the bed and stood in front of him, wagging his tail, seemingly fully recovered. I'll admit to a twinge of irritation. Bonzo seemed to prefer Lavender to me. Come to think of it, he preferred everybody to me.

"Well done, Harry," said Lavender. "You're making a connection."

"We don't need one. Our relationship is just temporary."

Lavender shook his head. "And I'm supposed to be the heartless bastard."

"What do you want?" I asked, arm across my eyes to block out the beginnings of the sunrise.

"Get up and get sorted, we've a decent drive ahead of us and I want to be on with it. Breakfast's in the lounge bar."

"Give me fifteen minutes."

"You've got ten. I'll feed the dog." He switched his attention to Bonzo. "Come on, boy." And then they were gone. I willed myself to rise. If I didn't move now I'd fall back to sleep.

I desperately wanted to get some more shut eye, but then I'd have Lavender to answer to. I went downstairs.

Lavender was halfway through a fried breakfast with a steaming mug of coffee by his elbow. The smell of eggs and bacon made my stomach lurch. He nodded towards a nearby table. "You can sit there," he said. "I like some space to myself in the morning." This, even though Bonzo was at Lavender's feet, nose in a bowl, wolfing down some meat.

"Very social," I said. Lavender ignored me.

There was a young woman behind the bar with Jerry. She was in her teens, the red rash of acne across her cheeks, a ring through her nose and several in her ears. Her hair was hidden under a beanie hat. She crossed over to me. "What can I get you?"

"Just toast and lots of coffee to wake me up before I go-go." I grinned.

She didn't. "White or brown?"

"The toast or the coffee?"

"Cut the crap jokes, Vaughan," said Lavender with a glare.

"White bread, black coffee," I said.

"I'll be right back," she told me.

I slumped on the table while I waited, ignored Lavender and Bonzo. She returned within a couple of minutes carrying a plate and a large mug. "Excuse me," she said. I might have nodded off. I sat up, she put the food and drink down.

The toast was four triangles slotted into a metal holder. There was butter and several types of spread on the table in small bowls. I picked up a pot of strawberry jam, but it reminded me of O'Neal, the scrapyard owner Gregory had told me Hennessey squished in the compactor. I put the jar back, wondering what fate awaited me today and whether I was bothered or not.

Bonzo was done eating. He sat side on to me, staring expectantly at Lavender, obviously waiting for discarded bacon or sausage. Lavender tossed him a chunk. Bonzo caught the piece neatly, licked his chops.

"You forgot to feed him," said Lavender.

"All his stuff was in my car."

"Good point." Lavender pointed a dirty knife at me. "I'd suggest you get eating. We're leaving shortly."

"I'm not feeling great."

"Then wrap it up in a serviette. We won't be stopping."

"Maybe I'll try then."

"Christ, you're like a kid."

"Yes, Dad." I spread a piece of toast with butter, using a whole pat. "How long will the journey take?"

"Two to three hours, depending on traffic. And the Land Rover isn't the fastest."

"Great."

"You're map reading, by the way."

"No sat nav?" I'd got used to the technology remarkably quickly.

"No sat nav," confirmed Lavender.

I nibbled on a corner of the toast. When Lavender laid down his utensils and pushed his plate back, Bonzo switched his attention to me. I tore off a piece of crust, held it out for him. He eyed me, stepped forward, gingerly accepted the offering. I patted his skull. He licked my hand.

Lavender drank his coffee in silence. The waitress cleared Lavender's breakfast things. I got through the toast by sharing with Bonzo, surprised how much I enjoyed doing so.

Soon Lavender set down his mug. "Come on, time to head off." He stood, turned to Jerry. "See you later, sometime."

"Cheers, Noah."

I trailed Lavender and the dog. Lavender had the back of the Land Rover open. There was a rucksack inside already and my bag, which I checked. All the contents were still there – the laptop, the phone Six had given me, which I'd left turned off since, and all the paperwork. Bonzo leapt onto the rear bench. As I slid into the passenger seat I said, "So, you're known by your original name?"

"What else would they call me?" he said, twisting the key in the ignition and slamming his door shut.

"Where the hell did your pseudonym come from?"

"Can you think of anything less like me than Pomfrey Lavender?"

I looked him over. "Good point."

Lavender put the car in gear, pulled away and we headed out of Flash and into the hills. Just past the school, Lavender turned the car into a layby. He got out. "Come with me." Curious, I followed. He opened up the back, pulled his bag forward, undid the zips. Inside was a towel, which Lavender removed, revealing two handguns and a sawn-off shotgun. Along with a grenade.

I pointed at the explosive. "Where the hell did you get that?"

"I used to be in the army." As if that was sufficient explanation. Lavender pulled out a gun. "Do you know how to use one of these?"

"I've never even fired one."

"This is a Glock 19. Smaller than the 17 and easier to conceal. I could give you a whole spiel on the thing, but somehow I reckon it won't be a lot of use."

"You're right." Short attention span.

Lavender ejected the Glock's magazine. "Fifteen rounds. You won't need to learn how to reload. If you've fired them all and the opposition are still standing you're in big trouble anyway." He passed it over. I was surprised by the weight. Heavier than I'd expected. Lavender made to zip up the case. I handed the gun back.

"I don't want it," I said. "Not my style."

"We're going to be up against killers."

"My mouth is my best weapon."

"I suppose you do have a tendency to shoot it off."

"Funny."

Lavender shrugged. "Don't blame me if you take a bullet." He returned the gun to the rucksack. "Let's get going," he said as he shut the boot.

We were well up the M6 and past Manchester before Lavender spoke again. "Do you ever think about your family?" he asked.

I turned away from watching the countryside whip by and regarded Lavender. Wondered where the question had risen from. "Of course. All the time."

"What would you say to them if you saw them again?"

"That I was sorry I wasn't there for them when they needed me. That I loved them. Then I'd hug them and never let go."

Lavender stared at me for a long moment before returning his attention to the road and silence.

The Pier

St Anne's, Lancashire

The St Anne's pier marked the invisible point where the South Promenade became the North Promenade on the map. It was a long, straight road which ran parallel to the coastline, so I got a good view of the Victorian-era structure designed for pleasure as we approached.

The pier was effectively a long box, with white walls and green bay windows, stretching a few hundred yards out into the sea, suspended on sturdy iron legs which kept the building up and away from the lapping waves. Currently the tide was well out, the pier surrounded by damp land. About three quarters of its length was enclosed, the rest, at the culmination, was open to the elements.

Lytham St Anne's was the sleepy sister resort to the brash, gaudy wanna-be-glitzy Blackpool; home of the hen- and stag-do weekenders. I'd been to Blackpool once as a kid – maybe seven years old – to see the illuminations which was a big event up here. I remember it being cold, windy and nowhere near the level of fun my parents had promised. This was as close to the place as I'd been since. I didn't reckon I was missing anything.

Statistically, Blackpool was another depressed seaside town with more than its fair share of economic and demographic issues. St Anne's, in comparison, felt like a retirement village.

Slower paced and a high average age from the residents I saw out and about.

The pier was lost to sight as Lavender pulled into the car park out front, hidden by a large building which housed a café and a chip shop. Both were open, but trade was minimal. Lavender drew to a halt. We were early by half a day.

I stretched my aching back as the engine rattled and died, the sound of sizzling oil in the background. It had been a bone-jarring journey. Where the Land Rover suited hills, it wasn't built for cruising. The valves were loud, the exhaust smelly, and the shock absorbers absorbed nothing much at all. I missed the BMW. I was turning middle class.

Lavender seemed as fresh as a daisy, unaffected by the pummelling despite doing all the driving. He turned in his seat. In the rear, Bonzo was still asleep. That's all the lazy bugger ever seemed to do.

"What about the dog?" I said. I twisted my spine, felt and heard something crack. "I think he'll just get in the way."

"Ironically, that's my view on you, Harry."

"Hilarious." I slammed my door. Bonzo raised his head at the noise. He whined to come out.

"I'm serious," Lavender said. "Both of you stay here. I won't be long."

"Why?"

"No need to get yourself worked up. All I'm doing is a quick recce before tonight. I won't be gambling." He stepped out of the Land Rover, headed to the rear, opened up, pulled his rucksack forward, flung it over his shoulder. He threw me the keys, which I attempted to catch. They hit the ground with a clunk. "Behave both of you." And he was gone.

Bonzo distracted me momentarily, scratching at the door. I let him out and he relieved himself on the back wheel before raising his nose high and sniffing the air deeply. Then he was off too, following in Lavender's footsteps. I swore, locked the car doors, turning my head over my shoulder repeatedly to keep the Hound of the Bastardvilles in sight. But by the time I was done he was around the corner and heading for the pier. I pocketed the keys and ran.

Entering the pier building was like stepping back in time. Immediately within the entrance was an unmanned ticket booth, the pier was free to enter and open twenty-four hours a day. Just beyond, a glass roof hunched over some slot machines, a couple of punters were dropping coins and generally losing. I'd bet Lavender would refer to them as "civilians" or "bystanders". Maybe even "collateral".

Bonzo paused in a patch of sunlight, his head turning. I caught up with him and grabbed hold of his collar. I tried to drag him away, but he was having none of it. He stayed where he was, checking out the area.

I'd no idea how I was going to move him. He was unwavering, and I was without a leash. Then, for once, I had an idea. The borrowed trousers came with a belt. Using one hand I unhitched the buckle and fed the length of leather through Bonzo's collar. The trousers were loose at the waist but so long as they didn't end up on the floor, I could live with it.

I pulled on Bonzo's makeshift tether, but he didn't budge, still snorting. He dragged me forward a couple of steps, lowered his nose to the floor and sniffed. I tried to pull him away, but he decided we were going into the next section, a boxy structure crammed with leisure games, so we did. I was power-less.

Some of the entertainment I recognised from my youth: Arcadia, Pac-Man, Space Invaders. There was an old horse racing game and a mini bowling alley too. Along the perimeter the periodic bay windows faced out over the beach and sea. Two narrow corridors either side of the space. Bonzo carried on, me following like a reluctant water skier.

The third area housed more modern entertainment, also crammed together. A snowboarding game, motorbike and car racing, that sort of stuff. Then I was outside. The wind whipped at my hair. There were gaps between the floorboards and I could see the sand twenty or thirty feet below. There were some wooden benches on the periphery for taking the air. But no Lavender. Where the hell had he gone?

Bonzo was wondering the same and dragged me back inside. It was in the middle section that I saw Lavender. He emerged from a gap between two games consoles pushed against the wall. He didn't have the rucksack any more. I strained on Bonzo's makeshift leash, keeping him from moving forward briefly.

Lavender got walking, eyes forward. He was out of the section before Bonzo decided we could move once more. When I reached the entrance area, Lavender was already striding back to the car. Instead of doing the same, I manoeuvred Bonzo towards the beach. He resisted at first, but when he spotted another dog he threw himself forward with abandon. I let go of the belt before I ended up on my face.

Bonzo dashed around on the sand like a puppy, bouncing like he had springs in his legs, playing with the other dog for a few minutes. When he was done, I picked up a stick and threw it for him. He brought it back. I chucked it again, surprised how much fun it was. I was actually laughing when Lavender found us. He stared at me like I was mad.

Shootout at St Anne's

The Pier, St Anne's

It was nearing midnight when Lavender and I returned to the pier. The tide was up, and the sound of breaking waves carried easily on the calm air. Lavender had moved the Land Rover from the car park a distance along the promenade, and Bonzo was asleep on the back seat so the belt was once more around my waist and there was no danger of losing my trousers any time soon, which, frankly, was the least of my worries.

We'd burnt the intervening hours wandering St Anne's, playing with the dog, getting something to eat. Finally, we'd stayed in a nearby pub drinking coffee until last orders. With the amount of caffeine zinging around my system I was bright-eyed and brisk. It was all very English, being at the seaside; and weird, considering we were about to meet the man who'd been trying to wipe out my family.

There were still a handful of hardy speculators playing the slot machines in the first section, even at this time of night. They could have even been the same risk-takers from this morning. But this wasn't Vegas. The pay-out was just a few pounds.

Lavender, coat zipped up to the throat, took the right-hand passage. A couple of lads were throwing balls down the lane of the mini bowling game in the second area. It was in the final section where I spotted someone I recognised. Two of them, actually. Jason and Stan, riding side by side on a motorbike game. They were really into it, leaning over on the animated corners, head down on the straights, as if wind resistance was a factor. I tugged on Lavender's arm.

"I see them," said Lavender, pausing a few feet away from where he'd stashed his rucksack.

The door opened at the far end. Hennessey and four men entered from the outside. He rolled along the passage in his wheelchair, bearing a huge grin of success. Two of Hennessey's guards remained at the doors maybe fifteen feet away, blocking them, and the other pair flanked their boss.

Hennessey whistled. Jason and Stan swung legs off motorbikes and made their way through the consoles. In the process they hustled out a pair of bystanders and barred the doors on the other side. We were hemmed in. Seven against two. Not good odds, though you wouldn't have known from Lavender's face, which was serene once more. Just like the first time I met him.

"You're punctual, Mr Vaughan," said Hennessey as he paused, leaving a twenty-foot gap between us. Hennessey placed his hands in his lap on top of a blanket which covered his legs. His bodyguards stood a pace behind him, arms loose at their sides. "I like that." Hennessey switched his attention onto Lavender. "So, you're him. You're the Nudge Man?"

Lavender stayed mute.

Hennessey continued. "You've no idea how long I've waited to meet you."

The pair stared at each other in some macho, let's-not-blink contest until the spell was broken by Hennessey pulling a handgun from under the blanket and shooting Lavender in the chest in one smooth movement. The noise was shockingly loud in the tight space.

Lavender had no chance. He hit the floor, arms splayed out, eyes open yet not seeing. It was over in a literal blink. I didn't even have chance to flinch. My ears rang as my brain struggled to make sense of the fact that Lavender was down.

"Ah, that felt good," said Hennessey. He crossed himself.

"Fuck," I said. Rather an understatement. I couldn't keep my eyes off Lavender's corpse. The burning smell of the gunshot residue hung in the still air. Make that seven against one. Terrible odds turned to impossible.

"Quite, Mr Vaughan. Well done, by the way, for bringing him to me." Hennessey lowered the weapon, and wiped it clean with the blanket across his lap.

"What about the money he stole and you redistributing it to the needy?" I asked. "And finding God?"

"I lied." Hennessey shrugged in a *What can you do?* way. "I wanted the Nudge Man for putting me in hospital, bringing down my empire and stealing my money. With some outside help I'd worked out Maddox, Lavender and the Nudge Man were one and the same. He'd put himself in prison, cooking up a charge the police arrested him for, then via selective violence against his fellow inmates, ensured he was permanently in solitary. So I needed him out and I needed someone to track him down and bring him to me. And in that, Mr Vaughan, you've succeeded admirably."

"What about Jack?"

"Your son, yes. I was very keen on finding him in the early days. Less so once the case was dropped. That being said, I'm a vindictive bastard. One day I'll deal with him, Mr Vaughan. When someone like you comes along, someone I can manipulate for my own ends and take the blame."

I threw myself at Hennessey, but his two protectors reacted fast, bundled me to the floor in a rugby tackle. I was buried under hundreds of pounds of muscle and unable to move before I'd even got halfway to the man. Then the pressure was released, and I was dragged to my feet, held in place by an iron grip on each forearm.

"So, Mr Vaughan. Onto the final act. Would you be so kind as to accept this?" Hennessey held out the pistol, grip towards me. I knew then what he intended.

"I don't think so."

"Bring him over," said Hennessey to my captors.

I tried to back away. Instead the hulks dragged me to within reaching distance of Hennessey. I kept my arms down by my side, fists clenched.

"There's no point resisting, Mr Vaughan. This is going only one way," said Hennessey. "As it has been since the very beginning. You're right-handed, correct?"

I didn't answer. The guy holding me yanked up my forearm and squeezed until the pain sliced along the muscle and I was forced to splay my fingers. Then I was holding the weapon which had killed Lavender. It was cool to the touch and was in my hand for a mere moment, not long enough to point and shoot.

Hennessey took the gun back, using a handkerchief to keep his own prints off, laid the gun in his lap. "See, we got there in the end."

Hennessey turned to my captives. "Deal with Vaughan and the firearm first, then get rid of Lavender's corpse. The police will be on their way."

"Does this mean you're going back on your deal, Eric?" I asked as the heavies began to drag me towards the end of the pier and a presumably watery grave. "Who's going to trust you now?"

Hennessey chuckled. "Cracking the jokes, right until the end." He spun his wheelchair round to watch me being propelled forward. I'd no chance of fighting back. I glared at Hennessey over my shoulder, my last weapon of resistance. Hennessey slowly followed.

Behind Hennessey was movement. Lavender, back from the dead. He rose off the floor, pulling out the Glock from his waistband.

"Boss!" shouted one of Hennessey's men in a warning.

Hennessey threw himself from his wheelchair and out of sight behind a games console. But Lavender wasn't aiming for Hennessey.

My would-be murderers let go and reached inside their jackets for their own weapons, though they were too slow. Tough guys, but not trained where Lavender was. A quick pair of double taps by Lavender and both were down. For the second time I was standing stock still, people being shot around me, the projectiles whizzing by, just inches away.

However, Lavender was still in action. He loosed off another couple or three bullets, taking out a guard by the door, missing the second who ducked, returned fire.

"Get down, Harry!" shouted Lavender, breaking me from my impotent state. I copied Hennessey and dived behind a console as a couple more bullets flew. In the brief pause Lavender shouted, "Harry, are you okay?"

"Wonderful!" I said.

"Don't get yourself killed. Elizabeth would never forgive me."

I wasn't going to argue. Somebody whistled from behind, must have been one of Hennessey's remaining men. There should be three of them left. I heard shuffling. I lay down, my cheek on the floor. There was a small gap between the dirty lino and the base of the machine, full of dust motes, and a pair of shoes inching their way towards me. If I stayed here I'd be found. I crouched, heart in my mouth, took a deep breath then ran for my life across the corridor and hurled myself behind another machine.

Bullets followed me, fired rapidly, deep judders. Then a single blast from a shotgun and silence. I gingerly poked my head up. The game I'd first hidden behind was ruined, a huge hole ripped through the top. I inched forward. Hennessey's man was out, half his face ruined. A machine gun lay beside him. I glanced over my shoulder. Lavender was crouched, making his way in the other direction and paying me no heed, heading towards danger.

I had two choices. I could leave this to Lavender or help. Against my better judgement I picked up the machine gun, made my way slowly across the other corridor, flanking Lavender. My heart was beating fast. Copying Lavender's crouch, I moved forwards. In the centre was Hennessey's wheelchair, but no Hennessey. I made progress in fits and starts, glancing out from cover before darting on.

Suddenly, Lavender reared up a few feet away, brought the shotgun to bear and fired, racked the bolt, fired again. Another of the bodyguards flew backwards, his chest exploding. It was Stan. Lavender dropped the shotgun and dived as Jason returned fire.

I slumped behind some cover, my breathing fast, shallow and hard. Like having acrophobia and standing on a high, narrow ledge. That urge to step off, the body fighting the impulse with a huge heave of adrenalin.

More shots, single reports. I couldn't tell who was firing at who. A scream. Somebody had taken a bullet. I squeezed my eyes shut, held onto the machine gun for dear life. Until Lavender said, "Harry, where are you?" He sounded in pain.

"Over here," I said, like that was informative.

"I'm hit," said Lavender. "In the leg."

"That's good to know." It was Hennessey, and he was on his feet, walking. So even the wheelchair was a scam. He loomed over me, gun back in hand. He was grinning again, fully in control. "I'll return for you shortly." And he was gone.

That phrase, now or never, had always sounded like bullshit to me. Until this particular moment. I pushed myself up, trailed after Hennessey. Lavender was sitting on a bench beneath one of the windows. His trouser leg was stained red. His jacket was off, exposing a bulletproof vest. That was why he was still alive. The Glock was beside Lavender, but he didn't go for it. Empty, presumably.

Hennessey was raising his own weapon. Lavender seemed to have given up, ready for the end. I ran. Towards Hennessey, lifted the machine gun like a baseball bat. Hennessey turned at the sound of my feet, but I was faster, and the butt caught him on the outswing, all my fear, aggression and shame focused into that arc. I cracked him on the neck and Hennessey went down, hard.

"Jesus, Harry," said Lavender with a weak grin. "You're not such a wimp after all."

For once failing to return with a retort I inspected Lavender's thigh wound while he unclipped the vest and let it slip to the floor. I'm squeamish and cringed at the sight of blood, torn skin and muscle which did little for my stomach. Yet again I removed my belt and cinched it tight around Lavender's leg just above the wound. He hissed in pain. Sirens cut through the shocking silence, distant but definitely closing.

"Time to go," said Lavender.

"Not without you."

"You'll never make it in time," said Hennessey, sitting up, leaning against a games machine and its cheerful, flashing lights. He was laughing, while blood ran down his head. "You're finished. And I'll keep hunting your family, Vaughan. I'll never stop."

"Leave, Harry," said Lavender.

"No," I said.

"You've five seconds."

"You're hardly in a position to argue, Noah."

"I think I am." Lavender held up the grenade.

"Don't do it," I said. I couldn't take my eyes off the explosive.

Lavender grinned, pulled the pin. "Five seconds."

"Go."

"Bollocks," I said.

Lavender rolled the grenade towards Hennessey.

"Ah, shit," said Hennessey as the explosive came to a rest near him. He scrabbled forward, trying to reach the grenade. He got his fingertips to it, but the bomb rolled away at his touch, towards Lavender and me.

I grabbed Lavender, got my shoulder underneath his and, suddenly energised, lifted him off the bench and out.

We went through the glass as the munition went off. The concussion was a pressure on my back, shoving me forward a couple of feet, lengthening the arc Lavender and I took towards the sea. There was a brief moment to hope the channel beneath us was deep enough before I had the presence of mind to pull in a half gasp of air before we hit.

I hit the brown water hard, the slap knocked the wind out of my lungs and I sank. The water was so cold, my skin felt like it was being pricked all over with needles. I felt a momentary panic. Which way was up? I looked around, saw the lights of the pier. The pressure in my lungs was already building, my heart rate high. I kicked, scooped water with my hands, fought my way to the surface.

I broke through, rising a few feet into the air, sweet as a pregnant dolphin. I breathed in, out until the spinning in my head receded. Then I realised I'd lost Lavender. I twisted, left, right. There was a bundle of clothes floating about ten feet away. I put my head down, swam hard, the inward flow of the tide helping my cause.

Lavender was the wrong way up, taking in water rather than air. I turned him over, grabbed hold of his shirt and kicked for the shore. It wasn't far, just a few hundred yards, but it seemed like miles. I kept flailing my legs, inching forward, Lavender a dead weight. When I could put my feet down, I walked the rest of the distance, pulled Lavender out of the water, laid him on the sand twenty feet or so from the pier and in the shadow of the building out front.

I put my ear to his lips. I couldn't detect any breath. I started applying CPR, first blowing air into his lungs, then a chest compression, back to giving air. Nothing. I repeated the process, but Lavender remained seemingly lifeless. His skin was white, his lips bloodless. I bent down to have one last go but suddenly he coughed, spluttered, rolled onto his side and vomited seawater. I flopped down beside Lavender.

There was a large hole in the side of the historic pier. The window I'd jumped from was gone, a ragged hole in its place. Black smoke billowed upwards, and inside a blaze raged. The sirens were close now. There would be cops everywhere and Lavender a wounded and wanted man. It was a case of being blown out of the fire and tossed into the frying pan.

Or some shite like that, which I was pretty much in. Then there was a weird, unexpected noise. It was my phone. I pulled it out of my pocket, amazed it was still working. Like me it was dripping with water. I tried to swipe the wet screen with a wet finger. Nothing. The ringing stopped, began again seconds later. I tried swiping again, this time the call connected.

"Hello?" I asked.

It got worse.

Much fucking worse.

Six is a Bastard

The Beach, St Anne's

"Mr Vaughan, you don't know me." It was a woman, American. I'd only met a single person from the other side of the Atlantic since all of this had started and that was hardly a pleasant experience. And once more somebody was aware of me, but not vice versa. "My name is Melody Blessing."

"I'm very pleased for you." I wasn't in the mood. Lavender was bleeding on me. The sirens were getting closer. I didn't have much experience in escape and evasion. My patience was as thin as a slice of graphene.

Molecular.

"Excuse me?" she said.

Americans, they have no ability to recognise sarcasm. This was going to be difficult. If my personality style was measured on a continuum, one end would be labelled, "Acerbic", the other, "Highly Scathing". So this conversation was probably doomed from the outset.

"I'm short of time here," I said. "What do you want?"

"To help."

"That's nice. I don't suppose you have an ambulance?"

"No."

"Then you're not of any use."

"But I can get one." Maybe Americans did do sarcasm after all. "Where are you?"

"Look for the fire. We're beneath it, taking the sea air."

"I'm on my way."

"Be quick."

"The cavalry's coming, Mr Vaughan," she said. Then was gone.

Trouble was, so were the cops.

A minute later and the sirens finally arrived. I checked on Lavender. He was unconscious. Blood loss, maybe. But what would I know? Something else I'm not is a doctor. In fact, I struggle to be a well-rounded member of society most of the time.

I'd been expected to be many things recently and I was sick of it. Fed up with being dragged pillar to post, manipulated, beaten, lied to, driven off the road, shot at, blown up. The next person who did anything to oppose me was going to be sorry. Extremely sorry.

I left briefly. Sparko Lavender wasn't moving. I crept round the side of the building; stayed within the shadows. There were uniforms everywhere in shades of Day-Glo. Three fire appliances. A hose was already unreeled and snaking into the pier. Another engine was extending a ladder, presumably so the blaze could be suppressed from above.

And the police. They were crawling around, milling like ants. For now, it appeared to be a search and rescue effort. Secure the area, save anybody who needed saving, figure out what the hell had happened, then act. I snuck back to Lavender. We had a little time, perhaps.

Four more minutes I waited. Two hundred and forty intensely long seconds. Until torches flashed on the beach to my left. Where I'd come down with Bonzo half a day ago, yesterday now, and thrown a stick. Five individual lights, headed straight for me. Not probing. They knew. Melody whatever-her-name-was, or the cops?

I could leave Lavender, hide behind one of the pier's legs or dive into the sea until I was sure. Run the other way along the beach. Retrieve the Land Rover, even, and drive off. Not stop until I reached Thanet. Forget all about the Nudge Man.

I dug around in Lavender's pocket. Found the car keys. Almost went. The lights neared, a few yards, they'd see me in a couple of seconds. But I couldn't leave. Why? Because despite it all, Lavender had been there for me, my kids, my ex. I owed him. I wanted to spit.

A beam fell on my face. The person behind, a short silhouette. "Mr Vaughan?" Female and American. Melody Blessing, my saviour, my hero. Unless she'd voted for the President.

Lavender was hooked up to all kinds of gadgets. I recognised a drip and the regular bleeping of a heart monitor. Everything else was jargon and wires. I perched on the bottom step of the ambulance while a couple of paramedics worked upon Lavender. They were Americans too, in fatigues, perhaps from the nearest military facility, or something. Who knew? Who cared?

We were parked up a short distance from the pier, far enough to be unaffected by the activity around the pier fire, which seemed to have taken hold across the whole structure. Lavender had probably destroyed an antique. The locals wouldn't be pleased. Likely be a few heart attacks in the morning when the OAPs saw the state of their pier.

Light from the interior spilled onto Blessing and me. Now I could see her properly I was impressed. An African-American

– she was business-like in her mannerisms and speech. Cute too. About my age, curly hair, an attractive quality to her features that I appreciated. Even though I'd nearly died my *"must be a man"* inner self was trying to assert itself. So, I feigned indifference.

God, I needed a girlfriend. "You're American, then," I said. I could have done with a coffee too.

"Last time I looked," said Blessing.

"How do you like your eggs in the morning?"

"I'm vegan."

"Oh."

"Awful chat up line, Harry."

I raised my hands in surrender. "What's your involvement in all of this?"

"That's classified."

"Very helpful."

"I just saved your friend's ass."

There was that. "We're not friends."

"Oh-kay."

"The last of your kind I met threatened to kill me."

"My kind?"

"From the wrong side of the pond."

"You're being kind of a dick, Mr Vaughan."

"It's a self-preservation thing. Have you got any coffee?"

"No."

"What about gas and air?"

"Focus, Mr Vaughan. We're not done here."

"We?"

"I assume from your derogatory comment that you're referring to Mr Six?"

"That's him, scary bastard."

"He works for me."

"So, I've got you to blame for his late night, shit-my-pants visit?"

"I use the word 'work' loosely, Mr Vaughan. He's in my reporting structure but Six has always been a loose cannon and since this latest administration came in he's literally a law unto himself."

"That's reassuring."

"And I lost control of him."

"Better and better."

"I've been tracking you for the last week."

"How?"

"I work for the American government. I've all kinds of methods at my disposal. Even here, your side of the pond, as you put it. I've followed your every move."

"Why?"

"Too many questions, Mr Vaughan. We don't have time to go over everything right now. I assume Six told you he wanted the Nudge Man?"

"Jesus, I'm sick of this. That's all everybody has said to me all the way through this ridiculous episode." Except for the lawyer, Conn. A million quid to stay away. I should have taken the money and gone on holiday somewhere hot. Let this bloody lot sort things out for themselves.

"Six is making a demand. He wants the Nudge Man. Tonight."

"Look, Melody, I'm tired, wet, and need to go to bed. I've had enough of everything to do with the Nudge Man. Lavender's in the ambulance, Six can have him."

"There's the rub. Mr Lavender isn't the Nudge Man. Thankfully Six is currently unaware of that fact."

I put my head in my hands. Just when I thought I had all the answers. "So who is the Nudge Man?"

"I think you know already."

I paused, considering. I'd had my doubts about Lavender, but pushed them to one side, focused on dealing with Hennessey. The Nudge Man was strong on morals, possessed excellent IT skills and was handy with his fists. But maybe it had been two people? Brains and brawn. If so, there was only one person left who fit the bill ...

Blessing was talking again. "Six has a bargaining chip which he wants to exchange for Mr Lavender. Your daughter."

I did say it got much fucking worse.

Showdown With Six

C hina Street, Lancaster
Atkinson's Coffee Roastery was on the busy single carriageway of China Street in Lancaster, just a few miles north of St Anne's.

It was rush hour. The smell of diesel fumes hung in the air, trapped between the high walls of the buildings either side of the road constructed in blocky sandstone which would once have been yellow but were now stained brown from exhaust gases. The sound of revving engines was almost as loud as the scolding voice in my head. Bonzo, who was trotting beside me to keep pace, could feel my mood. He repeatedly glanced up at me.

I had the phone Six gave me the time he broke into my house. The one I was supposed to ring him on to supply updates. The one I didn't even switch on until this morning. To arrange with Six where to meet. Then I'd called Gregory, asked him for command. One that Bonzo would react to immediately.

I pushed open the café door. Ordinarily, I'd have been delighted to check out an establishment which roasted its own. Here was an artisan's dream. Stripped wooden floors, mismatched benches where people shared space, old machinery against the walls, huge hessian coffee sacks. And they brewed their coffee in vacuum flasks. Who does that? It was a bean lover's haven. But I was here for love of a different kind.

Maddie was sitting with her back to me, though she didn't turn when I entered. She was rigid, as if her spine was an inflexible rod. Six, however, rose smoothly to his feet, arms loose at his sides. There were cups and plates between them on the table. And a gun within Six's reach, the barrel pointing towards Maddie. Six's drink and Danish half consumed, Maddie's untouched. There was nobody else in the shop, no customers, no staff.

"What's with the shades?" asked Six. I wore thick, dark glasses.

"Bad eyesight," I lied.

"He's ugly for a seeing-eye dog." Six indicated Bonzo.

"I wouldn't know, due to the bad eyesight."

Six picked up the gun, crossed to the door, clicked the Yale latch so we were all locked in. "Sit down, Mr Vaughan." All so polite, these Americans.

I shuffled forwards until my shins hit the bench. I parked my backside a few feet away from Maddie, got Bonzo underneath the table. I let go of his leash, hoped he would stay alert, feed off the atmosphere. As you know, his tendency was to sleep at the slightest opportunity.

Six retook his spot opposite, regarded me for a moment, reached out and removed my glasses. He tossed them over his shoulder. I blinked in the brightness, they really had been dark. The black hole which was the gun's barrel pointed straight at my chest. From here it would blow a hole right through me.

"Enough with the bullshit, buddy," said Six. "I followed you for weeks. You can see just fine."

I shrugged. "I was after the sympathy vote."

"Ultimately, I don't care. All I want is the Nudge Man. Where's Lavender?"

"Why, Six? Why all this effort?"

Six's features adopted a zealous fold. "He insulted the President, my President. Nobody does that to the most powerful man in the world who's there by the grace of God." Religion again. Six continued, "If the Nudge Man were able to get away with the slight, then so would everybody else. From the Taliban to the Koreans to the Canadians. It's not acceptable."

"What got your man so riled?"

Six pulled out his phone, tapped at the screen with the thumb of his left hand. All the while the gun stayed rock steady. "Here you go." He turned the screen to me. I leant over, read the words. A tweet which said, "The President has a tiny dick".

"Is that all?"

"It's more than enough. The President is a great man, who should be revered as such."

"People have died, Six."

"Happens every day, anyways. Just a bit sooner than they expected, is all." He shrugged. "So, where's Lavender? Where's my Nudge Man?"

"Getting medical care, under armed guard."

Six's expression darkened. He leaned across the table. "I told Blessing, the deal was we swap your lovely daughter here for Lavender."

Now was my turn to shrug. "I don't know what to suggest."

Maddie reacted at last, throwing me a worried glance. God, she'd grown up. The same features and expressions as when she'd been a kid, still young, but older. She was an adult now, striking out on her own. Did she have a boyfriend? Where did she live? The only aspect of her life I was sure about, she was still a computer nerd.

"How about I shoot the girl, then?" Six slowly tracked the gun towards Maddie.

The moment Six shifted his aim I shouted, "Bite!" There was the snap of jaws, the heartbeat of a pause, then an almighty scream from Six. Unsurprising, as Bonzo had latched his powerful jaws around Six's nether region and squeezed. No man wants that.

I launched myself across the table, scattering the cups and plates, grabbed Six's arm, forced the barrel up. Six pulled the trigger, an explosion close by my ear. Momentum carried me forwards and Six backwards. We went over the bench, hit the floor hard.

I lost my grip on Six, who rolled across the floor like a football player hoping to get a penalty from the referee. Bonzo, had been forced to release his jaws but he was a different dog now, one I hadn't seen before, in full-on attack mode. Snarling, bared sharp teeth, ears flat against his head, snapping at Six's face while he writhed. Maddie was rooted to the spot, caught unawares by the sudden change of events.

"Maddie!" I yelled. "Run!"

She clicked into action and pelted for the door. Six smashed his elbow into Bonzo's nose, the dog yelped and backed off momentarily, giving Six enough time to swing the barrel towards Maddie as she struggled with the lock on the door. I launched myself into the air once more like a fleshy cannonball, a feeble attempt to get between the bullet and Maddie.

While I was mid-air there came a heartrending scream, cut off by a gurgle. Six had exposed his throat to Bonzo and the dog exploited the opening with deadly effect, sinking in his teeth and tearing out a chunk. Six fell back, the gun firing as I hit the boards. Maddie was outside and gone.

I picked myself up, felt my body for any new holes. There were none. But the ceiling had seen better days. Bonzo was standing over Six, head down, his jaws a bloody mess, ready in case the American moved. But Six wouldn't be going anywhere except the morgue.

I patted Bonzo on the head. "Good boy." Bonzo sat. He'd figured Six was done too.

Outside and the road was quiet. No traffic at all. Maddie was standing with Melody Blessing and a distinguished-looking man with a shock of white hair. As I neared, Maddie ran to me, threw herself into my arms. My first contact with my family for five, very long years.

And it was amazing.

Lavender is Dead and Buried

The Police Station, Lancaster

The distinguished gentleman turned out to be a man of ermine. He was Lord Dennis of Wetwang, no less. I'd never met an actual Lord before. He played the part, too. Imperious, very sure of himself, used to getting what he wanted – all communicated via his stance and speech. For once I was too tired to rail against privilege.

We sat in one of the police station interview rooms, obvious by the décor. Getting here had been a blur, a vague recollection of a patrol car, whisked away from the scene, sat in the back with my daughter in my arms. She was with me now, holding my hand. Opposite us were Dennis and Melody Blessing.

I'd no idea where Bonzo was, which bothered me. "Where's my dog?" I surprised myself, stating ownership.

"Does it matter?" asked Dennis.

Blessing said, "Next door. He's fine." Dennis rolled his eyes. "You'll want to know what's next, of course," she said.

"That would be a first," I said.

"From the British side," interrupted Dennis, seemingly keen to move the process along, "there's already a clean-up operation underway. The press will be told that the escaped convict, Pomfrey Lavender, has been found dead. Committed suicide. Six's corpse will be cremated and what's left will be buried in an unmarked plot somewhere remote. As far as the world is concerned, Noah Maddox, Pomfrey Lavender or whoever is dead."

"Six will be quietly forgotten in Washington too," said Blessing. "The President doesn't like failure or to be associated with embarrassing events, so I'm certain I can get that to fly."

"And all of this over a tweet?"

"I'm afraid so."

"That's what politics is about now?"

"For the next couple of years, at least, yes."

"Where's Lavender?"

"In a secure facility, awaiting you both," said Dennis.

"What about Hennessey?"

"As far as we know he died on the St Anne's pier. The fire is out now, all that's left are the iron legs. The building structure was gutted." Dennis rose, clearly better stuff to fill his time with. "Anyway, I must be going. The wheels of government keep turning."

"And the Nudge Man?" I asked.

"I don't know who you're talking about." Dennis stood, extended a hand. "Thank you, Mr Vaughan, you've done us a great service. I'm impressed you came through. Six was a dangerous man."

"I didn't do any of this for you," I said. Dennis blinked, dropped his hand, departed.

Blessing, who'd proved time and again she was the person with the comparatively higher emotional quotient got it. She said, "Let's get you both home."

We were led through the station out to the rear car park. The Land Rover was there. Bonzo was already on the back seat, sitting calmly. "You'll have an escort until you collect your friend, then you're on your own." Blessing held out the keys. "I strongly suggest the Nudge Man retire. No offence, but I'd rather we didn't see each other again." She nodded at both of us, disappeared back inside.

Maddie and I got into the Land Rover. There was a smell of damp dog hanging in the air. Someone had washed the blood off Bonzo. I gave him a pat. He wagged his tail, settled down to sleep. As usual. I opened the window.

A squad car turned on its lights, filling the yard with a wash of blue, and headed out of the car park. I started the engine, fell in behind the bumper of the cop. I glanced in the rear view. There was another patrol car close behind, lights on also. To reach Lavender all I had to do was take the same turns as the car in front.

"I'm sorry, Dad," said Maddie. She looked like a little girl again, chewing on a cuticle. "All I wanted to do was help people." She'd always been the same. But her power had been through electrons, key touches, social media blasts, not her fists like Lavender. She'd been a computer genius, but I'd never realised. That's what a five-year absence does for you.

"Why?"

"At first Noah was working on his own. He started in Mersea, with the guy who hassled Jack."

"Mourtice."

"That's him. But it was easy to figure out the bad guy in a small town. With Mr Purcell and the streets of London it was a much bigger job. He asked for my help. For example, with a little guidance from Noah, I was able to access CCTV. At first, I just gathered data, left the rest to Noah. But it became addictive, looking out for others. I couldn't stop."

"Why call yourself the Nudge Man?" I asked.

She gave a weak grin. "Every good superhero has a name, right?"

"It's a bit of a crap one, though."

"I suppose so," she laughed. "Like a hitman, but less violent. It was Noah's idea. Our actions were getting some attention, a few websites were starting up, people beginning to make connections. A title gives people focus." Which had certainly proved to be the case.

"Is that all now? Are you done, as Blessing suggested?"

"I'd no idea I was going to cause this much pain. If I'd realised I'd have never started."

"Maddie, you did a lot of good. I met Mr Purcell. The man has his medals and his dignity back. You and Noah achieved that. Nobody else."

"Thanks, Dad."

"I assume the lawyer, Aaron Conn, was sent by you?" There was nobody else it could have been, frankly.

"I hoped to keep you away. To ensure everybody was safe."

"You should have just come to me, told me what you needed."

"I'd forgotten how to, Dad. It's been a few years. And I was used to dealing with problems via my computer. Moving individuals around the board as I wanted."

"Humans are awkward things."

"Especially you."

I laughed. The cop car dropped onto the M6 motorway. We were heading south. "Where did you get the money from?" I asked. A million pounds is a lot by most people's standards.

"Stole it from Hennessey."

"Poetic justice."

"We needed cash to survive and it was Hennessey making our lives almost impossible. So it felt like a fair trade. And there's plenty more left."

"It didn't work. The inducement that is. Money has never been a particularly big motivator for me."

"I know, Dad. I'm the same."

"Everyone has been dancing me around like a marionette."

"Sorry."

"Doesn't matter." And ultimately, it didn't. "I'm just glad you're safe." Maddie grinned. A comfortable silence fell. As much as it could in a rattly old Land Rover.

Though there was still one question unanswered. Who framed me six years ago?

Reunion

Flash, Staffordshire

With Lavender and Bonzo stretched out in the back and Maddie curled up on the passenger seat beside me, I drove the Land Rover back to Staffordshire. The old engine was sluggish on the motorways and I stuck to the slow lane. But once we hit the inclines, twists and turns of the Peak District the Land Rover came into its own again.

Lavender directed me through Flash, out onto the unnamed road I'd traversed just a couple of days ago. "Here," he said. I took a right between two large gateposts made of local gritstone. A sign said, *Quarnford Farm*. The rough track dropped down at a steep angle to an isolated, white painted farmhouse.

Somebody was waiting in the doorway, wearing jeans and a light blue shirt. I took my foot off the accelerator when I recognised Elizabeth; older, with a lot more grey hair and a few extra worry lines, but just as beautiful as the last time I'd seen her. So much for my family being a long way off. Another smooth line from Lavender.

I rolled to a halt, pulled on the handbrake. Maddie was out of the car and running to her mother before I twisted the key and let the engine die. The pair hugged fiercely for a few moments, Elizabeth's face in Maddie's shoulder. Eventually Elizabeth looked up, stared straight at me through the windscreen with tear-filled eyes.

Lavender eased himself off the back seat, popped the door and slid slowly out, favouring his uninjured leg, followed by Bonzo. "Come on," said Lavender. "Time to meet everyone."

I got out of the Land Rover, left the door open, walked slowly towards my ex-wife. As I neared, she and Maddie parted before drawing me in.

"I'm sorry," whispered Elizabeth. "I'm so, so sorry."

Their arms around me, I began to cry for the first time in five years. Something nudged from behind, it was Bonzo, pushing his head into my leg. He barked. Maddie separated from me, knelt down and stroked the dog who'd saved both our lives.

Keeping me in her grip, Elizabeth said, "Jack's waiting inside."

Elizabeth pointed me to the door third along a corridor which ran the width of the house.

"What do I say?" I asked. I had no idea how to deal with a teenager on the cusp of adulthood. All my experience was way out of date and hardly relevant.

"He's a quiet lad," she said. "Likes his music and spends a lot of time playing games over the internet with his friends."

"Okay."

"Best thing I can suggest is just to go for it."

Suitably vague advice received, I knocked. No answer. I turned to Elizabeth. She waved her hands at me in a *"go on"* fashion. I tried again before turning the door handle and entering. A typical teenage boy's room. Double bed in the centre below various posters stuck onto the whitewashed stone of current bands and films. A large window took up one wall.

Jack, my son, sat at a table, his back to me, wearing a pair of headphones and staring at a computer screen, killing aliens. He hadn't responded because he couldn't hear me. The chair was impressive, like something from the deck of the Starship Enterprise.

I crossed the floor, leant against the wall so I was in Jack's eyeline. He removed his thumb from the controller, lifted a hand, pushed the headphones off his ears. "Dad?" His mouth hung open. "Mum said you were coming, but I didn't believe her." Jack's voice was deeper than I remembered.

I had so much I wanted to say but felt ready with so little. "I got your letters." I held them out.

"They were stupid."

"Just the opposite, your words were a massive help. Without them I wouldn't be here."

"Really?"

"Really." Jack gave a shy grin, an expression I recognised. I pointed at the paused game. "What are you playing?"

"Destiny 2."

"Any good?"

Jack handed me a spare controller in answer. I sat down on the bed and we killed aliens together. No more words needed.

Jack and I played for a couple of hours. We spoke little, just being together was enough. Eventually, I left my son. I found Elizabeth by herself in the kitchen, sitting at the table, sipping a mug of tea.

"Where's Noah?" I asked.

"In bed," said Elizabeth.

"I need to talk to him."

"I'll show you." She stood.

Lavender's room was beside Jack's. Elizabeth knocked, stuck her head round the door. "He's awake," she said. "When you're done, let's go for a walk."

The curtains were part-drawn. Lavender was propped up in bed, pillow behind his back, his bandaged leg outside the duvet. He appeared tired and drawn.

"How are you feeling?" I asked.

"Pretty good, thanks."

"Something I want to know."

"Sure, what?"

"When we were talking in the pub before heading to St Anne's I asked why you'd targeted me. You said somebody paid you to. That was when I believed you were the Nudge Man. Which you're not. Nobody paid you anything, did they?"

"No, sorry. I needed you to believe me."

So I still didn't know who'd set me up for my big fall six years ago or why. "I understand, Noah. Look, I'll let you get some rest."

Elizabeth was standing outside. "Everything okay?"

"It's fine. You mentioned a walk."

"You'll need something more than just shoes. It's muddy out."

She led me across the fields on a path she must have known was there but was invisible to me. I skirted a puddle. Elizabeth had scared up some stout walking boots, as essential footwear here as flip flops in Broadstairs. Elizabeth walked fast, clearly used to the hills. Thanet was pretty much entirely flat, and I struggled with the incline.

"Noah told me you know everything," said Elizabeth when the ground levelled out and I had some of my breath back.

"Pretty much." I panted. "I'm sorry I wasn't there."

"How could you be? I'd left."

"I know, but ..."

Elizabeth stopped, put a hand out, touched my arm. "I was wrong."

"About some stuff, not all. I was a childish idiot too absorbed by himself and his own little bubble. Still am, most of the time."

"I meant about the accusation of being a child molester."

"There's that."

"I should have believed you."

"It doesn't matter now."

"Who framed you?"

"That's why I got involved in all of this." I frowned. "To find out. And I still don't know."

I got walking, Elizabeth trailing after me. She said, "I can't thank you enough for saving Maddie. And Noah."

"Are you and Noah happy?" It killed me to ask, but I had to.

"Yes, I think so. We've been through a lot together."

"Good, I'm glad."

"Are you?"

"Yes." And actually, I was.

Elizabeth linked her arm through mine and we trekked in silence for a while.

I stayed at Quarnford Farm for six days. I didn't want to leave, but it was time for us all to return to our lives. Maddie back to university, me to whatever I had in Thanet, Lavender and Elizabeth to their peace here, and Jack to school.

I hugged Elizabeth, Maddie then Jack. He held onto me the longest time.

"I'll remain in touch," I said. "You won't keep me away now."

"Great." Lavender rolled his eyes theatrically. I was only just beginning to think of him as Maddox. We'd even been to the pub a couple of times together. I quite liked him. He held out his hand to shake. "Be good, Harry."

"Not if I can help it."

"Come on, let's get you to the station." Elizabeth opened the Land Rover door. With Lavender's leg injury and, being officially dead, he could hardly drive me. I guessed he couldn't and wouldn't venture far from Flash ever again. Elizabeth whistled and Bonzo ran over, leapt into the front seat, his tail wagging, tongue hanging out.

Lavender turned to me with a grin. "Seems like you're in the back."

I sat where the dog had decided. Elizabeth started the engine and drove up the hill. I stared over my shoulder until we crested the peak and Quarnford Farm, along with my children and Lavender, were out of sight.

As I didn't have a car I was taking the train back to Broadstairs. The nearest station was in Buxton, where I was planning to buy a ticket using almost the last of Hennessey's money. There would be enough left to get some food on the way, then I was skint again.

From Buxton I'd head to Stockport on the edge of Manchester, take a fast train on to London Euston, make a half-mile walk along Euston Road for St Pancras Station before riding a South Eastern train down to pretty much the end of the tracks.

All in all, about six hours of journey time. It was going to be a long day. But I had my laptop. There was a story to write and some thinking to do.

We drove in silence the whole way. I'd run out of sensible words to say. The drive took all of fifteen minutes. We skirted the edge of the town before we pulled up in the station car park. I got out. Elizabeth left the engine running. She popped her door, said, "If you don't mind, I won't come in with you." She'd never really done goodbyes.

"I was going to say the same."

"What about Bonzo?"

The dog sat in the seat, barked, knowing we were talking about him. "I think he should stay with you. There's loads of space for him to run around and I'm not really a dog person anyway."

"If you're sure."

"I am." I wasn't.

Elizabeth gave me a quick smile. "I'm sorry it all worked out this way."

"There's nothing either of us could have done about it. There were bigger forces at work."

"Thank you."

"I'd better go. My train's in a couple of minutes," I lied. I had to leave.

Elizabeth nodded. I turned away and got walking. I didn't think I could watch Elizabeth drive off. When I reached the station doors I heard Bonzo's bark. I twisted on my heel. He was running towards me. Elizabeth was waving from the open window of the Land Rover. "He wouldn't stay," she shouted.

Bonzo leapt up, putting his front paws onto my chest. It seemed I had a travelling companion.

I rang Gregory from the platform. "Fancy a pint?" I asked when he answered. "I've got a tale to tell you."

"So you're okay then?"

"Ah, yes." I'd forgotten to call him. "Everything was fine. Bonzo attacked Six at my command. You were right."

"You're welcome. When are you thinking?"

"About five o'clock, in the Flag. The beers are on me."

"I can do that."

"I'll call when I reach Margate."

"See you then. Safe travels."

I disconnected. I had my family back and a friend or two. I was a rich man after all.

Grinned like an idiot while I waited for my train.

Return to the Flag

The English Flag, Margate

Dick, the landlord of the Flag, was pulling me and Gregory a pint. He'd argued about serving a cop and having a dog on licenced premises, but he shut up and started pouring when Bonzo growled. Dick was onto the second glass and Gregory was selecting a table when the door banged open.

"Hello, you bastards!"

I couldn't believe my eyes. It was Les, who'd sent me off on the wild goose chase to the breaker's yard right at the beginning. The cause of everything else which followed. Larger than life. Not dead.

"Les," I said.

"That's my name, don't wear it out, H." He grinned, like that was a brand new joke. Bonzo snarled. Les' expression as he took in the dog was one of puzzlement, as if he'd never seen an animal of its like before.

"Where have you been?"

"On holiday." Les returned his attention to me. "All expenses paid. To Majorca." He pronounced it as Ma-jaw-cah with a hard J. "Partying like it's going out of fashion. Once my joints eased up anyway." He waved his arms in the air like an ageing raver. "I told you, don't you remember?"

"No."

Les tapped his temple. "Your memory's failing you, lad." Les glanced around, ignoring Bonzo's continued low rumble and Gregory's bemusement. "Anything been going on?"

Lots. But I said, "Not really. Though you might want to have a chat with DS Gregory over there before you go home."

Les made a pfft sound. "More important matters first, H. A mate of mine's got a run on an exclusive. Interested?"

"You've got to be kidding, Les. Of course I'm not. I got arrested last time."

"About that ..."

I held up my hands, cut Les off before the flow started. "I don't ever want one of your leads again."

"You're making a major mistake, H." Les stepped forward, getting into my personal space, using his bulk in an attempt at intimidation. Bonzo stood, barked twice, each huff deep and dark. The pub turned. All eyes on Bonzo.

"Whoa, whoa!" Les stepped back, arms up again, this time in surrender rather than mock merriment. "Calm down, mutt."

"He doesn't like you."

"I can't imagine why."

I could. "Anyway, I've got an investigation underway." I still needed to know who'd framed me all those years ago, and why. The event was back in the open again and I was burning to know who. I was going to ask Gregory for help – once I'd bought him a couple of pints.

Les raised an eyebrow. "Paid in advance, is it?"

"Speculative," I mumbled.

"Ah, that kind of effort! I'm sure you'll be fine." Les turned to Dick, said, "Pint, landlord."

"Harry needs to settle up with me first," said Dick. He held his palm out for payment for the beer awaiting me on the bar. I patted my pockets. Pretty much empty. I spilled some loose change onto the bar, the last of Hennessey's cash, which Dick pushed around with a finger and sniffed. There wasn't anywhere near enough. However, my wallet held my bank card and the one from Hennessey. He wouldn't be needing that now.

"Try this," I said, handing over Hennessey's plastic.

"Don't be ridiculous, son," said Dick, an incredulous expression on his face. "*Cash only*, you should know that. Have you had a bang on the head recently or something?"

Les grinned, he knew I was always short. "Same as ever, eh, H?"

"You'll have to go to the cash machine," said Dick.

"I'll be back in five," I said.

"Give me his pint then, Dickie," said Les. He stretched his hand out to take the glass. Les smiled like he owned me. Bonzo glanced up, I gave him a nod. As Les raised the pint to his lips Bonzo opened his ample jaw and lightly clamped his teeth around the newspaper editor's crotch. He froze.

"That beer is mine, Les. Get it?" I said.

"Sure." The reply was a squeak.

"You can put it down."

Les did. "Tell you what, H." He gave me a sickly grin. "How about I buy it for you?"

"I'll get my own thanks. I'm never taking anything from you again."

"Fair enough, H."

"And it's Harrison to you, not H or even Harry. Maybe even Mr Vaughan. I haven't decided yet."

"All right, whatever you want."

Gregory was keeping his head down, concentrating on his phone. There was a tiny smile playing across his lips.

I turned to Dick, who was standing open-mouthed, staring at me as if I'd grown a second head. "I'm off to get some money then I'll be back for these beers. Bonzo is going to stay here and keep an eye on them, all right, Dick?"

The landlord nodded. I patted Bonzo on the head, said, "You can let go now." Bonzo did. Gregory winked as I passed by.

The cash machine was over in the New Town, a good five minutes' walk away. I was still buzzing by the time I inserted Hennessey's card, tapped in the pin number. The card was blocked, and the machine swallowed the plastic. Must have been cancelled after Hennessey's death.

All I had left was my own card, which followed Hennessey's. I was given a series of options. If I remembered correctly, I had a quid and change in my account. I also ran a small overdraft, so I'd be able to get some money, at least. Having won an altercation with Les for once, the last thing I was going to do was return empty handed. So, I took out thirty pounds.

I began the walk back to the Flag, huge grin on my face. I was in touch with my kids. I had a true friend in Bonzo at my side and a human one in Gregory. Perhaps he'd properly introduce me to DCI Hamson if I asked nicely.

Maybe I was going to be okay after all ...

Don't miss out!

Visit the website below and you can sign up to receive emails whenever Keith Nixon publishes a new book. There's no charge and no obligation.

https://books2read.com/r/B-A-BGNH-BNRX

BOOKS 2 READ

Connecting independent readers to independent writers.

Did you love *The Nudge Man*? Then you should read *Dig Two Graves* by Keith Nixon!

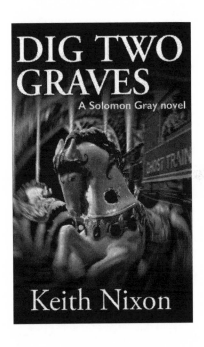

Was it suicide ... or murder? Detective Sergeant Solomon Gray is driven to discover the truth. Whatever the personal cost. When teenager Nick Buckingham tumbles from the fifth floor of an apartment block, Detective Sergeant Solomon Gray answers the call with a sick feeling in his stomach. The victim was just a kid, sixteen years old. And the exact age the detective's son was, the son Gray has not seen since he went missing at a funfair ten years ago. Each case involving children haunts Gray with the reminder that his son may still be out there – or worse, dead. The seemingly open and shut case of suicide twists into a darker discovery. Buckingham and Gray have never met, so why is Gray's number on the dead teenager's mobile phone? Gray begins to unravel a murky world of abuse, lies, and corruption. And when the body of Reverend David Hill is found shot to death in the vestry of Gray's old church, Gray wonders how far the depravity stretches and who might be next. Nothing seems connected, and yet there is one common thread: Detective Sergeant Solomon Gray, himself. As the bodies pile up, Gray must face his own demons and his son's abduction. **Crippled by loss Gray takes the first step on the long road of redemption. But is the killer closer to home than he realised?** Set in the once grand town of Margate in the south of England, the now broken and depressed seaside resort becomes its own character in this dark police suspense thriller, perfect for fans of Ian Rankin, Stuart MacBride, and Peter James. *Dig Two Graves* is the first in the Solomon Gray series. Pick it up now to discover whether Gray finds his son in this thrilling new crime series.

What Others Say

"... deeply emotional, a dark rollercoaster ride." **Ed James**, author of bestselling *DI Fenchurch* series "A stunning book and a new series that has become a must read." **M.W. Craven**, author of the *Washington Poe* series "Keith Nixon is one hell of a writer." **Ken Bruen**, author of the *Jack Taylor* series "A compelling murder mystery with a multilayered and engaging new hero. Great read." **Mason Cross**, author of the *Carter Blake* thriller series "Dig Two Graves is a smartly conceived introduction to a new series, and there are a good number of loose ends just waiting to tempt you to continue the journey." **Crime Fiction Lover**

What Readers Say

"It's just too damned good, I loved it.""I haven't given 5* for a while, this deserves it.""Read it, you won't regret it.""What a joy.""Could not put it down.""Grittiness seeps out of this book from every pore.""The author has hooked me in yet again.""OMG loved this book!""This is a must read.""A dark, uncompromising tale of loss, murder, and revenge. Glorious noir, which takes the police procedural elements and gives them new life. I can't wait to read the next step in Solomon Gray's journey for answers ..."**Luca Veste**, author of the *Murphy and Rossi* crime series

Also by Keith Nixon

Caradoc
The Eagle's Shadow
The Eagle's Blood

Detective Solomon Gray
Dig Two Graves
Burn The Evidence
Beg For Mercy
Bury The Bodies

DI Granger
The Corpse Role

Gray Box Set
The Solomon Gray Series: Books 1 - 4: Gripping Police
Thrillers With A Difference

Harrison Vaughan
The Nudge Man

Konstantin
Russian Roulette
The Fix
I'm Dead Again
Dark Heart, Heavy Soul

Konstantin Box Set
The Konstantin Series - Books 1 to 3
The Konstantin Series Books One to Three

Standalone
The Solomon Gray Series: Books 1 to 4: Gripping Police
Thrillers With A Difference

Made in the USA
Middletown, DE
02 August 2020